BURNING SECRETS

Dr. Rajeev Madhavan Menon

PUBLICATION

Delhi - 110089 (India)

Edition : 2024
ISBN : 978-93-6210-237-9

Price : 650/-

Burning Secrets
Dr. Rajeev Madhavan Menon

Cover Page & Book Layout
Jyoti Singh

Published by
PRAKHAR GOONJ PUBLICATIONS
Reg. Office: H-3/2 Sector-18 Rohini, Delhi-110089
Office : A-4/57 Sector-18 Rohini, Delhi-110089
Email : prakhargoonj@gmail. com
info@prakhargoonjpublications. com
Ph. : 7982710571, 7838505899, 011-42635077
Web : prakhargoonjpublications. com

BURNING SECRETS

Your fears may loom when it is dark. Let them expand so the absolute horror can unfold.

A book on horror drama that talks about the cultural order, the secrecy of the family, and a certain community that guards the honour to ensure everything works in the right fold.

DEDICATION

The book is dedicated to all those who like fantasy as a genre, want to enjoy suspense as a core part of it, and wish to explore more in the realms of cultural heritage.

The work is set in the backdrop of the glory of a community known for its pride and the influence of fear connected to it where people try to catch up with royal treasure, so it is also a kind of thriller.

It is dedicated to those who believe in the cultural stretch in existence saving the heritage as the work talks about the coin and role of the order who vanguard it from all threats even if they have to sacrifice their life, imprints as ghosts and no matter what they would restore the actual functioning.

PREFACE

What do you think when we talk of ghosts? Shapes that looming shadows or fear that can grip you suddenly from behind? It is part of being horror that it has a mystique to create, a secret of its legacy and it may give you surprise to behold.

'An imprint of something that may come to foresee everything to have a dip down in shadow' is the core perspective that is associated with the cultural realm and the author tries to unfold the narrative with hints on how shapes become complete in their form as the story progresses in backdrop with a lot of personal fear.

with ghosts of the forests who like to invite or chase people, the existence of a community in such a backdrop that may look after those who cause mayhem, and chaos and stand as their counterpart who bring the balance that holds the whole story around.

The bad spirits shall finally be sent to the nether world by practices connected to them by local powers as peace is being brought back by the efforts of all the members who want to make it a better world.

Mainly the ghost of a son dead by unfair means had to play a huge part in the process as it kept appearing loyal to his father as a secret who feels for his untimely demise due to a backfire. They all came together to seek the needs of the hour and finally led the charge with the guidance of a positive spirit who came by a legend and helped in achieving control in the city.

There is one more child who is not given equal priority by the family. Nastika is a tour guide and photographer who has a busy mother who works as a lawyer and a father who is connected to the order, always being away with rare guidance to her at Upendera's place. Her position is simply left to her hands as she tries to find treasures to showcase, ghosts of the woods, and a lot of crises take place while she tries to bring balance amongst people who visit as tourists.

The work also brings nature into the background as hilly tours that are connected with tales of their legacy are brought into vision as a core element of the work on its whole scale. You may find ghosts lurking after their love was rejected, social turmoil, and restricted to women which all brings a society as confined to the progress of the narration making it more spicy.

Further, the wishes of global people to get hands-on coins become more intent as they too start to plot conspiracy. The conditions of threat in the form of disease and ghosts with social problems make it equally touched as the work goes through with more changes in places with more involved. The calamity both by nature and humans, the trouble of family with more damage, and its effect make things more critical.

No country is different when it comes to your own loss or being taken, which is the ultimate message of the work as more deaths happen, people get injured and the work spans to more chaos itself.

Finally, the twists of life come to a close with the birth of a cute child who may come as a guardian to solve problems. The arrival brings true joy, and happiness to be part and a global event is held to mark the moment when the previous guardian will hand over the coin to the new generation to take over and it becomes quiet after so much which would take years to heal in the mind of people connected in the story.

FOR READERS

This book is based on the true imagination of the author. The work is filled with challenges, tracking the treasure or trying to fix the personal problem as a whole. None of the characters mentioned or portrayed in the book has any direct connection to real events, people, or cultural legacy in life. If they are found to be connected through any certain reference or with effect to similar activities, it may just be considered as a matter of coincidence as the story depends on what the author thinks rather than touching on a real-life element of it.

The plot twists mentioned in the story are highly risky or come with absolute danger in real life. It is advised to readers not to try such stunts, spy roles, or creative actions at home or anywhere else as it can lead to tricky incidents or matters of chaos in life that do bring damage so they must be avoided at all costs.

The thoughts presented in the work have no intention to hurt, offend, disregard, or make bad remarks on any community, country, or global standards working in the fold-It is just based on the pure imagination of the author and shall be subjected to his creativity.

Lastly, readers who feel fear of ghosts must not connect the plotline with the presence of them in life or another possible effect. Spiritual influence remains a matter of different viewpoints, but the story is only created to entertain them rather than make them feel frightened by regular twists or suspense. It is up to them how they take the plotline being of essence and appreciate the creative realm of it and the author is hopeful that they will enjoy the work by reading it.

CONTENTS

1

SHADOWS IN THE FOG

It was a chilly and frosty day, as it just struck 4 in the morning, but Upendera due to his habit took up his stick to go for a morning walk. He heard the alarm, slowly limped to close it, and then started to walk. He was the first who gets up this early, taps his old stick, and turns away to walk. He is new to this city of glory and greats but his habits haven't changed. In the previous city, he used to go walking and he hasn't overturned his lifestyle.

At a late age, you do get troubles due to less sight, and body not moving but he has been shifted to this city where a lot of people have become famous. Upendera used to have a son who was a sharpshooter and had met his faith with his deadly skill. He was once trying to get the best shot but his gun backfired and he has simply died. This led to the old man getting weak from the inside and broken. Upendera used to work in a government place and had been at a very high rank. Some say that his son's soul goes with him as the ghost of it is still on his face with cruel emotions as he saw his son lying on the floor last time who was no more.

It was still too dark but he carried on to his vigil. He can hear the voice of an owl in the far distance, the shout of a few cats, or it may be some sort of illusion coming through to his ears. His pale face can be seen and it started to fade as pink dawn appeared showing him in the light of a man. His wife doesn't dare to talk with him when he awakens so he keeps walking alone with no fear in the shadows trying to find more about the place.

It is not safe sir, a quiet voice came from the shadows. Two men had come suddenly, their hands raised with guns loaded in their belts. Who are you to tell me it's safe or not? I can find my place fine, the old man taunted them quietly. The voice was so sharp despite being quiet, that it gave both of them certain chills. We are sorry, we shouldn't disturb your vigil. you may carry on, With gestures of hands on a new person to each other, they turned away not asking a single question further to him as they can feel it can become a sign of trouble.

Intruders always like to find secrets of life, the old man whispered to nature. It was suddenly very quiet. To his dismay, a figure bloomed out from the shadows this time. He cackled in the same way but had a skull in its white hand. Who are you to me now? the old man used that ethereal voice again. I like fresh meals, you are not my target as it is my sleeping time now, the man with the skull whispered to him with his bloody teeth shown wide and fierce, This night is over so I am going back, I will come to see more hunting options being on motion soon, he spoke and has gone away from were it came.

It would have surely been horrible to any other person, but to Upendera, it was just like facing a rival, someone who wanted to challenge his reign. He smiled at the words spoken to him as there was a sound of taps of his stick close to his house. By the smell of it, his wife has woken up and is surely in the kitchen. she must be preparing his morning potion which excites him the most. Hoping to have a hot liquid soon to his throat, he slowly climbed the stairs and he was soon inside the dining table of this place handed as a government quarter to him and his remaining family to live a peaceful life.

There was a sound of a few coffs, children yawning as still in sleep and all looked quiet here. It could hardly be any kind of disturbance, but there is a certain whisper in the air. While the old family grappled with their life, a cry could be heard from far across. It came from the place where Upendera had gone for a walk and had faced the white figure. He had guessed by the sight of policemen that something may have been fishy. He told his niece not to go and stayed in her bed as she yawned. The place has a lot of secrets and somehow Upendera doesn't want anything to happen to certain children in his company right now.

A few of the cops surrounded a family who was crying. their only kid had gone missing and hadn't come home for 3 days. After a lot of investigation, the night guards found him dead last night in the forest. As they had to face Upendera while they were trying to bring back the body, they decided to do it later after his counter word to them. Now early morning around 7, they brought the dead body which was slashed by a monster. Half of the face was crunched, one of the eyeballs was not in the socket and it was absolute outrage in the form of a death.

As the cops tried to explain they tried their best, a few nods made them lower their voices. The parents received the body folded in rags, took back the FIR with their signature to affirm it and the cops were gone as more cries could be heard becoming louder in the area which is mostly known to be peaceful and welcoming to others. Death has changed the mood totally and the air has gone quiet for a while.

NO morning strolls for you, sorry dear, Upendera's wife spoke back at their quarters strongly. The niece had a habit to poke or find out what happened to others. Ever since they came to this city, there has not been much to do for her as she is a photographer but has been restricted to close quarters. I want to see what may be so interesting. it will help to make a cover-up, she spoke in half yawn with her hair everywhere. She stood up, finally folded them, and looked for a new story . No, not yet. It is time you get ready for your workshop. The clock is almost striking 10 her aunt reminded her and she jumped holding a half toast in her hand but then had settled back to her chair.

No word from Digvijay, is there? Her uncle came in,

sitting on the old chair and munching a toast to himself. If you like, it shall be good to go back home after the workshop dear, he raised a sugar-wrapped finger towards the niece who shook her head. I want a jungle trip, in your company, she added, shaking her head in denial. The old man sighed, rolled his sleeves off his shirt, and started to enjoy porridge and bread. There were only three people seated, but this home was filled with more people as shouts started to come from lower rooms where the rest of the members lived.

I may quiet them, the niece stood up in calm excitement. I have told a few of them to take them to the zoo but couldn't, so they are getting angry. She started to step down at a fast speed with half-finished toast still in her hands. Two of the younger brothers stopped her, took the bread, and started to run away. She called them back so one of them got tripped but had a rye smile on his face with a tear in his eye. Let's come upstairs, call all of them, she said and the both boys turned back to their place.

We will share the horror story, the first one whispered as all 5 of them started to climb the stairs. It was not a story, it happened Vidyut, the younger sister said with terror on her face recalling it. Have it our way, we are not going to face a red tongued, great-headed monster, do we? few of them laughed at the description as Aisha flushed as her face to face encounter was being slammed to a fairy tale by her brave brothers. Come quick, the aunt told them, stopping their conversation in the middle and they got assembled round the table looking hungry and unslept.

What did you say to Aisha? The eldest niece has come back. Any stories you wanted to speak of right now Dushyant? he shook his head eating his potato fritter. I am not in the mood to talk, let me fill in, Vidyut gestured with his fritter in his hand. It's always ghosts, shadows, wolves, or vampires if you get beyond it, the eldest smirked wondering what they had got for her this time as she admired them for being fit for her photo magazine with the glory of it. What did you say? A Vampire, how does it look like, Aisha stopped him before he could say a word but watched him sip coffee, she had to raise her hand too so she could get it hot being earnest.

A red tongue creature. it has thorns coming out, she claims it was approaching to attack it, the eldest got more concerned but excited. I wonder where it came from? Maybe shadows, isn't it? they all had glazed look on such words. Vidyut has finished his potato fritter and is now munching the toast. I wish vampires also like bloody fritters, don't they? Good for your front cover, a decent design would do, it made the eldest laugh. She checked her watch and started to get ready, leaving them to have fun. It was time for her workshop and as they knew, it was no good to stop her so the children let her go and started to pull each other's legs for the happiness of the moment.

This is not good for all of you. She is the youngest. You better not make her frightened by pulling your face or wagging your tongue, Abhi and Vidyut stopped as they heard the voice. Their only fear was the great uncle and as he entered Aisha got settled with more calm on her face. These were sons of Upendera's younger brother Mahendra who was abroad due to which the children liked to stay here. They lost their mother due to cancer last year after which Upendera's wife decided to take them here as they needed a family and this was a perfect option. All of them live happily and the children have been admitted to local schools for their bright future.

Be hurry Vidyut, we don't want to be late in the evening, the aunt said loudly as all of them started to run down seeing their uncle in front. I will make a cartoon based on the fear you face, Abhi said as they reached the bottom stair and there was still a lot of laughter on their faces. You see, I can bring a real dummy of the vampire you know,

Dushyant added as they turned the doors and Aisha ran away from them looking for her school dress and she felt disgusted at her brother's jokes.

It was a sunny day with no white figure being cut loose. The night guards were sleeping and they woke up when a suddenly strong-looking man hit one of them on the back. NO sight of the ghost. You idiot, one more failure, it has again cheated us, he scowled looking very ominous with his broad face and open shoulders with a prominent moustache. The crime has gone to its height, you know. You both can be sacked if we don't catch the right person soon, there was a kind of pain spread through his face. We are not able to trace him, they both showed equal disgust with their faces low in profile. There is also an old man roaming around early in the morning . What can we do boss, there is no direct evidence for it. It was all going the wrong way.

they got one more thump on the back for complaining as they stood to have their afternoon iced tea to get fresh for the night coming ahead. We can't wait for the darkest hour. it is the worst day, they started talking. Are you sure it is more prominent on the new moon night with the best shape to absorb? they nodded, gulping the remaining ice tea so fast that made the boss worried. Those who have seen it say that it's more powerful that evening, we don't have any clues though, there was a strained-looking expression on their face as they said. Let's get back to planning how we can catch it. no intruders today or they will die too, they punched their fists in anxiety.

Back at home, Upendera was talking to his wife. Sweet girl, she had gone on to her mother, his smile started to stay dim as he spoke. I presume we should solve the matter before she starts to fall in Devasha's footsteps, what do you say to it? she nodded. The children's mother also used to have visions when she felt possessed by the devil's vision and then she started to get ill. Upendera's wife agreed, thinking about what could be the best way to solve it.

A bell rang and their niece appeared on the top stair before they could answer it looking unhappy. No perfect session always bore front angles as I don't know them, she expressed her disgust in the workshop. I am going camping uncle, please don't say no? she put a hand on his shoulder so he couldn't deny and he slowly put his head down. she went inside to wash her hands and saw her face in a mirror in front which made her worried. Her bones were strangely sticking onto her cheeks, for a moment she couldn't realise why she had gone so thin, but ignoring it she went back and started to gulp her juice to calm herself before going to the campfire with her friends.

She was meeting with them after a long while as she only came here for photography workshops. She is simply niece to Upendera but she belongs to his wife's family. She is the daughter of his wife's younger sister who is a lawyer by profession and comes by the name of Upama. It looks like that her daughter is fond of nature or scenes so whenever a new quarter is provided to her uncle she decides to go or find workshops happening there and call old friends to camp to have an excuse so she can visit their home.

Call me Nass, she mostly tells her friends as her name is Nastika but she likes her short name to be her favourite as she doesn't understand what this name exactly suggests. We will soon have fun, but don't be late or we can be caught by strange figures, she would be heard talking as they all found her walking around them with her camera and finger pointing at the lens. A new one, good for you, a few of her friends whooped but she gestured to them to turn and they were all ready to go boom and make noise with the party.

They were heading to the same place where the dead body had been found last night. Little did they know that the wood and bones they were using did belong to a death that happened here. a whisper came as evening drew closer making Nass getting chilling with its sensation. She burnt a few logs but when it couldn't overshadow the voice, she decided to pack up. From the light of the fire, they saw a masked face, with one eye open and tongue lashing as it caught her camera making her shiver with fear. they all covered the leader as the voice became loud and it made them run with their hands on their head to save each other.

Smoke filled from somewhere and it made a few of them cough but Nastika survived the attack. She found the lights of the local police vehicle coming closer as they shouted at them and they retreated with 1 of their members missing amongst them. NO chance, we can't help it, the boys said hoarsely, By now he could have killed him. The best chance is to bring his body back the next day, help please, one of them threw an ID proof towards the driver of the police and he simply understood. Don't worry, we will find him, a few voices spoke from inside and Nasthika had a horrible evening never to forget in these dense woods.

She stepped on not so fast as she had done in the early evening asking permission but thought not to go to the top floor. Upendera could see her from the lower window but he kept walking on to his room without a word. I am sorry uncle, I couldn't take your word or how serious it was, she whispered to herself and collapsed into a sofa chair. Aisha slowly came to her as she could feel what may have happened and offered a glass of water from nowhere to make her feel better. It was a perfect way to calm her nerves as both females understood each other and comforted themselves with words so they wouldn't have to face the fear again that was so sudden in nature.

Good bloke, that driver was, she said to her aunt at the dinner table. We could have died if they didn't come at the right time, she was feeling sad because the news spread on how the police were not accurate. You sure it was a ghost?

it could have been a person planning the trap, an old enemy? Nasthika shook her head and brought the camera from her bag lying on the other side of the table to show something. She opened the lens and smoke came making all of them shriek. Burnt. I surely took the image of it, she sounded worried, the aunt tapped on her shoulder asking her to dine out and then sleep so she could feel better as her uncle didn't bother to ask any further questions.

Everything was quiet as the children were sleeping, and then a movement took place close to the window. A strange sound came disturbing the night as the lamp went out. No one moved as they didn't wish to face the fear of the deadly night. It smelt the air like trying to withdraw the pain or uneasiness but then it realised the mood was quiet so it simply left the place with no further damage to anyone. The alarm clock rang again as the night reached close to dawn. Upendera took his walking stick, wrapped it in a muffler, and went out as all were silently sleeping.

It was very still with a little bit of breeze wafting outside. No one was going to disturb him today, not even those ruddy guards, but would they? A voice was coming from the place where he had faced them the previous day. Someone was crying, it was visible with light as a hand could only be seen with a diamond wristwatch in it. Looks like these ghost-like jewels to collect and Upendera spits on the place turning away from there wondering what else he may find if he continues his walk in the jungle going deeper in it.

He took a few steps backward and heard the crying get louder. He had no wish or intention to find all the mess. Cries always bring him back the memory, the pain of his son on the floor, and all that followed the night. No one understood his sorrow that day so why should he bother to feel pity for these unknown bodies on the floor? He tapped more vigorously on his stick, somehow managed to push his mind away from the past, and turned back. It was somehow a prickling emotion he had, the day when his son missed his skill and died with a cruel response. It is unbearable, something he may never forget in his life.

One more death. This time it's one of us, the remaining guard said to himself. No more answers. what may happen in these woods? he punched his fist onto his belt and fired in the dawn to summon the jeep. NO movement took place except a strange wind blowing across his face. He turned to feel that a cut had appeared on his right cheek. thinking it was the night's mischief, he started to turn away. He checked for his gun and started to count as he had fired only 1 shot. All of the bullets were missing so he released a smoking bomb from his inner pocket, let the air fill with smoke, and ran as fast as he could from the place.

What's this? Not a hint on how he died there? the pompous man said, watching him on tiptoes. It is happening daily now. we need to ensure who is behind it, he looked with a benign smile as he looked at the man's face closely. He took out a cotton pouch from his inner pocket and dabbed on his cheek politely. I am sorry at least you have survived. Now put this ointment, your wound will get better, he looked bemused as the cut was somehow familiar to him. Most of the persons who have died had to face this jungle crunch. He was concerned now, wondering how to solve the problem of the ghost that is absolutely hungry

The laughter was again coming from the lower rooms of the government quarters. Upedra's family was having pure joy as children were now frightening Nasthika on her adventures in the jungles. Shut up, not a word. Did you feel how it was last night, we are lucky to survive, Aisha intervened trying to speak but the eldest stopped her from doing so. Fear will be tackled with light, they all spoke together at the food table and it was somehow looking calmer now due to the happiness they all were sharing.

Are you going this Sunday then? Vidyut asked with a longing to the eldest. I may wonder why go so early? as he was reminded by their aunt that she has already been here for 1 week and it is time to go back home. We will certainly miss the fun and miseries too, Aisha stood up, taking the bread piece from Nasthika and munching it. You didn't take us to the zoo, what about that? the other boys asked with more longing as she shook her head in dismay. It was time to get relief, to find what she could do for the person missing, but the fact is that she did not even know who was dead from their gang with true honesty.

She is not sure whether to go or to stay but thoughts prickle and disturb her so she is not able to decide yet as the group circled her. This is not fair, we want to go to the zoo, her one look made all of them quiet but she promised to take them to visit the place as she finally came to decide to stay one more day here at her uncle's place. His prominence may help them to somehow tackle the fear and she had total belief in his strength.

It may be a fear to see, but the trouble has been avoided for the time being. The evening was cool as the family members were seated together eating their favourite fruits. nobody knew how that fear had spread around and how long it may stay. One thing was sure, Nasthika was certain to recognize the moment and she would soon be gone from here to find out more about it. Her promise to take the other cousins to the zoo came to her word the next day with no trouble to face at night. They all were laughing as Vidyut mimicked a monkey, Abhi reminded Aisha of the coils of a snake and they were cheering on a giraffe to jump inside a cage.

Back home they had a few rides, the eldest spent some money to buy sweaters and it was all over when the bell rang and the door was opened by their aunt with a gesture of welcome. She was leaving early in the morning the next day from here and she is going to miss it all, including the company of younger ones. They forced her to play Antakshari with them, tricked her into singing the false word in the night, and with a lot of snide remarks on it, they all went to sleep as she packed her bag and dawn circled around. The chirrups of the birds meant the time had come with a blissful morning to face and be part of it.

She had a hot water shower to get fresh, lifted her things to be thrown inside her trolley bag in a hurry and it was time to go to her place. Before any of the children could say anything as they were sleeping, the horn of the car sounded in the courtyard, and Nastika was gone. A sigh of relief could be heard from upstairs as she had taken away all the horror along with the glamour connected with her.

Everything was quiet now, at least for some time before the ghost returned and turned it all over with its fierce white glow towering upon all of them strongly. A smile became visible on Upendera's face as he finished his lunch and saw his wife going down to pass the children for lunch as it was a holiday. They all were still together and hardly anything was going to change as these young ones were under them so they had to care for them or try their best to make them happy.

2
HAUNTED VALLEY

It was very cold, the wind was fluttering strangely as people were trying to go back home. They say this place is haunted or belongs to some strange spirits who haunt the road at night. it is better to leave this place before they come or anyone who stays back becomes the toast of their night party as they swoop hungrily on human flesh. The way they do may give in to a creature, but they are not living sight as their bones stick out or the popping of eyes could tell how they are truly such cynic ghosts disturbing others.

This place welcomes people with a great turning spot every afternoon, but as the shadows lengthen, the fear starts to speak for itself. The young lad who fell from the roof last summer and died can tell how critical it is to stay here at night. Morally, a lawyer was able to prove one of his female friends guilty, but when she was also found hanging from the same roof with a strange expression on her face there were no answers. The place has some hidden secrets which belong to a charming figure who holds the key.

The authorities have cleared the place with no apartments except one towering tourist villa so it has been turned into a deep valley after breaking off such places for stay. It is a kind of place that is welcoming but has its fears to accompany it. Simply, people don't want to stay here but the natural beauty of the area is enough to invite them from all outdoors. It drives people forward to come here to reside in it and be part of the eventual delights with some risk if involved in its backdrop. Cases do come regularly but police are not as strict in dealing with them and let things happen accompanied by ghosts.

Call me Nass. this way, don't go to the left, a shriek

sounded as two young girls tripped in their roots and fell into a valley so deep they somehow wouldn't survive. I am so sorry, it's not my fault. I told them not to go wandering off at night. , she called the police to investigate smirking to herself in a calm way. One more good coverage for my magazine, isn't it? Her face was white at night with few lines but nobody noticed it. A quick glance on anybody being present or not and she walked inside her place to comfort her problems looking a bit confused.

A fire was burning in a mental furnace. she took some ash in her hands to make it more intent as she pushed the sleeve from the arms to get a better feel of it. It was much more terrible to practise dark arts being the affected soul, but she was one of those who believed in its strength. The reason her face has become so pale is the fact that she has been indeed using it constantly either for defence or directly attacking her opponents. No one knows of her secret, or why she does that but she may have control of dark spirits or may summon them for her pleasure allowing them to possess, kill, or even crush others brutally with their force.

There was a knock on her door as one of her teammates for the next trip tried to come inside. She covered the fire inside her cabin, put the ashtray in the corner, closed the lid, and put on her jacket. What's the matter? she asked, looking into the other girl's face with intent and worry. |Anything I can help you with? she shook her head and asked to come with her. With some daring to face the unknown, nass stood up, opened the door, and started to follow in her wake.

I heard their voices, I don't know how but it has been happening for the last hour or so, the girl whispered finally as they came across to the point from where the 2 girls had fallen and died. It is not bothering but it is like they are whispering to help andI am sure they can't do it, the girl looked seriously worried on the subject. An echo! It happens at this height, doesn't it? Nass tried to pinched her onto the shoulder, taking her back towards the entrance. Now, you get some sleep, we have to go on the next day for camping for thrills, the girl agreed to her but reluctantly and nass let her go inside the tent to help her feel the presence of true warmth.

The next morning was truly cool. All the friends have recovered from the incident they faced. A few jokes were happening in the crushes of girls and Nastika quietly slipped amongst them without anyone noticing her. She found some of them were still unnerved so she stuck the right cords to her advantage. This way, please, she said calmly, We don't want any other tragedies, just follow me, ok? they all nodded and tried to walk in a straight line. they could see the cliff above with its twisting path but no one dared to climb it except the girl Nass had met last night who quietly started to step upwards

Off we go, shall we? she encouraged others in her following steps. One by one please, don't make a group busy, they could hear the voice as they started to go towards the towering target standing so tall. Few of them were soon out of breath. Suddenly they stopped in the shadows from where a dark figure bloomed powerfully. It has white teeth and is completely made of smoke. For a moment it made everyone scared, but then they realised it was smoke billowing from a chimney which was enough to take their chills away in the tough climb.

They thanked the god and kept climbing with sweat pouring hard till the girl on lead reached a turning fork and Nass commanded everyone to stop opening a can of water with disposals in her hands. She could see a few of them also had water bottles which made her calm as she was thinking whether the water would be enough for them or not. After getting fresh, they collected the disposals and wrapped them in polythene safely kept by Nass in her bag. She took her whistle out and asked everyone to turn around carefully.

Finally, they were in sight of a place as the sun was also climbing upwards in the later afternoon.

A song was coming from somewhere with voices of water falling in a soft but supple stream. Everyone admired the beauty as they tried to go closer. No, not allowed. I can't take any risks for you, Nass stopped before they could step down in rock pebbles to feel the water. They understood why she had said 'no' very soon as the stream turned into a waterfall and it gurgled past a few feet as they survived somehow from its natural might. They thanked the leader who laughed and started to click on the waterfall. For a moment she saw a diamond-like shape coming in its fork that made her fear but then it was gone. They were all enjoying the sudden arrival of this point in their trek.

what's there? It looks like a rock broken in some past or is it a tomb? one of the boys asked the leader. Her eyes were still closer to the beautiful scene folding around. Don't touch it, there may be some dark power with it, she spoke from a distance without turning her head. the person touched it with his foot and it made him cough hard. He was a bit curious but it suddenly brought a dark cloud into the sky making them all worried about what might be coming further.

There was a burst of dust close to the rock and a ghastly figure came from the earth. It demanded to get his treasure back to which nobody had any idea. In response, Nass has thrown a burst of flame which she has just illuminated from her lighter. She threw it towards the blueish white figure and it went back into the rock. Everybody watched her with admiration but it was not good. More such copies of the figure were coming so she gestured to them to pack or be ready for the strike for the hidden fear of the rock.

One of the boys reached for pebbles affected by water and threw it towards the copies as all of the sand covered them so they were sent back to their resting place due to the effect. The girl in the lead was looking pale as she watched from the backyard with all such events folding in front of their way in fear and elation. All of them were told to step back so things could be cleared and Nass did it on her own so they could return to their place safely.

We are not going trekking. It may prove risky, she ordered in a silent but strong leading voice. Follow me, everyone, in the path where I show the burning of my lighter's tip, she ordered them to go with her so no spirits may affect them. She kept talking to a person on the phone as they followed her up towards the cliff. They finally got a view of a road, a small bus standing there and passed in Nass's hands as she told them about conditional service. You can pay for the ticket for me later, understood? For now, safety is more potent, she asked them to be seated and they all felt relieved but shivering due to what just happened in front of their eyes.

What exactly was it? Have any of you seen the faces of the copies? a few of them shook their heads as Nas asked about them after reaching the spot. Due to a heavy climb, action in them, and a typical hilly bus ride, all of them were seriously tired. She collected the payment of 50 Rs from each which was not much but it was enough for the bus ride as a local charge. It was good for her smoking habit to suit as her cigarettes were not expensive. She keeps this secret hidden even from her strongest uncle who may be wandering back home about her. She simply saved the money collected in her pocket and left for her fire routine.

Inside her room, she opened her camera which once smoked harshly. It was good that she shared files in her cloud this time as she didn't want to miss out on the fun of the waterfall and diamond shapes in it. They looked familiar to her, those that had appeared in front of her while camping a few weeks back at her Uncle's place. She thought to plan a visit but is not in such a mood to do that right now. There is a lot of magazine work left for her as she opened her online platform and saw requests for ghost clowns coming to portrait soon with faces of them laughing.

A knock on the door made her come out of the old thoughts. The same girl was standing there with a bottle in her pale hand. Yes, what can I do for you? Nass replied with gratitude on her face. We have by mistake ordered one extra drink, I would be happy if you accept it as a friendly treat, Nass turned to say no but after seeing the look on her face, she didn't deny it and took her offer. Thanks for your kindness this late, I am more than elated about this, both of them shared smiles and she was gone.

Secret is hidden in the kindest words, she whispered to herself with no one present. Nass knew it may be a trick but to content the girl watching from the back door of the main gate, she lifted the drink and drank it. The girl's shocked expression was visible in the mirror of her back door as she gave her the bottle coming out sharply. It is nothing but water from the stream, she said, finally turning off the lights and gesturing to her to go now. A smile broader than the stranger came to her face as she put all the lights in the area and the unknown girl vanished with total darkness.

An eye for the hidden one, is it? I can handle this, she lifted her hands to see red lines in them. It was not painful but she knew the effect of sand water as she had guessed it right. The girl had been acting pale, while everyone was trying to calm down the fake copies of ghosts, she had been busy collecting them, which meant she also had found the secret of diamonds connected with the mystery of jewels. Let it be, she can't be that daring to face death in search of rare jewels, Nastika said to herself and finally toppled onto her bed deep asleep after enjoying water

A strange dream came to her at night. A girl was holding the torch aloft as it was much brighter than her lighter. She claimed herself to be from a community of ghosts, following Nastika as she went everywhere in her footsteps. One by one she took a few lives, throwing people down, stabbing them with a knife and even throwing her torch to burn a heart. This all changed into a golden light where diamonds were visible and the female ghost wore them onto her one by one. She took them to the remaining members, forced them to wear the diamond necklaces and the female bodies turned into dead, burning their throats. It was so scary that Nastika woke up in sweat and was worried by its glimpse.

The next morning was peaceful again as horns could be heard on the road close by with busy traffic. Nastika looked for a visual focus but she was still worried about what she had seen in a dream. She held herself calm after taking a pot of water and looking at things in shadow as she poured it down a plant outside. When she could see nothing or no sign of anything dizzy, she turned back as a bird flew forcing her to look up with surprise for it. She thought it to be a coincidence and simply went inside with thoughts on what to do today to help the gang.

Morning, May I help with anything? The boy approached her, one who had attacked copies last night. Not much to worry about, we are heading to the top again, aren't we? he inclined his head with his cap bobbling a bit. Let me think of the final schedule. I shall be with all of you in an hour, he nodded and went away leaving trails of his footsteps behind. I guess it is better to close the tour down. I can't afford to face pale girls daily coming in my dream, Nastika whispered to her and went inside to get fresh so she could feel relaxed from last night's vision and the fear accompanying it.

A phone rang and she stood suddenly. It was from her aunt, maybe she was missing her Yes, how are you dear, all fine? she said but not with polite interest to her. You are looking angry, what happened aunt? the niece inclined her head towards the window. Vidyut is playing tricks on others. it's only you he listens to, what should I do to him? Nastika took a sigh and told of her fearsome experiences to her beloved aunt while talking. She promised to come back soon and disconnected the phone in a hurry.

She came out fresh after a hot shower, found her lighter, and started to smoke for a moment. The smoke rose close to her window as she could see it turning into visions of strange faces. For a moment, she tried to have an eye for the pale girl but there was no one. Apart from the sound of water going down through pipes, there was not a single voice. She texted the group to be in the main quarters in half an hour and sat there smoking for a while. After she was done, she checked her bag for coins, filled it with a few napkins and a water bottle, lifted it, and went to face whatever came in front today.

Two members are not ready right now, the owner of the quarters responded to her, Shall call them here or do you want to go inside? Nastika shook her head showing that she had the pass but she wanted them outside for a better plan. The owner called and all of the people who were staying had come out including the girl and her two helping cronies. Let's go to a new place today, shall we? a few of them demanded, to which Nastika agreed, checking for the local mapping they had done for the tour.

Who amongst you is brave to lead me to the tunnel caves? Let me be honest, there are wild creatures there too. any chance of daring to go there? The leader checked for the map locating the tunnel root. We are on for it. Just let us know the plan, will you? they whispered not shouting but in a plain and crisp voice. The leader handed them a cave map showing the entry and exits to the place mentioned with red dots. Be careful, I don't want any of you to be missing in this, she said firmly, holding her map and checking the watch on her wrist.

Any Pearle vision we can expect? the boy in front asked as they marched away from the quarters. Nastika smiled with thoughts firmly on her magazine. Oh yes, I said there are wild creatures. People have been killed. They say spirits roam at night making people get confused and get lost in the tunnel, a chill spread through them but the pale girl was not affected by it. they all were starting to laugh at another night prank as Nastika could understand and kept marching close to the tunnel with excitement of what lies ahead.

This is the beginning. Like I say, stick to the map. One wrong move and you are done, it made all of them a bit frightened by such words. Are you willing to take the challenge or do you have the option to back away, no one moved so Nastika bent low, and pressed a hanging cave stone and with the sound of a roar, the gate opened making all of them more worried. Let's go, we are in for a treat or become its part, she said, stretching her hands towards the entry with her lighter pointed in her upper pocket and gleaming. They all followed her for a while and then turned to choose their direction.

For a moment it was quiet, no voice was vocal except the hussle of boots or twirl of a jacket, but then voices started to come. It was like night inside, bats were swooping from all sides, and few torch-like eyes. Nastika knew the way so she could walk very easily. However, at some point, she heard a shriek on foot falling onto a pit or even a hoarse voice of someone. She knew what this cave looked like and walked without being disturbed. This was not the same for others, few of them were facing challenges to hold the map straight. One of the girls had her right leg tangled in a bush and she was in pain. It was no good as it was like absolute dark and they had to find their way through.

A hand appeared, it was a wisp of smoke like a glove dipped in a water tub and white. the girl tried to move away but it clasped onto her throat pressing it tight. Nastika had felt it so she had come before it could happen right here. She burnt a cigarette and dropped it onto the floor with purpose. the hand withdrew looking disturbed but not shaken by light. It was a fire that forced it to withdraw and it has gone back as with the help of two boys Nastika pushed the girl back. She calmed her and then went back to the way from where she had turned to them in an outer stone way.

Nasty plots. these demons are everywhere, she stopped whispering as one more noise came. It was a trap, maybe, or a real one. Nastika touched her pocket but this time she didn't bother. it was a kind of foul play as those who trap create such voices to remind you what happened here recently. She has found a creature facing her as she turns the next corner. A giant river slug was belching on a frog but as soon as it saw a human, its tentacle started to open trying to catch her. The fire did drag the slug back and it withdrew just like the hand before.

The next concern was not so good as she heard the voices of two people arguing loudly. It was the two boys who were thinking of tracking the leader. They were stuck and were making noise that would surely wake the reptiles. There was a whisper of 'hea' from behind one of them. A sudden crunch sounded and the 1st boy felt his throat broken by a strange creature they had seen never before in life. It let the other boy run to survive as Nastika tried to find the source of the noise. The spirits whispered from the shadows, One for the night, we are thankful. It left her feeling disgusted and deep chills sending in her heart but she had to continue the walk.

Few of the group members were easily seen, they have survived the challenge. Nastika came to the exit point but the stone connected to it was moving. She wondered for a while why it was happening but then she had that vision. It was rumoured that the exit forces you to see the worst dream. The ghostess's face appeared in front of Nastika, lifting the light, diamonds in her throat and for a moment she was going to shout. A hand came this time helping her, she put her foot on the stone and she came out safely and in perfect spirit. She turned back, laughed at what she just saw, and started to count the members present in the group.

A few of them were in tears as they knew one of their best friends had gone. The boy who was called Marud has been well known to help them. He was the one who would serve the drink, and bring breakfast to their rooms and he has served well. There were few pensive faces in the group, some were wiping their eyes and the leader understood how big a shock it was. It was strange that tough trips take your test and if you fail to perform well, there is no chance of going back from it despite your best efforts.

We have lost one more, the pale girl said, this time she was in real pain. If you hadn't been there, I would have died too, the girl Nastika, protected from the watery hand, spoke in some calm. Let's get back to the main road. We need to recover from this and the loss we had, Nastika obliged all of them. Their boots were not making much noise as the excitement had gone. They have lost one more friend and no investigation is possible here in this tunnel. They would surely go home with a lot of sadness to accompany this tour and the shocks it brought.

They all gathered outside the quarters where they had stayed most of the tour with laughter and pain. It was not looking well even in the sky as it was going to rain hard. I shall come with you at least till the mountainside of it stays as a force, Nastika said firmly before anyone could comment. They didn't have much to say but the group photo session went on for a few minutes. A boy called Pranay stepped in front handing them lemon and orange juices depending on who wanted the variety. Nastika took an orange one with extra pepper salt and started to suck in the straw. She was quick to finish as few of them were taking photos as their last moment here. There was no chance of them coming back, it had been a lot to spend or sacrifice and the leader knew it too.

It was nice to have your help boss, the main team member shook hands with her. With the loss we have, I can't say whether we can come next time or not. I express sincere gratitude for all the efforts you did for us, he paid her for arranging all the outdoor camps including safety coverage for them. Nastika smiled, holding the empty glass in one hand and the bundle of notes in the other. She didn't say a word except Coming as they waited for her. She paid for the stay at the counter as she felt they might have paid less, saved the rest in her pocket, and came out.

We are going, here is the vehicle, she gestured to them to sit first. When all of them had seated, the front seat was left which she occupied telling the driver that she was coming for a ride around the corner just where the waterfall ends. The gang hasn't been able to cover it due to the shadows of the trek, but they are now going to enjoy watching it as a beautiful scene. You can take a photo now, Nastika told the pale girl who finally said, Glad to have your help, I am Mritanjali, It made Nastika shiver, the name sounded loud in her ears but she couldn't do much for it now. The vehicle stopped where a waterfall was falling into a river and she stepped out saying all of them goodbye simply.

Mritanjali was her classmate, 4 years before while guiding a trip alongside her, the best friend had fallen from the top of a cliff where despite her own life being at risk Nastika couldn't protect her. Nobody knew whether she was alive or a ghostess. She was the reason why Nastika saw the vision in the night. It frightened her as she stood waiting for a local taxi to come and pick her up. After 15 minutes of chattering in their teeth as she recalled the pale girl with the same hairstyle and dominating emotions to accept what she offered, Nastika got into a taxi and went back home as thoughts kept disturbing her with strange emotions.

Why you had to come back, now? she spoke to herself, lighting a cigarette with its puff flying up. She could feel that sad emotion, the hopelessness of not being able to help, and all that had gone through while a few members died on this trip. it was very true of her to take to the spot where 2 girls fell from height as she had the experience. The pain was certain and even when she wanted Nastika to sleep, there was something like a pinch of disgust, like she wanted to make her feel how much it costs when a person dies, which was certain in human nature.

I am not going to forget you. Neither as a person nor as a ghost, she whispered to no one in particular as the lights outside started to dim. There was no fear in the leader's heart for the group. It may be tough to recall but somehow the rest of them will survive. She called the police to trace if anybody or a human corpse was deduced from the cave, which they reluctantly agreed to. They have sent her post-mortem reports of both the girls who died which she sent to the main touring party just as a consolation for visiting here. it was not looking good there, all this mess and people dying, there's a certain connection but she wants to find it by herself and solve it.

The night proved more fierce than the evening as Mritanjali's face was still swirling in her mind. One more dream appeared where she was holding hands with her childhood friends. All of them were laughing except a pale girl. It turned into a bit of an older reflection. They were standing close to the tree where they had first punched the foreign student for sneaking into an old shop owner and threatening him. It became more dark and Nastika woke up with a dream ending in the fall of her best friend from height with a loud shout unheard to anyone inside her mind like a deep tunnel.

She looked for some water and found the same pot filled with it to calm her nerves. It was not looking good so she thought to go back to her uncle where it was more safe and comforting. She picked up her phone and saw three missed calls from her aunt. A message was also popping up with a request from Vidyut to come back as it was getting weird. She thought all things into contention and quietly started to find her things to fill in the bag and ready to go.

She looked at the clock ticking as it had just struck 8. She called for her mother who had been busy outdoor watering the plants. Hearing she had woken up, the mother turned inside, and in 15 minutes Nastika was holding a hot glass of coffee with bread to comfort her mood. . I want to go back to uncle, the dreams are becoming nastier, she told her mother without any personal talk. Yes, I noticed you have been concerned with them, a sharp reply came like Nastika was not well greeted with her thoughts. His father has not been home for 1 month and the mother is still worried about what may have happened to him. I am going, maybe for 1 week, the daughter said firmly and she agreed with no other choice left

She got fresh, texted Vidyut with a smile, See you soon, and checked for money remaining after she handed some notes to her mother who took them smiling like it was gold and Nastikaa was gone from the place. She was going back to camping, to find her friends and probably to save the day for herself against the ruddy ghosts who couldn't leave her alone at night. They kept disturbing her for the last few days, laughing, sneering, and trying to get closer to her from the shadows like they wanted to destroy her hopes.

She wants to calm herself with some emotional treat, to find peace or a place that can refresh her mood. She is now missing all the moments she spent last week with her siblings and the way they all made her happy. She has to check out for a workshop to happen but nothing popped up in her timeline to excite as a funny moment to accompany. She just needs an excuse to be amongst those younger ones and she can't wait to have the fun or creative moments on ghosts, tales, and fears surrounding them to get the best joy possible together as a group.

3

WHISPERS OF THE WOODS

It was a cool breeze at the corner of the woods. Upendera didn't come to know there existed a lake but now after a few vigils a bit late in the morning, he has finally located it. This was the place that was made in honour of a famous social activist. They say his ghost takes care of the place and protects it from outsiders. Upendera did have a strange feeling to come when he crossed the site like someone was pressing him forward. It was not frightening or causing trouble, but a kind of stint that works with the heart making him feel relaxed with its presence.

Surely, who wouldn't like to come here? I realise why those ghosts stop others from coming, he took a long breath watching his reflection shining in the backdrop of water. He clasped his hands in a salute, picked his stick back, and started to turn. Wait, you can't go just like this, a voice intervened. He turned to see an ancient power illuminated in reflected waters. Those who are brave enough to come here are honoured by me, a flash of light appeared in the sky and a small diamond coin fell which Upendera clasped in his open palm. Keep it safe, not a word to anyone or you can regret it, the great soul said to him.

I will keep your word, don't worry, Upendera promised as the water started to gurgle in the background of his voice as he spoke. It is so calm here, You won't mind if I come to have a good time here in the future? a sudden rush spread over the voice as Upendera tried to talk it over. I don't talk much to humans, but it's fine if you come I will be pleased to have company, the voice rumbled within the wind blowing hard and water splashing in nature harshly. it was sublime for which the old man thanked and felt closer to nature.

With a wisp of smoke, the power had vanished and Upendera thanked leaving the place as the sun started to bloom outside in the area, marking the reflection and making him smile. For the first time in years, he felt gratified as after his son's death, he had no one to accompany him. He looked at the gleaming coin for a while, then safely tucked it in his neck pouch and started to walk away with it. A vehicle had approached inside the woods as he was passing but he had no fear of anyone. All of them saluted him for crossing the threshold but he didn't care much.

The old man kept walking with a stick, sounding harsh but respectful in the local area as he couldn't find any morning ghosts to encounter. He has arrived home and can smell his potion again with the hope of enjoying it as he hears the sound of utensils being cleaned by his wife. Nastika arrived here last evening due to which children have started to gather for food and entertainment. Again their ghost stories never end but they have respect for their uncle so they don't talk much in front of him. He went in quietly, found his ancient leather bag, and put the coin safely in. It would somehow prove handy, maybe one day when he might have to be in action again.

A bird flew very close to the quarters with a dead mouse in its beak. It happened so fast that Upendera could only see it. For a moment he felt the memory of the day when he first told his son how to shoot intruders where they were tricked by a bird flying past. Now it looks only past where he knows he is not going to come back. the old man looked for a white towards the top glass from where he had seen it but then just tapped his palm on his forehead. It is somehow connected as he can feel but he is not interested in finding out more about it. Searching for ghosts or looking for secrets has gone out ever since he captured the love of his dying son and he is not willing to release it again no matter what happens.

The slow noises were coming from the low rooms as children were running inside it with something to chase upon. Their footsteps can be heard but Upendera had found his moment to keep things together. He pushed the bag away as his wife came handing him the potion to sip. A nice one, he said while drinking it and she smiled. Nastika has no workshop today. I wonder if she should be going for some fun in the area to find more? she shook her head as she had already said no. We don't have trouble unless she wants to create problems for herself. Quite a nasty nature she has when it comes to outdoor activity, they both agreed as he finished his potion.

NO news of her father. Can you be of any help? the wife continued further drinking the potion herself. What can this old man do to comfort the royal people of such high calibre? she laughed as he said this waving his hand You are known at the government for services. can they help search for him without much trouble? Upendera shook his head as most of the time his status was being taken for granted. Sometimes you are bound by a stronger power than human status, he obliged and it was calmer as the sunlight fell onto the upper windows and they opened the curtains wide to greet it as the room got filled with the light all around.

I heard this family talking about me, Am I correct? a sleepy voice came from the next room. Nastika was talking half asleep and had stood now. She turned towards the sink to wash her face. There was not much of a change in her as her hair spread across when she was sleeping and she pulled them up and covered her face. Go to prepare lunch. we are not going to make it for you today, her aunt said but stopped her before she could go to the kitchen to do it. Yes we are talking of you and don't you dare give us a fright with one more nasty tour again, all of them started to laugh at it.

You have grown a bit. I didn't think you were so quick to go to the kitchen in the past with such moves, Upendera recalled the time when his son used to greet all of them with chocolates, present gifts and it looked like ages to him now. Don't worry, he will be blessed and maybe watching, Nastika said when he had come to find the news of her elder brother dying. That time she was not much grown but now she knows the value of him going away. better be off and prepare so the children can have the groove to do a party with us, she tapped her uncle on the shoulders and went inside the washroom to get fresh and feel good afterward in a better mood.

There were a few jitters as the children climbed upstairs. One of them slipped one step so he was watching his ankle with a concern on his face. No twist, it's fine Abhi, Vidyut told him with a smile but also a relaxed expression on his face. It has nothing to do with feet. I was thinking of an idea so I got a slip, he also smiled, tapped him on the back, and climbed the stairs with equal zeal. They all were happy again with hopes of finding more stories stored by the eldest for them with spice of daunting threats.

Come along then, she was watching from the front chair as the open window hinted her to come down. It is looking a bit grim. what happened to all of you? she greeted them with arms splayed open. A bit of a headache, I guess. Aisha is not happy with her notebook too, they all started to complain one by one as they reached upstairs and started to turn their voices into shouts of laughter as they saw her seated quietly. Now it's not going for a while, is it? I insist you stay a few days with us here, Vidyut could be seen jumping up and down bouncing on his feet happily as other children demanded for more food.

After breakfast, the children wanted to have some fun with her, but she told them on a walk she was going alone. they wanted to know about it, but they didn't get any answer to it. Simply she took her camera, checked the lens, and filled it with a new reel to get a good picture for herself.

A chimney could be felt smoking in some portions of the area. She crossed the main quarters and turned towards a more quiet place. There she sat on a stone bench, took out her lighter, and smoked a few cigarettes. She knew it wouldn't be hidden from them for a while but nobody knew for now so she could do it peacefully while sitting here.

A figure burst from the smoke in which she was surrounded as she felt something touch her hand in which she had held the smoking pipe. It transformed into a shape, a glowing burst of fingers, and turned into a silent humanless hand. She knew it may belong to the ghost who she stopped in the cave, but didn't use fire to throw it off. She searched in her pocket for some ash, threw it and the smoke became quiet leaving her alone to enjoy her morning with her lips turning by smoke filling close to her nostrils.

No sign of her. will she dare to come or stay with the groups who arrive to experience the worst? Nastika spoke quietly as there was no one except her. She looked at the backdrop surrounded by trees. One more voice came suddenly as she decided to leave. A soft wind blew across but it couldn't pinch her like it did the guard who had to run off in the past. a decent figure popped out in the breeze quietly and pale as it started to speak. I haven't gone from here, you see, it whispered and the pale girl started to move without any footmarks or noise of her walk. Come, let us have a stroll. You shall be safe with me, she encouraged Nastika and she started to move around with her.

It has been years since we used to walk this place alone. No one was better than us, Mritanjali's ghost spoke in a voice so calm only Nastika could hear it. I know you have the memory of me in this living world, that's why I made you realise who I am, she had the laughter of a ghost across her empty face. You scared me totally with that dagger ghost dream, I know it was your trick. Nastika had a happy expression while listening to the old voice. She checked for her lighter and it was safe inside her pocket. For a moment she thought the ghost was taking her upside down on the cliff, but then she turned, taking a shortcut that would lead to the quarter where Nastika lived with her uncle and aunt. Farewell for now. Will be in your dreams. Take care of the children, you are the eldest, she raised her humanless and spilling hand to say goodbye and she was gone leaving her alone in the mist.

Back at the quarters, children were having fun with TV as they watched horror movies, cartoons, and aliens or tried to pull each other's legs. Look Dushyant, he looks like you with a tummy bulging hard, Aisha said as others rolled with laughter with more noise. Add a few dark eyes to the flying bat it would do for a monster, Vidyut commented before the first boy could answer, making the girl frightened with fury. Don't you say a word, you are afraid of pandas, she countered him as others laughed seeing Vidyut in sudden fear. He has got in the habit of running away even in front of a woolly teddy bear due to which other children bother him.

What's all this noise? Come on, shake hands. show me you are good kids, Nastika entered without anyone noticing her, and she got settled. She had a look towards the TV where an alien was killing a shadow rider ghost. She switched off the TV as it could be frightening and told all of them to sit quietly as she had brought mango juice for all of them. They tried to ask about where she had gone but no one could bring it out. For a moment she felt that Abhi might be trying to look into her inner pocket but she had carefully hidden her lighter upstairs as he could only find a toffee inside. Go on, willing to sneak through like a ghost? She made other young ones laugh with her words.

A shrewd expression came to Abhi's face as she said further: Just make sure you sneak to your level, it's not worth it here, she smiled, handing others the juice and calming him down with a touch onto his head. Let's find more on ghosts, what do they look like? Dushyant said changing the subject as Aisha looked up from her glass worried. No more fight, if you want to know it, Nastika intervened, looking around everyone with hope. I feel you should see the cover of the next edition of my magazine, she showed them a photograph of a few shadow imprints chasing a long cloak figure and it gave them a few chills but it wasn't fearful as it wasn't real.

A message flashed onto her phone and she asked the children to excuse her for a while to cover it. She saw a request for photography of the jungle by a Turing group that made her feel excited. She came down and told them she might get late as it was time to do some outings in the evening. Be careful, there is a fear around with fog, Aisha told her as she turned with her head bowed in the hope that she wouldn't have to encounter any fears coming as she knew it is always associated with tours happening around her.

She came out with her usual travel bag on to her shoulders as a jeep appeared suddenly with a few dashing cops sitting inside. Back up, We have been told to follow the touring gang, the driver spoke from inside with relief too. A car followed the jeep moving as Nasttika could hear a few mantras played in music within the police jeep. She approached the car from which 2 girls came out. Hi, we are Disha and Dasha, twin sisters and fond of hiking.

they both shook hands with one being fair and the other being light in colour when it came to faces. Shall we go for the safari or do we have to wait? The twins asked, leading the car as the jeep followed it with Nastika being seated in the first vehicle moving and the lights were on due to the weather in total fog as they started to turn towards the tough lanes, the conversation began. Is it true or only people mention it? Disha asked Nastika just out of curiosity to calm down her nerves. We shall find out soon by ourselves, won't we? the helper obliged without much interest in those ghost shows people ask to relive while travelling with her.

Please turn right behind the police jeep, we don't want to miss the trail, Nastika gestured to Dasha. She was not familiar with how many other persons were inside the vehicle to accompany them as it was just told to join the group and have fun with them. We shall know others soon, don't worry, Dasha replied as she guessed what was coming. We are a total of 6 members but one of us got infected by the local flu so she is at the hotel. We are still 6 with you included, all 3 females laughed but Nastika kept a close eye on the police jeep. The vehicle in front had stopped and so their car had to. All of them stepped out of the car and started to spread out in the place arranged for them by official ranks.

Here you go with the food services you wanted, a person has come holding a tray of hot soup and fritters. Time to munch, would you like to join Disha? the other twin sang in her strange but familiar voice. Yeah, it shall be good to enjoy them, you too join us, the twins offered soup to Nastika. For a moment she thought it better not to have it but seeing the guard close by she decided to take it and felt warmer. Not so fishy in this. is it? The twins laughed as the boys around them started to play music or pulled each other's legs n who could be more brave to go on without a vehicle to cover the best fun.

You are not allowed. it is not perfect weather, the helper told them in her firm voice. I can assure you all to be brave, but if you go alone, it may be foolish rather than being kind Nastika smiled as the policemen agreed. No more chances to have real fun for us then, the tallest boy shot back but he got quiet as Nastika looked at him. Well played dear, a voice whispered closely to her and she felt Mritanjali's ghost present around. She couldn't see it due to the fog and smoke of the hot meal cooked in the furnace but she knew it was there as a few of them started to get chills due to it.

Let's get back, I am sorry there is not much adventure today, Nastika responded as Disha and Dasha paid for the food. It's good to have a few scenes captured, I was doing that while being in the vehicle, Disha told the boys. They cheered in unison, thanked all the members and the car turned back sharply. The police jeep was still in front but suddenly the car felt a bump, one of its tires got stuck in the pit and it made Nastika worried as lightning flashed in the sky at the same time.

We do have the choice. No issues, Dasha replied, stepping out from the driver's seat as the same was repeated by the driver of the police jeep in front. They managed to replace the tire with some difficulty but in the process, two other boys had to come out too. For some moments they worked quietly but then one of the boys flinched as A creature bit onto his thumb and he scoffed inside whirling in pain and spit. Not much worse, I can fix it, Nastika told him, turning in her seat to offer an ointment and he felt better.

It happened as they were getting started to move again. A white smoke covered everything including both the vehicles. A voice boomed from inside and it spoke crisply, It's not the day or you all have died. I request not to come here again with the full moon coming soon, the smoke filled largely with dust making girls in the front seat cough with disgust. Nastika threw some powder into the air but it was also swirled by the stronger power. . there was a flip and a sudden jerk, and the car got started. Dasha felt frightened but she took her role to drive and they had to take speed with a police jeep rattling over stones and the car following in its wake at top speed.

We are sorry to bother you. it had to happen like you said, Disha remarked as they reached the spot. It's fine with me. I am accustomed to these things in tough life, she received her guide payment and didn't complain about how much she had been affirmed. Will you come again tomorrow? Dasha asked in a polite gesture as both the boys shook hands with gratitude for helping their roommate from that bite. Will See what can be done. Think of something else, the forest is not safe right now, Nastika replied and they nodded to her words in calm.

We shall go to the tourist spot, one that is famous for lovers, shall we do that? Disha asked the police jeep driver who gestured towards Nastika. Yes, this can go well. Your other partner shall also recover by that time, Nastika obliges once more with lights of joy in her eyes. See you the next day, will you be ok to go back home with them? Dasha was eyeing the policemen with a bit of worry as Nastika showed a note to the driver and he let her be seated with word of dropping her home safely and there was no need to be worried.

Knocked on the door around 8 in the night and Upendera went downstairs to answer it, holding on to his stick. Come, I was starting to get worried, he said not in a polite but greeting voice. You should come upstairs first, he asked her to follow in his footsteps and she did quietly with fear of something worse coming soon. There was an envelope resting on the front table. Open it, I have some news, he obliged Nastika to follow the word. After checking it though she found a few photographs in it, they belonged to adventures in caves, and a few of them related to heights. The policemen have sent your adventures, I am not worried but this looks dark, he said nodding to a letter attached with it.

It was from her mother, who is a lawyer and knows how visuals can be used to blackmail. The letter clearly stated to limit the night activities or she would be locked in her home for good and her safety. It explains how her father has already not been home and there is no need to put herself on to such risk. Nastika had a smile as she read it further but seeing her uncle's prominent eyes, she kept it to herself. After reading the letter and scanning the photos for her cloud storage, she went to her room with Upendera's wife following the lead to let her feel better with some juice

You must be protected, she told her, Ever since our son was lost, we can't afford to lose that much, Nastika agreed with flashes of gunshot very clearly coming back in her memory. It seems your mother has got some time for you finally, but regardless we can't let you be in such pain or face tough times, she nodded and didn't say a word as she knew it was coming someday from her mother. It is never easy to hide things you mainly do in life from parents or relatives. This was the moment to bear the truth and simply accept the threats she had to face in such adventures being a tour guide to others and trying to care for them herself while she tries her best.

She has told it to her aunt already in the past but seeing those photos made her look more horrible than it may have taken place. While looking closely at a photo, she can see how closely that slug has turned away just in time. She could see the faces of people after the trip as they were going off and her own whitened face once she waited and carried herself back in the taxi. It was a certain fear that loomed but she wanted to be part of it. her soul does not allow her to go away from the ghost of Mritanjali as she has become part of her journey. Be it trying to survive the threats as a human faces them being bold rests on Nastika's own hands for now as she has to decide it.

The next morning she started to find something in a bag. After waking very early as she knew her uncle would be out, she started to find paper and a pen to write a letter back to. For some time she kept thinking about what to write. Then she started to describe her case, the trouble she was accompanied to, and her defence. As her mother was a lawyer, facts must be sharp and she had to stick with them. She has promised the twins about the ride and she is going and with that, she closed her words ensuring her mother would understand.

After a brief sigh, she attached it to an envelope and printed a positive photo for defence. her aunt was a bit surprised to hear the noise of it coming from her open room. yOu are not that early to rise, are you? she said, poking into her room but there was no reply. The cling sound meant that the photo had been printed and she made sure it didn't come in large sizes which she attached with a letter to her mom. I am going out to send it. When does the office open? I would have done this by email but this is just for print records, she handed it to her aunt so she can help it be delivered for her and went back to her bed feeling better for it.

Upendera has taken longer today as he felt peaceful at the bank of the lake. The wind seems to whisper to him which he likes. it is that someone is telling him the truth of life. He sat there for half an hour without any disturbing noise except the pricking of twigs and whispers in the air. He thanked the good spirit for letting him stay and stood back to turn finally. As a routine, a few guards would salute him while he would return through hard clumps of natural creation while going back home. He is still on his own and doesn't care as he feels that these men are expecting something from him so he ignores them while walking home with pride of connecting with the positive spirit.

You are sure this ride is safe? Nastika was requesting her aunt to let her go for a ride close to Lover's Point. I have been assured. We weren't disturbed or threatened as they also have police cover, she said, getting annoyed by the way she had been stopped frequently. After all I am a grown-up, you think of the younger ones. They are safe here, she finally spluttered in anger with hair all over again. Fine, I won't stop you. But be safe, that's what we expect from you grownups, The aunt slammed back bringing her a piece of toast as she went inside to wash her face to get ready for the trip coming today.

What's all this noise? Haven't I been told not to disturb the charm of morning calm? Upendera has stepped on the top stair without them noticing him coming through. Your niece wants to go out with risks associated usually with her he sighed sitting on the front seat with his wife going in to bring him the potion he cherishes so much. I say let's give her a chance today. If she fails to protect her friends, then we might have to think for her safety in the future, he said with his throat steering due to the hot potion and voice being muffled due to it. The wife shook her head but then turned to see as the niece came out and seated herself next to her uncle.

Now, I must set standards for my ways if the chances are going to be limited here, she said to her uncle. You have the right to your own life but safety is crucial to live it, he replied without looking at her. The noise was coming again but not from downstairs but from the sky above. It is not safe to visit natural places at night. Keep yourself on guard, it was an alarm by officials of the local police to protect others and Nastika's stomach slumped further due to it. Her face had the feeling to bear the fact that she couldn't take risks or roam on her own in the dark.

Her uncle saw her face become more gloomy and took the attached letter from his wife. It's still late morning, I can deliver it, shall I? He checked for the spelling of the address, took it from his wife, and stepped down to walk for a stroll. It may also help him to find out why people are not allowed. After all, he also goes in the dark to have a walk in the morning so he wants to know further. it may be dawn but it comes as part of dark so he strolled away waving his hand with a smile.

It left his niece sitting quietly wondering what it was all about and she realised that her coffee was getting cold so she started to enjoy the food with adventure coming for her in the afternoon. In a few minutes, the children started to come upstairs and they made loud noises when they came to have breakfast. I am not going to school today, one of them would say. Yeah giants may be hidden in that cupboard, I am not going to, and the girl would think to make her excuses. No more complaints, I will put you in the cellar if any of you say no, Nastika stood up forgetting her misery, and started to make all of them laugh.

One game of chess together shall we? Abhi asked, lifting her glass of milk. I will beat you all If I like to, Aisha laughed loudly as he said this. Have a dream, it is sweeter to defeat the eldest in it, all of them cracked with glee at such words. it has certainly been good company, Nastika fears what may happen if she is locked in doors for good. They felt something fishy so Dushyant asked, Any games going in your mind? with his samosa pointing towards Nastika's nose to throw out. She raised her empty hand while sipping coffee from another one and they started to mimic the hand making her smile with shrewd gestures.

It doesn't suit her to be left alone or to go away, she wants to find out more about this world. A place where she belongs with her dreams to chase and she reminded herself to update the social media page of her magazine or it would be late. Vidyut tried to aim a kick at Dushyant but missed and they all continued to stay happy while munching the food and copying each other's hitting techniques.

Put that down, now, the aunt came wanting to take the plate away from all 3 boys. It is not a war to duel with strength, a smile came to her. Dear, your water is getting hot, if you would like to, Nastika stood up taking the plates suddenly from all of them, and handed them to aunt with a smile. She went inside her room, checked for new clothes, and was off to get ready and soon she will be out of sight.

4

A JOURNEY BEYOND THE SHADOWS

A car arrived at the main gate which separates the woods and the outer city. It stopped and two boys stepped outside holding a packet of chips and a cold drink in their hands. Nastika walked slowly towards it as Dasha came out from the driver's seat to greet her. We are going to have fun, don't we? she enquired with her eyes looking excited. NO forest trips, you must have heard too? all 3 inclined their heads on the word as Nastika settled inside the vehicle and gestured to go to the outer world with thrills waiting for them.

It hasn't been easy driving here for Dasha is it? the other twin told Nastika as they swapped chips amongst each other. I have been wondering about the police, it's not there today? The guide asked them and saw Disha raise two fingers in a gesture of their time to join up. They will be there with their safety protocol, Disha said, further wrapping the chips and thinking to throw them from the windowpane simply. Nastika stopped her, took the packet, and put it inside her bag. No waste on the road, it's bad, at least for us, they all smiled.

A quick intro to the place, if you can? the boy who she had helped has spoken up. We are new in this place so it's hard to say which way is right or not, he added looking outside with the scene changing with every turn. Just known for the scenes, what else? It is famous for having a love marriage which was rejected by the family leading the couple to flee and stay there for a week before they were killed, the last words made Dasha lose her grip but she has turned in the right time or they have been done including Nastika who spluttered in her water bottle seeing the turn and the fear it had produced to all.

Careful now, these bends can make you frightened, the guide told them as they had to look out one longer turn. specialty of hills, isn't it? bends and scenes, isn't it? the boys spoke in unison So we can certainly enjoy such a famous point, they stopped as there was a pause and the car stopped to a halt. What's the matter? Nastika witnessed the reason before they could say anything further on why they had to stop the car.

A creature has appeared sitting on the stone with tall legs and an ugly body. it bounced right over the roof of the car and suddenly went out of sight. What the hell, they are everywhere, even in this part of the world? Dasha commented as she saw it pass through and she started the car again to continue the drive further as others laughed on her shrewd expression. Yes, they are amphibians. Can live in all parts of the world without much fuss. Nastika commented as the car kept moving.

Nasty start, wish it could be a better one, they all smiled at these words spoken by a trecker. He was looking tired but wanted to continue. Why don't you come with us? it will be easy, Disha offered as Nastika shook her head at such a drive. NO chance, I am a trecker, I will do it myself. Thanks for your help, all of them smiled as the trecker vanished and they started to move towards the point. The place has changed over a certain time, we used to be only rocks and woods, now it is a decent one with shops in line and few stalls offering hot and cold food items for tourists.

Let's get out, as we are approaching, the twins said and the back doors of the car opened as all 3 boys stepped out to have fun. Nastika followed the twins coming outside and started to check for a jeep. She located it hidden close to a clump of bushes. There you are, we are back to help you, the jeep driver spotted her as her eyes kept whizzing past and all of them were in fresh air once more cheering each other on. The boys walked towards the samosa stall, asked for 3 plates, and stood there as 1 samosa came to all 6 members with 3 plates consisting of 2 in each of them.

Good noise, these tourists come every year? the first boy asked. Not really, it depends on the weather. The rain is not much so it's been a good pack Nastika obliged by throwing her plate in the bin and taking out the chips packet to do the same to clear up. She felt something in her pocket as she did so and her finger naturally turned towards her lighter but she has good control now. Let's have a tour, would you mind doing it? the twins asked the guide and she nodded, coming back to her senses.

All of them slowly turned towards the place from where the smoke was coming. Someone was warming his hands in the fire, and when they explored it came to be the same trecker. It was strange that he had reached this place so fast but Nastika didn't want much to do with him. this is the place I was talking to while we were driving, she let them pass through the large rock and showed the symbol written with it. don't dare to challenge the lover's point. it's the last thing you would do, they smirked understanding the meaning of it and were just thinking of going back not feeling comfortable.

A cold wind approached suddenly, making all of them shiver. It lifted the hair of few, touched past the soft cheeks, and whispered without much strength. Not the time when I am at my best. I really mean the sacrifice, it made them frightened as the voice felt always existed here within the natural strength. The story is quite long, one trip is not enough to know me and my love, come again for delicious words, it rasped making Nastika feel like going for her lighter inside her pocket and burning through but she even couldn't dare to cross the line. It has gone as soon as it has come through which made all of them worried for what else stays here as secret.

This way, we need to get something hot, the jeep driver instructed approaching the gang with the hope that no one could be hurt. They were surprised to see a cut that appeared on his left cheek and the gun on his belt loaded. We may have to leave before they both rise or it won't be easy to survive here, the other cops muttered as Nastika led the gang to a stall that was selling tomato soup. Six cups if you please, she said, raising her purse but her hand was brought down by Disha. It's our duty, let us do that at least when you are here with us, she smiled as Nastika didn't look offended but it did make her surprised to see them recover so quickly from the natural effects of the threat.

The tracker came again but he was not looking tired now. How was it? A whisper from the air? he sneered looking at all of them with some hunger to dine out. Surely, what happened to your nose? Is that broken? a boy commented before he could say a word that made him get the temptation to throw him down but he tried to control it. Not scary, am I? You better hurry before the evening covers everything here, he taunted instead, using his smoke-like hands to clasp the human figures around him.

It's no good to talk with such power or spirits, Nastika stopped the boys from arguing with the element as they were getting heated due to the effect of hotter soup. We better get going. Give me your disposal glasses to throw down. It's now or never for us, She understood the panic of the trecker who was looking truly in joy to taunt them. Be smart or it would not be what it is right now, he laughed at them as the gang turned without much of a word to him as they recognized the threat coming closer in his form.

You are lucky, I don't feast on those who are wise enough not to cross my last rights or the rock where you were standing firmly, he sneered as all of them went away. A few of the tourists were shouting but he didn't care. It's fair to say that if I was not invited to live then why should they? He got hold of two strangers but then released them as he found the soul was not good to be cleared off at such a young age. Get out, all of you, his voice boomed and they all ran towards their vehicle in urgency and panic as Nastika's gang did earlier to avoid him.

It was very close. Lucky you rounded it fast, the police cops followed suit speaking to Nastika. I tried to see why he kept following us from the beginning. get in, no words now, she told the gang to approach the car silently. Where's that pendant you had in your hand? Dasha asked her twin, thinking about something that may have been missing once they were inside. She showed it to be lying on the front safety box of the car and did a thumbs up. Everything has been in control for now as they have escaped the first fear in front of them.

Drive smartly. will you? the police driver told her with eyes thinking about what happened last night. I am aware of the turn a bit more now. Let's hope it goes well, It sounded strange as suddenly nature started to clasp them strongly. it got absolutely quiet, like it was about to snow but it didn't. Instead, raindrops started to lash down on them from all sides as Dasha turned the car around and the police jeep followed them downwards covering it.

Rain was falling thick with cat merlin and howls from the scene that looked beautiful in the afternoon. Due to the cloud and overcast, it was not easy to see and Dasha had brought speed down as they started to go below. It was easier as you didn't have to press on the steering. Suddenly Nastika shouted, Watch out that stone pillar. A slow turn made them safe as they were almost going to fall off once again like they did during the arrival. One more close shave. it's much closer than last time, the boy whispered as the wind blew and rain continued to pour heavily on the roof of the car.

The twins somehow managed to come on top as the car jerked but kept moving forward. In a certain place where the light was dimming, the police jeep overtook it and the car followed suit for the safety of others. Nastika could see the hollow place where once it used to be a bridge but it was shattered in the last landslide last winter. She could hear those strange voices that only answered to her and she could feel the emotion of those who may have died. The other members sled strangely but once they had come to the road with low turns, the jeep let the car go in front with a bike passing very close but the car managed to negate through and get back to the main lane.

We can breathe a sigh of relief now, Disha heard the jeep driver open a window behind their car. It is not over yet so keep driving at low speed or we face the challenge ahead, he shouted to which Dasha nodded. As they came in light of the broader sight, a strange vision met them. A hoard of people was passing, they all had garlands in their hands with the front vehicle playing music. What does this all mean? Is it the day they got married? the boy from the back seat asked but Nastika shook her head in total disbelief at what she was witnessing in front of her eyes.

The voices are hollow like we can expect. they don't sound polite as they sing out, Disha whispered as her voice had also gone dry in the sound of harsh musical notes. We better turn away from this or it can be serious trouble for us at night, Dasha drove out as one of the vehicles with lamps passed closely to them moved around. A small lit lamp touched the smaller pane on the car's window but it didn't cause any problem. It felt positive to Nastika and they kept driving away from the band that was still in the mood for a night chorus enjoying a certain festive moment together.

We are here. it is somehow good that we haven't faced much chaos till now or it could be worse you know, The boy seated at the corner said while opening the window as the car stopped. Put that light off, will you? It is somehow painful to my eyes, Dasha told her twin as she switched it off and stepped out in the calm of night. The tour ended as they could hear the horn of a jeep sounding just behind them, patrolling the best they could in these harsh places on request.

Nastika took charge of guiding them through and thanked all as they had the final clicks of the tour. I am sorry I can't come with you as it's already night spreading. You better go the next day as it may not be safe, she told them as final words and paid the jeep driver to drop her home easily. Good work, they are safe for now, I thought we were gone to the point, He softly smiled as they trudged away with the gang laughing in the night spread with lights and smiles as it was their final day in this place.

A sigh of relief in the camp as all of them turned. Disha called out to Avantika and she appeared. The girl looked much better after the treatment at the hospital. Sorry we couldn't take you to the tour dear, Dasha said walking inside the room. My visions were more exciting than your tours, maybe, any scary moments? she asked. All the gang laughed as they started to find their bags to pack and return home the next day.

Disha told about the lover's point, the ghost, and how they survived narrowly from the fierce climbing face. They also recalled the momentum, how the car kept getting stuck and Avantika smiled like she knew all this already and looked calm as everything unfolded by her gang members. She asked about weather, pitfalls, and a lot more things but nobody asked how he knew it. They just said 'yes' and 'no' as she enquired and it made her feel relaxed to hear it

What she has seen has come to reality, her stable form in hospital finally lets her feel that she is capable of seeing things through and cherished to experience it inside. We bought you a few pastries if you like to eat, the tallest boy said with a smile on his face. No, you haven't, it was totally scary, how could you do that? Disha told him and knew it was just an offer to let Avantika make some noise for food, she is well known to have a hot temper and a liking for sweets. They all started to laugh harder as the night approached and the gang would be finally gone once the sun appeared on the top of the mountains the next day.

Nastika has simply come closer to her uncle's building but she didn't dare to go there. However, for a fact check, she visited a gothic website that explained about ghosts and fairies in the place. She found what she had been looking at on the 2nd notice as a curious fact which speaks about the couple who died in [lover's point getting married on this day so the guess has been confirmed. She further came to know that those who can listen to their music won't get affected by the fear of their presence as it is a symbol of prosperity and glory. She felt relief as a text flashed and it was from her mother asking her to return home whenever she was free from her task.

The practitioner sat on a bench with the wind blowing quite hard. She took out her lighter and started to smoke as no one could see her around. There was a certain alarm too for people not to roam at night but she didn't care. A pleasing sensation gripped her like her best ghost friend may be circling and she tried to imagine her pale shape in the puff of smoke rising. A strange feeling came to me like it doesn't matter even if she dies or doesn't belong to this world anymore. Then she was taken aback by such emotion as she knew the children wouldn't be happy, nor those who call her their niece and she felt miserable thinking it over.

She may have to go home soon and she stood up looking to go to her uncle's quarters throwing the empty packet into a dustbin lying close by. A figure came suddenly as she turned, opened its mouth with sockets instead of teeth, and started to laugh. Nastika could have been worried but all that had happened at the lover's point made her smile and throw the pinch of powder which made the figure choke in the air. After a smile not like her own, she spoke a Mantra, turned her wrist with a flick and the towering figure had to turn away feeling quite weak in front of the chanted words.

Thank goodness, you are here, the aunt opened the main door as she knocked to enter. I was in the company of pure hearts this time, the niece replied, climbing the stairs as the door closed behind her. Vidyut jumped on his chair but she was not in the mood to talk with them right now so he turned back. The children were already having the night's dinner and Nastika felt hungry watching them eat fast. Let's go upstairs, I want some food to get warm too, she said, climbing up and being greeted well by her uncle as she started to go towards her room to empty her overloaded bag.

There you go, come and sit on the table or it will get cold, the aunt called so Nastika came out wearing night clothes with a smile. We did have to face weathering but we were lucky to come out safe, she told her uncle as he had a questioning expression on his face. Thought they did well to drive out and the police jeep kept following to have huge help to protect us, she continued but her uncle was not listening now. he had something in his hand which was the receipt of the letter she had requested to send and she felt happy asking it to be put down as she enjoyed the best of food that made her feel comfortable for now.

She didn't feel good at night, the fear of certain dreams kept looming and she finally dozed off. A room with a golden door was opening in her dreams. Someone was calling her name and it felt like her papa calling from the corner of the room. In her dream, she felt moving towards him but he was tied by cords. A voice whispered to her, very familiar, Bring her your best friend and we will release him, a cackle of laughter, sounded loudly and she awoke feeling nauseated.

Not this bad, I can't bear the thought of him being captured by a ghost, she shrugged off looking outside. it was still dawn, she could hear the tap of a stick with her uncle going for a walk. I can't follow him, it would be the best way to get the ticket to shut down, she told herself checking the clock, the items on her table and feeling dizzy at this point. The dream had shaken her terribly and it may take time to recover from it as her eyes remained open feeling what she had seen.

There was a sound of zing that surprised her. It was the vibration of a message from her mom. I have been told of your good behaviour. Keep yourself out of trouble, it made her a bit irritated but a smile came onto her sleepy face. It's been a long time since her mother complimented her on purpose. Recalling the last day, she feels decent to protect others and also have better company, but she was not in the mood to think it over as the dream kept popping into her mind troubling her fiercely.

There was a knock on the door. Her aunt came followed by children who were acting like they had fallen sick badly. She is not well, we shall have breakfast downstairs, Aisha started to sing with glee and frustration. No more words, you shall all be put to sleep by the musical ghost, it made them double with laughter on these words and 2 of them flushed on such emotions. Nastika stood up and looked at the clock with glazed eyes. She had overslept after the dream and it was almost 11 with sunbathing at the whole dining table as she gestured on coming to eat soon so children went back to the table making too much noise.

Upendera didn't go to the lake today, he just circles from the inner lane to the one that ends in the forest and twists inside the hidden secret passageway. His thoughts were disturbed as he was worried for his niece. It is a kind of pressure that sticks to your throat and makes you gulp or spit the emotion out. For a person like him who has lived most of his life without being bothered and only crying out for his son, the emotion seems to be tightening. it may be a kind of strength when you associate with spirits, if they can't make you frightened, they try to possess you by making a strange vision come in front of your eye or give such shivers that it breaks you.

It's not my fault that she landed with us in the first place, he muttered as an owl flew past his head. We need to figure out how many times she wants to play with the fear or out with it, he gripped the stick more tightly, thinking it over shrewdly. After turning one more fork he decided it was better to leave the thoughts away as he started to hum something like music. With the sun spreading its light with a peaceful glow, he felt a bit calm as nature always helps him to get in a better mood. He saw a turn where a few police cops were coming to do their work and decided it was time to go back and have his potion so his throat may feel better.

It was not good for guards as they had not come to investigate but to collect a body. it felt that someone had crossed the warning they had sent a few days back on the speaker. They have told people not to wander at night but a teenager may have thought it's not wise and may have tried to cross the line of his strength. They looked for marks and saw the same crunch-like mark on their left cheek. it has been identical to one of the police personnel who felt uneasy matching it over. Search the woods, don't you listen? it's an order, their leader growled in the morning as they spread and started to search for more clues regarding the person dead in these woods crossing their rules.

An ID card master, one of them shouted from a few yards away. he has been permitted by city officials to search and explore, they spoke, coming closer with a few documents in hand clasped tightly. It looks like he didn't read the warning on these documents, it is mentioned here, one of them sneered holding the certificate signed with no chance of survival in woody nights. The leader checked the documents and felt the person to be a nature lover as there were photographs too. Sent Him for post mortem and also advertise with his photo or send it to the city, we shall find who he is very soon, they turned looking disgusted on such a death.

head of culture and tourism speaking. Thanks to your report, we have identified the man, a voice officially came on the phone. You have found all the documents? Good, he was trying to have a run, the main charge smiled with surprise. He was thinking of claiming extra money by saying he has caught some illegal charges against us, was a clench of a fist behind but it was not heard by the cultural head. Send the details after the scrutiny, and we shall send to the resident to where he belongs, have a good day. he said and with Yes sir the phone got disconnected and it became an absolute outrage on how people can trick their field of expertise in search to gain more lust or become popular.

A few hours later, news coverage was running on TV downstairs in the main room. There were no children as all of them had gone to school. Nastika was watching the news when the man found by police was shown with a brief on how his mission failed. We would advise not to visit the forest in the night the next week or so, It can result in a pure suicidal if you do, the spokesperson continued gesturing to mark on the person's cheek. Nastika looked at it and felt shocked to see that she had seen it somewhere before. It was a sign of horns, a signature power of a movie character who transforms into a ghost at night and kills its enemy.

She felt stunned to see the mark and felt she must do something about it as it could spread very fast amongst whoever was trying to plan it with mass killing to offer. It has been said that this mark has the phonetic power to insist on forcing one who becomes part of it to have brutal behaviour with others. It is a cosmic instinct to be a ghost who can kill beyond its limit and continue the onslaught. This is what frightens Nastika as she thinks of the sign of the horns as it becomes an absolute sign of admiration for the ghosts of the jungle to kill and fill their appetite by hunting out humans in large numbers.

Wait for a trip to come, you will get the chance to find why this mark keeps appearing with bodies, she said at the same time as the spokesperson mentioned that in the past this mark has been a core connection with deaths. Why does it come frequently? Are these ghosts fond of something or is it just a coincidence? Stay tuned for further coverage, we will bring it first for you, he closed the show and Nastika turned the TV off looking for such a sign wondering where she had saved it closely attached with great fervour to add it someday.

She has saved the mark to be part of a ghost character for a magazine cover in the future and she found it as it was hiding in her back pocket. A pierce look in it made her feel that this was not a human mischief and it had been driven by a death in the past which was unfair. Someone more powerful is involved in the deaths and wants to make human life miserable to take revenge for all that may have happened. She felt disheartened as she was not able to solve it with her strength. There may be time to think all things over, not for now as she has to focus on safety cover so she has no plans to wander at night and accompany the risks that come with it as you try to follow the adventure.

The house was filled with noises again as a bust stopped and all the noise makers entered the room. Abhi was holding a paper with a cartoon, Aisha was also holding a drawing, Vidyut was looking unhappy with something and Dushyant was trying to hide a plastic lizard he had brought to scare them off. Behave, won't you? What's all this fun about, Nastika told them as she opened the door to let them in. They were in some sort of mood and she told them to change first and then let them explain the condition to her.

We took part in an art contest, Abhi spoke as they all threw their school bags onto a table with socks tossed in the air that Nastika caught and piled in the corner. It was a gothic contest where we had to make faces that could frighten anyone. ' Nastika took the drawings from their hands. What happened to Vidyut? Why are you not speaking much? Dushyant threw one more drawing, he had nicked it made by the child who had come first. A teddy? It's not that scary or is it? Nastika obliged but Vidyut looked grim so she threw it back to Dushyant with disgust.

Time to get you out from this silent fear once and for all, the eldest said, speaking to other children about their performance in drawing. Only Abhi has managed to get a consolation prize. To make Vidyut happy, he handed over his money so he could buy something scary. This is how you got the sticking lizard, don't you? she asked simply looking back. A feeling of joy came all around as the aunt appeared suddenly from behind. She called for the order to the local sweet shop asking for jalebis and they all got excited hearing her speak out.

They were back at the top room, sitting one after another as the uncle saw Abhi's drawing with elation. He didn't ask much but felt pleased that the children were up to something positive. Better eat them or it will get cold. the aunt told the eldest as she was explaining the chaotic part of the design made by the child. Yes, let's dig in. It's one of the joyous days coming to us. Deep down she thought it was the time to take advantage of the smiles. She may think later on about her father's dream and the mark that keeps popping, for now, she can have fun with children dancing around her offering more sweets to munch on with them.

5

FEAR, POWER, AND REDEMPTION

It was dark with a few owls hooting in the night's sky. They flew across a window with their eyes shining and a voice was heard. It was a groan of the worst kind, someone was in real pain and it felt like this person had been captive of some certain group. A few figures bloomed from nowhere, their hands empty with no mass of blood and white. They towered on him and removed his chains without much effort which made him feel surprised as they turned into his worst fear that night. .

You say the wife is a lawyer. Will she be able to defend you? one of them cackles with glee. I bet she won't believe you have been captive of the ghost, how does it feel? a cold slash fell to the man's cheek as he shouted but it was not going to be of any use. As long as you don't tell us the secret of the good spirit or location of the chamber, we won't kill you, get it? he nodded in a deep understanding and then shook his head like he wasn't going to tell them anything as he felt more screws on his face making it tougher to face out.

It is certainly a fact to consider. the marks you make are popular, he snorted even in such pain. My wife may not be able to, but someone else. People in the news or media will and your reign will end, the ghost felt pleased with his daring. Very brave, but what reign sir? Surely we won't go to hell as our lives were miserable already. We are dead already, aren't we? What else we can face, we are not bound to live, they sneered towering over him and taking him back to the captured place.

He has been brought under a trap. A salesman had told him of better food stock at a corner of the jungle. It may have been an imposter or part of this gang who lured him. They waited till the captive came to the end of the forest where the lake was situated. In pretence to take him away from the dangers of the lake, the gang of ghosts swallowed him like a sword over him and made him unconscious. when he woke up, it was this place where he was tied now which was under the red light of greeting but it soon turned into blue and he is facing this unknown brutal torture daily now by the ghosts as they try to find about treasure.

You won't be immortal even if you are no more human, he said to them when they started to leer and made it a hell of a life for him. My daughter won't leave you for good, you hear me? one of the ghosts turned on him, gesturing that they could also bring me here but the man shook his head. She is facing ruins with a lot of dead bodies regularly. We have made sure it becomes tough for her to digest your absence, they snorted as the man slumped down on his knees from the pain of daggers inflicted on him wondering how he can skip this terrifying place somehow.

This is my most crucial gem. I am handing you. Promise me you will keep it safe, the social activist had said to him years before while in his last moments before death. I shall try my best to protect it, the man had promised him to keep it guard. He had summoned Pandits and tried a lot of fire practices but he was not able to keep the secret hidden. bad spirits can cross the best emotions on hand as they somehow came to know he owned the spiritual gem. The effect of the gem can make the city go into chaos so it was a perfect one for them to steal and finish everything once and for all.

They tried to search for it using their demon powers. They used creatures, smaller to more threatening ones, to trace it at home. they turned themselves into lost cloth, torn envelopes, and other elements to effect. Even they tried to use meat eaters with the darkest of emotions to trace but the gem was not found in his home. Finally, they decided to capture the person and torture him. After a food distribution function where they sent false intentions to people so they could finish the food. The salesman lured the person to follow him and he landed there.

Back on the other side of the lake, a few people were marching round the corner together. They have caught a young man, not more than 21 years of age and wanted to hurt him badly. They shouted a lot as they claimed to have insulted the idol made in honour of the activist. How dare you, that blue-coloured portion is not fixed just to entertain, they all shrieked in the sky. The ghost on the other side felt one more member join their party soon. In a few minutes, the crowd had gone out of control as the person was beaten up badly. They left him wounded with a bleeding nose and left with peace so suddenly like nothing may have happened in this place.

A figure emerged, closer to rocks splashing in the lake. It came closer to the young man on the floor and lifted him gently. He took some strange natural material and made the boy feel relaxed. His pain was gone as the hooded figure asked him to walk along. This way, we can fix it back, he said with his voice only audible to the young person being a sole guardian. The figure kept closer to the idol, raised the broken blue remark, and attached it like nothing has broken here in the past. How did you do this? He raised his hand from inside his cloak and it was white like a gleaming pearl. He spoke to the man not to fear him as he is connected to the glory and told him to go back with some fortune and the figure had vanished.

Who was there? I can't see the power. You think we should capture that boy for fun too? the taller ghost asked the dwarf. Not to worry, he didn't show any money or gold that we were after to excite us, the dwarf replied in his innocent tone like he was singing. We can wait for our time, till this man doesn't speak out, they leered at night and the fear of it looking back with the intent to do more damage to innocent people who may approach with greed of becoming rich and die here.

If you are ghosts, why do you have such a lust for gold and riches? a voice echoed suddenly in the wind not recognised by native ghosts. As the ghosts were turning to torture the man captivated, the figure bloomed suddenly in front of them with light dazzling in his ghostly hand. |So pathetic, you are dead but the reason for which you died still looms in you. , a blinding light smashed through as the ghost felt worried about seeing a strange identity. Who are you to play with us in this light? Please close it out, they started to beg and fly off for safety, even though a few of them hid for cover feeling the intensity of the spark.

I am... the true keeper of the gold, he said whooshing past with a few of the ghost assistants clasped into his fist and he crunched them as they cried like babies. You shall not harm the person, he is crucial for the success, he continued and smashed all of them into an empty but open cauldron. The pain you have passed wishes me to make a soup for all of you and enjoy it like a tasty gas, he looked into the place in outrage as everyone feared. He found the person tied into a corner and released him by offering a glass of white potion so his face could heal. I am leaving for now, stay safe, he said to the man who expressed gratitude and the light faded again.

It made a few of them scared of the way it happened quickly. It didn't give them time to plan, prepare, or strike back in motion. It can't be a human, it was so deadly, they whispered, shaken badly due to the sudden event. We must not push this person far who we have captured or it can make matters worse, the ghosts who have been thrown in cauldrons with brutal power felt uneasy or did not want to talk about it so they muffled their ears with wind flying across. it has certainly made things better and stayed in control for the humans living amongst them after it took place with such fierce intent.

The response changed for some while as these ghosts who used to torture the man started to become polite to him. Please if you can let us know, where the diamond is, we will honour you, they may be heard talking in the evening as some of them force local people to bring food or they would take their souls away. It did sound good but for the human being captured, he doesn't like to have meals in exchange for torture or threaten someone so he doesn't eat them properly. Try to become good and it will make you a lot calmer, he kept talking to them but the ghost won't accept the fact of honesty and pride in life.

You are aware why we are so good to you. If it hadn't been for the cloaked figure, we may have broken you into pieces earlier, one of them started to begin shrewdly. Easy now, the light can be visible from the topmost glass. He may be around us, the other shrewd-looking ghost warned him. I don't care, whatever may be the reasons but we are not your servants, he tried to latch on but a glove caught the white figure suddenly. It spat and squeaked for a moment but then its imprint went like it had been destroyed by a kind of strange fire.

I may warn you. He is required to accomplish the task. ' It brought a shiver to the ghost who didn't even feel anything but being burnt or frosted in ice. Yes, master, we don't intend to hurt him. I was telling him to get calm, the shrewd ghost with a pugmark on its ghostly face bowed. The mood has changed again from daring to fear and the ghosts were worried about what they may have to face in the process to find more about the gem as time was passing fast and they can only hunt at night to settle in their killing streak.

It shall happen on the full moon. I may call for your assistance, the cloaked figure said to the human a few nights before. You are sure I can survive even after doing it? he asked the cloaked figure who shook his head. If you haven't been handed the ownership, it might not need you, but yes you will be safe, he handed him more white potion so he could survive on these tough nights. I must acknowledge your help, this potion keeps me warm and quiet, the man said to which the cloaked figure waved his hand, but he was gone before any of the ghosts could sneak in to find out why he had been talking to the human alone.

People were still getting lost in clumps of trees and rumours started to spread that the forest possessed people who wandered at the wrong time, in the shadows, or at night. with deaths happening more fast, it was assumed that they must not visit it at night or closer to the full moon. The cloaked figure appeared one more night asking the human to come with him. I am sorry but this can be dangerous. I need to protect you the night before the full moon, he touched his cloaked hand with which he took the human away without telling anything to the ghosts who could just see it happen hopelessly.

A cave has come into sight of the man alongside the cloaked figure. A stone statue was standing in front blocking the view. With a touch of the cloak, it opened as he spoke, The owner of the treasure brings the protector with him, the stone statue shifted as the man started to step down. The figure didn't need to go down by steps as it bobbled and reached downstairs. It may be tough for you, but Yes you have made it, very well, he touched the feet with his empty but warm hands to a request to follow inside the deep cave.

The tunnel to reach the richest, the man spoke as the light illuminated by the golden chandelier hung high. The path became broader as they kept stepping up and it finally ended inside a cave beyond which water could be heard splashing hard. It may be a direct entrance to go inside the lake but the man didn't ask. The figure stopped as he threw a powder into a furnace close by and offered a salute: Sit down, have some good food, it's time you get filled in for pain you had to face, he said and the man felt obliged for receiving the honours in such a manner.

Your daughter is safe. we have managed to send a vanguard who can look after her, he explained as the man was handed some food of the living world. It's not chanted. The food is pure. neither taken by torture nor brought by false means, the figure continued. The man felt pleased to find all things falling in place now. I am not sure what I need to do for the great Guardian. One who certainly did everything for all of us, He said just in a whisper. In answer, the figure dug his ghostly hands inside his cloak and flicked a paper that floated on the clean but purple and blue floor and the man took it curiously.

A strange design was made with rough lines marked with blue. The man understood the blue lines to mark it as a lake. In between the blue lines, a white dot was strongly attached that may refer to the cave where they are currently. Beyond it, a few stairs and a glowing place were marked with a circle in black marks which may represent the moon. it couldn't get more confusing than this, but the figure took it back wanting to speak on it raising his hand so he could oblige the person.

This place only opened the day before the full moon, he gestured to white dots trying to explain. The secret closes itself on the next day after the closing of the ceremony. we shall have to get out as soon as it takes place, the man was getting the word of it now as the figure told of a ceremony. He has been part of those moments at a young age when social activists roamed the city with pride and valour. I got it, the ceremony of the blue novelty, is that it? I am excited, the figure raised his hand and threw out the sapphires which the man didn't catch.

Passed the test very easily, let's go further at the meeting point, he said and they stood up with fire being put out with a simple flick of the wrist. After two smokeless turns, a smell of something on fire came to man's nostrils. He kept her eyes sharper in focus as things started to reveal. The figure simply lifted the seal of the entrance covered in fire asking the man to go forward. As they reached the final turn, a creature sat there protecting the final inner cave with its leg stretched so false entries could fall and be killed by its strength.

It was similar to one Nastika and her friends had seen on the mountaintop. it lifted its leg to let them pass and the entrance closed with a thump as a few voices started to come from the inner side of the final passage. The figure asked the man to locate his gem being the member of the order. He could see that he was not the only human, few men and women were also present alongside ghosts, fairies, and strange creatures. The man whose name is Astitva reached for his gem in the jewel box attached to the passage and finally touched it, feeling the world of good by touching it.

In honour of the gold and diamonds, the main ghost spoke leading the march in front. We crave for those who know the realm to have the true royalty and be part of the glory, they all lifted their gems and jewels together. The sound of a metal tray came from close by as Astitva was asked to have a seat by an elderly woman. We are here to feel honourable by being part of the moonlight soon aren't we? she said, holding the hot cup and swapping the saucer to Astitva who felt joyous enjoying the hot soup. they all felt connected by a power, something that is ethereal and it was a true bliss.

Let's be honest. we can't deny that a few unwelcome guests may try to reach us somehow, the cloaked figure who had guided Aastitva spoke. He flicked his left wrist and it was imitated by other figures similarly. A blue light appeared in the passage and it expanded to blue flair spreading to all corners Thieves you are warned, if you dare to intercept that will be the end of yours, they all spoke in unison with their voices becoming an echo that expanded loudly and a blast happened with certain voices ending in a crash outside the passage for their relief so they can plan for the next night as full moon may approach here in night.

There was a sound coming from far away. Wolves had gathered in months to come across these woods and they were howling. It is said that they do get calm on the full moon so this has to be their night. There was the sound of a crushing throat, a deer had fallen and with a louder yowl, the leader of the pack summoned others to be a part of the meal to enjoy together. It may fall as a sacrifice as it used to happen when the social activist was alive throwing the party to the public. Everything was falling in place as the moon may surely approach here soon with its glow becoming brighter with its posture.

The news clearly showed warnings of tides in closer seashores so people must not go there to avoid any fatalities. People were getting angrier more frequently and children were having fights as emotions were high, the moon was somehow coming closer again as everything was ready at the base to greet the birthday of a long-dead social activist. No hands should raise the jewel till I allow, the main ghost requested and everyone agreed inside the cave to his words. A burst of white flame took place and a cup emerged from it leaving the humans mesmerised but it was gone with one more flick of the lead ghost. Now, you can start the discussion to offer wishes and execute the plan tomorrow, he said, leaving everyone in silence.

Back in the city, a procession was marching making it an absolute noise to hear. In the main temple, a Pandit was offering prayers as he lifted the pot to shower into the idol of a great person. He distributed sweets amongst people, craved for blessing, and told us it had been a blissful day for all of us. How come it is such an honour? a lady in her late 30s asked but he didn't tell her. He simply touched the forehead of the idol standing so she could read the inscription carved on it with words written in bold.

Birthday special, honoured in memory of the great icon of the city, it said and she turned to take the prasad from his hands with glee. The people kept coming, to grasp the influence, to see the time going, and finally Nastika had reached after a lot of scolding from her aunt to visit a temple. She bent low, clasped her hands, and took the prasad as the Pandit did Teeka on her forehead but felt somehow strange. He didn't know she was the daughter of the powerful person from the order so he simply handed her the plate and she was gone with a smile.

What kind of power was it? Did I mistakenly recognize someone and miss the golden chance? he muttered wondering what just happened. she must have forgotten her money or purse, let me check, there was nothing left and the excuse to converse with such a person went empty. A coin fell onto his hands from nowhere as Mritaanjali's ghost was watching him closely and smiled. He thanked the older members for showering with gratitude and turned away not looking for Nastika anymore as he had been obliged with riches.

Everyone was in a great mood as the warning announcement came again telling them not to go wandering in the forest in the dark. it was a true power that may swallow anyone who wishes to dare as it is going to be a full moon. All the guards were watching, alert, and on high duty, as their bosses kept instructing them on how to control the crowds in large numbers. Anytime a few people turned away to the forest, they would shower water cannons in the sky, confusing them and they had to go back. It has been a certain effort till the evening, but will it be the same at night? The time is coming for the moon to show its complete face finally.

People were running back home as the evening started to turn with lengthening shadows around the corner. There was a sound of horn as the bands were going back from where they had come. The dusk was filled with shouts of children looking for more food offers, people fighting for discounts that come only on this day, or a larger number of them coming out from cafeterias or canteens. It is a certain day to cherish and be with everyone, but for very few, it is a certain way to understand why it comes amongst them, thrilling all of them with pure joy.

Most people take the benefits it brings and simply forget the reason for which it is celebrated. It remains a duty handed over to members of the order who mark the time, fix the exact schedule, and try to balance it. However, there are also ghosts, false people, and others who consider it a perfect day to have their glory. They trap people, possess children, or try to read minds so they can find their chances and make them count. It will soon turn into night, the rise of the full moon of the month, and the patience will be over. Both sides will get a chance to have their prey or goodwill and make it a real treat amongst them.

Come, this is our night, the first cloaked figure moved towards the lake entrance followed by 2 humans. They made a circle in which all of them were standing. One by one all groups started to fill their pots with water as ghosts followed them around ready to spread out the honour. After all, having paid tributed into the final well that connects to the lake, they all looked on to the sky. They were outside the place and it looked royal in the night as crackers started to sound making it more clear and grand with its true colour.

What's all that noise? I wonder who shall be celebrating this late? A few people who had got late from shopping tried to find one but then they got reminded of the warning issued for the night's stroll so they avoided it. Nobody's a fool to throw their life on such a risk, a young man said who sounded half drunk but he has turned away from his friends who are shouting his name. They finally let him go as they know what may be coming the next morning and have turned back home with no hope of the drunk coming from the woods lately.

Back at the lake's outer circle, a few ghosts were glittering in the candles burnt by people who belonged to the order wishing to celebrate and express gratitude. Astitva raised his torch of flames high and bowed to the golden spirit watching them over. They surrounded the smell of light with their glowing eyes and it made the spirit feel the world of peace on seeing what they all just did. There are still people who remember him and know what he has done and it is a perfect honour made for him to happen on his birthday with so many noises spread all over.

Let's join in the feast, it's for him, the great and valiant soul, Astitva heard the main human leader shout, sending more crackers with blast into the sky. We shall go in to dig in and have a true party. Let's begin, they all went back to the tunnel taking their pots and key ornaments to be protected in perfect position. I can put it here, for the next journey? Astitva asked the figure who had helped him as he nodded 'yes' and he put the gem back. They all were seated in silver chairs with a golden table and were handed food. For ghosts gases were set to spread around with cold and hot smells as they enjoyed cheering on too. It was an absolute joy for all to be together in such a great fold celebrating the moment.

The other side was not so happy to feel as the drunken youngster was dragged towards the forest with the wishes of those who wanted to celebrate by onslaught. You are right, they are too scared, a young man's ghost told him but he simply ignored it. The youngster kept marching towards the forest but then felt his energy going down suddenly. He fell for some bushes, stuck his right leg, and toppled over onto the floor easily. Nice as it is for us. You are brought by the feeling that drowns humans, a sneering ghost leered looking at the fallen victim as it tasted blood in the air.

It raised a dagger and lunged from the air with top speed, for a moment the youngster didn't feel it but then he realised blood coming out from his cheek in the thickest of flow. The dagger went deeper cutting through and soon his hands were filled with blood piercing his white face that was numb and in a few minutes he had died losing too much blood. A perfect meal, one for the honour, the ghost who had attacked threw smoke from his bloodless hand as others came to find a man dead. They bent low and lunged onto the muscle to enjoy the feast. They tore the right cheek, crushed the left hand that was folded in the fall, and finally celebrated their remark of the forest by slaying an innocent life.

Both sides were quiet now but the people who had joined the full moon's glory were moving back. Astitva thanked all of them for being part of it and they exchanged gratitude. The figures left the march as they knew the ghost would attack them if they were left alone. Follow me, sir, I brought you here, so I should take you back, the cloaked figure told Astitva who nodded and started to go in the blue march. Through the sealed place they went out towards the open stairs. This time the man didn't need help as he easily climbed them, the joy of the completed process made him feel elated so he did much more easily.

The figure threw something into the air as he could trace a few spirits quietly lurking in the shadows to hunt. There was a squeak, Please forgive us, like words and the ghosts melted in the fire leaving them to go quietly in the dark knight with his enormous strength. you have done the job. I think we can send you back for the next 3 months. Your daughter may need guidance on solving the mystery of deaths in the jungle, Astitva nodded as they walked past the old tree stumps with secrets of them at night and the figure caught more ghosts hidden there which he easily sent back to the nether world by his power.

Nastika was sleeping in her room as it happened. She had a dream with golden light all around. There was no sign of the feeling associated with fear. People were singing, and shaking hands with each other, and among them, she could see her father seated with great honour. He was wearing his old chain which he used for celebrations, he held the royal gem connected to the old honour and it made her happy. Somehow they were known of movements through relations of family as she felt her father being released by a powerful spirit and he had joined the place for a royal process.

She could feel the power of the moon in her dreams, a bright orb coming under which people were showering water and it calmed her nerves somehow due to the affection in the morning coming closer with some happy news soon. The figure helped Astitva to drop in close to a station with noises of vehicles so he could take the ride home. He checked for his purse and found the old money safe in it like he had kept some change for future purposes and now it proved handy finally. Thanking the good spirits he took the bus and went away to his place, surprising his wife simply.

She felt elated after confirming it had been him and like usual asked him a few questions on life which he answered easily due to sharp memory. They went in, had a few jokes about where he might be and his wife taunted him for trying more experiments with ghosts leaving them alone. Right you are, I am not responsible to this small family, He smiled speaking to her over and she opened the Tv show to ignore him but the husband went inside to find some potatoes and has started to make fritters himself so the couple can have the best moments after his return back home.

I had an argument with your charming daughter lately, she said with a glass of tea in her hand. ‘kind of thing you may do, come on now. She is the only we have, he looked up in time to see her frowning. I don’t have much time to find out what she does but outsiders send horrible news which shivers me, he thought to talk this out with his daughter and had decided. I will go to meet her in the city. would meet your elder sister and Upendera ji too, they both agreed and with night spreading he has gone to bed feeling perfectly relaxed now after such conversation.

6
THE HIDDEN PATH

It was a blissful morning for all those who have missed Astitva. He called to Nastika as it struck 8 and she woke up with a shock. Hello gorgeous, how are you now? he tried to create a fake voice like he used to in the past. Surely, it's not you? I am really scared to hear strange voices, she replied, looking back at the window and the sun shining. They talked for half an hour as her aunt kept listening from the door outside. She couldn't understand the kind of talk they were having so she turned away simply leaving the niece to talk with the speaker from the other side.

I got company with my long lost friend. her ghost saved me from a lot of fears, she said in a low voice as her father asked about her adventures. Few ghosts are still lurking. They may look to go for an all-out attack, he responded, trying to stick to the things. They both shared words on how they were protected, the tough times and the good ones in between them and it was a certain talk to happen as the father only understands the harshness she has to go even in these wins blowing hard in the wood against her.

A few minutes later Upendera's phone rang. He has been feeling better today as he has managed to go across and sit for some while close to the lake on a stone pillar with ease. He checked the name and a huge smile came over his face. Bingo! Here he is, calling again, he picked up the phone and Astitva replied from the other side with a strong apology. Get my hands on you. It may be I who should strangle you, Upendera shouted and then turned his face into laughter as Astitva spoke something about the forest from the other side reminding the duties to the spirit and his role.

Are you back? This is a huge relief for Upama, you know that, Upendera's wife now has to talk with Nastika's father in urgency. It has not been easy for your daughter. She has put herself in trouble or fears, Astitva smiled as he responded politely. It has to happen as spirits were certainly after her, Upendera waved his hand wanting to say this has always been an excuse to get away but they kept talking and the joy had spread suddenly in all of them.

When are you coming? The family of ghosts you have been, indeed, Upendera said with a joke. He told the elders that after 2 days he would be back. There are a few things he has to solve regarding money received by his wife which she is not explaining right now. I can't tell you like you can't about the lake, they can hear her whisper from behind and Astitva disconnected the phone looking at his haughty wife with fury and amazement at the same time.

Funny enough. He is back. It's good for you, the ant went inside watching Nastika writing on a piece of paper. She was making notes of what her father had told her. yeah, he has a lot of offers with excuses on me too, she made her aunt smile, turning away and trying to go down to find whether the children were awake by now. Nastika folded the paper and simply tucked it in her heavy bag. She made sure the sign of horns stayed close to the note and looked outside. The girl stood up and started to check the functioning of her camera, turning it over and over.

It was all working well with its lens at accurate points to give her the best shots of the room. For a moment Nastika thought to call back and had a strong temptation to do it, but Then she stepped away, closed her door, and simply fell asleep for an hour to have a short nap. It will help her digest the return and she can get fresh from what she has been told by his papa back to his best with her.

In the forest, it was not polite. The guards were in action again, they had been chasing a thief who had decided to run towards the forest. We can leave him to the ghosts or we shall find him? a few of them responded as their commanding officer told them to be inside. It's morning you fools. Find him, now. He has taken documents with which we need, they started to surround him with a gunshot into the air. A few members were going away but those who were on the trail kept running behind till he came to the end of the forest. One more sound from the gun, a bullet struck his right knee and he fell as a bird shouted from behind.

What's this? How many secrets can this place hold? the officer said, watching the bird with its sharp claws trying to follow the man with its sharp front paws onto the floor. Blood! That is the most crucial element to attract, I see why they have come so quickly, he said, smelling his nose too. 'We can leave the body here sir! We have the documents from him, the commander looked at the pitiful thief on the floor and raised his gun in hand firing 3 more bullets. As the blood scattered, a few more birds surrounded him and the guards had left taking the documents with them that mattered the most as this person died being a victim of the many.

Thief murdered with brutal assault, the news was running in the afternoon. Nastika was in much relief as she had finally heard the voice of her father. What's special about this? It happens every day in busy life, she muttered, sipping the juice from her left hand and lowering the voice of the Tv with the remote in her right hand. the interesting fact remains why a normal thief shall try to steal high profile documents of the dept of culture running away with them? she raised her eyebrows as the newsreader continued further.

The investigation is underway, stay tuned as we bring you more from the mysteries of the forest, she finished the juice in pure disgust and turned the TV off wondering if what she just heard was true or just a twist of words as these blokes are paid well. She decided to find more and got an article on the murder further confirming the damage done by a wild creature.

What could be the concern? Should I let father be aware of it, she took out her phone and sent a text on the number from which she got a call in the morning. it replied, Have seen the news. I am digging in. She felt elated that this was indeed her father's old number working again. Got to see what we can do for this, she texted back and He easily sent an image of a bird clawing onto a dead man with words written around it, a ghost or a living creature? This is the main thing to know, she nodded to no one and put her phone down in relief as she could express her fears.

Back at the police station, the officer presented the documents to the security person who had been the man in charge. We are sorry you had to go into the forest for us, he thanked him, shaking hands with the main specialist. No worries, After all the golden treasure is crucial. It not only belongs to social activists but we who are vanguards of itt as soul charges, he smiled as they ordered tea requesting the PA to go and fetch it from the canteen. I will be in touch with you for its safety soon, if you like to, It has been a concern for them ever since the ghosts found out the ways to get hands on treasure.

The security person started to talk as they were handed tea with a few cookies from the canteen. It has not been just a few days, we need to get a better cover to simply protect it, what say you? The specialist wiped his mouth from the back of his hand and nodded easily thinking about the matter. As he could see the security loopholes that have forced such papers to be missing, there is a need for stronger protection. He doesn't speak much but has been in action lately. See you next week, I shall see what can be done about it, he stood up leaving his empty cup on the table as the security person sat there thinking hard about his words and the plan to execute soon.

A bus had stopped in an outer station as Astitva stepped out in his old official suit to match his presence. He walked past the famous sweet shop and stopped next door to have well-known tea. You are here, finally, good to see you, the shop owner said, being an old friend. Tell him I want 1 kg of barfi for my daughter and her friends, he whispered, handing the tea maker a few notes who nodded. Fifteen minutes after having his tea, he signed off with a cotton bag that had the sweets inside he had asked to buy for his family that made him elated.

He walked simply on the main road, stepping freely and easily found a taxi waiting to drop. One for the government quarters, he said as the driver agreed and he settled in. Once the taxi got filled with people, it drove away in a chilling but peaceful afternoon as he sat inside with thoughts on what happened in the last few months when he had to stay away. He likes these people, they have helped him in tough times but he knows people hardly believe in ghosts. He stepped out as the taxi stopped at his arrival place and he reached here.

Papa, it's been so long, Nastika shouted, opening the door and giving him a warm hug. Give it to me. I shall put it upstairs, she let him in as Astitva climbed alongside her, looking at his daughter in a completely different light after some time. She hasn't changed but there are a few marks on her forehead which means she has been living rough. The children were not home but he could see Upendera seated on a chair who recognised Astitva and welcomed him with a glass of water as he dropped onto an empty chair.

She has gone to bring fruits. It's been a while since we had a fruit chart together, the elderly said with a wave of hand. Had a brunch before leaving. she agreed to keep the money safe, Astitva replied, watching more of his daughter. Did you work on the bird image? he asked her as she nodded but the mood changed suddenly as there was a huge noise downstairs due to children coming back with some kind of argument happening again.

What's all this mess? Astitva saw his daughter going down to quiet them. No teddy fears or a lot of teddies to hand over to hit punches? Aisha cut in without getting calm. Yeah, it has a hairy beast, it was swooping in at night, Vidyut shouted but before they could say anything more, Nastika simply took their bags, making them realise her presence and making an apology to her for making such a huge noise inside the empty room.

Lots of fun to see you all again. Here are the chocolates I have bought, Astitva has come down inside the lower room with a message. Your aunt called up. She has come with a fruit chart, the children yelled with delight, holding chocolates and having a word on the fruit chart. Let's go up, that will be a lot of good unless there are ghosts inside the cabins, Nastika laughed with joy after a long time as all of the children felt scared but agreed to go up shouting about who got the better treat.

Back in the forest, an activity was taking place. Few of the locals who had lost their children were doing the last right ceremony of the dead. They raised ash in their hands hoping for the well-being of the dead and expressed how they could have lived a better life. It's been their work to take such a risk, one parent said while burning the dead started here. They managed to convince the temple pandit to come with them in the early evening as the wind blew across. The ghost watched them from a distance as they didn't like to come closer to the fire. They had got help from a forest bird as it had killed a running thief and felt to be filled for now munching the mass left on the floor for them.

We must have been sent with such grandeur. Look how lucky these children are, A ghost with a pale smoky face whispered to its next existing ghost standing closely. We wouldn't have been ghosts if we would have been honoured, do we? he replied, sneering loudly. they long for such activity as most of the ghosts had suffered a life of torture so they return the favor after being in such a state of life. Most of them have been hunted or murdered by officers to knick the active gold which they don't belong to. their cheats, trickery, and false standards let them fall short of good deeds so they roam this forest as their land of rights in the form of ghosts bothering and killing for their joy.

There were cries from the people who were forming the pack as the pandit started to speak mantras. The ghosts who were talking tried to fly away as it was surely going to affect them. They turned in with a wisp of smoke and vanished before anyone could come in their direction. The pandit asked for relatives of the body wishing for the positive send-off of the spirits and the strange sound started to come louder as he said the mantras. people kept remembering the names, family process, and other elements which he did and finally, the task was accomplished for which they had come here taking risk.

Shockingly, they have to die so early leaving us, Astitva whispered after enjoying the fruit chart. His daughter has gone inside the room to find something and show it to her father. I can't go to the last right ceremony, I am not allowed. he told himself as Upendera kept a close watch on him. They took out the old carrom left by Upendera's son, found the keys to strike, and started playing it so Astitva wouldn't feel bored. The night was coming soon and it would surely bring fears so it's better to enjoy the glories of the day until it has not arrived.

A hooded figure was walking with no voice in the grass. It had a candle in its hand covered in gloves. It walked past the trees, heard a few owls hooting, and went inside. He was in for a real treat as he could see the ash on the floors. He did a woosh from his left wrist as the ash was lifted. Who's there? We warn you intruder, a few ghosts came from the woods suddenly and then retreated seeing the flaming candle burn on the tip. The figure watched the ghost swoop away, took off the dagger hidden inside a clump of a tree, and started to look at it. Reveal your powers, it said, speaking with a candle tip burning the blade. I insist you tell me why you are here, in response a figure burst from the burnt blade shivering with pain.

My revenge shall only be over when I have killed 100 people. Not even the golden spirit protected me that day, he spoke in a sing-song voice rasping in the sky. My candle is not powerful enough to finish you off, the figure replied to the burst one in fury. They both looked at each other while the blade's figure was trying to catch the dagger. No, it won't work on me, You must know that, the first one threw the dagger with a flick and it fell inside the clump of bushes. Find it soon to do your bidding. I will come back to catch you on guard, the candle-lit figure said and it was gone with one more woosh.

The daggerless ghost was in true fear once the figure had left. it has never faced a power so tempting to throw him off balance or make him lose his dagger in such a way. I will have 101 strikes now. Mark my words, a flash of light went very close to the figure making him shiver as it bent low in its form to find the dagger. it was hiding in the bushes but the ghost was in shock to see him struggle. If there has been a human present, this could be a true sight of joy as the only true hunter has been disarmed for the first time. It has proved to be an outpour of emotions but being ghosts they can't shed tears so they could only make noises in the jungle unheard by anyone at night.

The ghost looks flustered by the way their main leader has been tormented by the figure. They were outraged as they wanted to do something. He is so powerful, we can't even think of touching this bloke. A few of them looked divided as the group was not forming due to the image of the figure who suddenly blooms and gives them huge damage with fire. What can we do? Let us tear his cloak, then he will be with us showing its ghost body, they rasped, looking angry at the outsider. The spirit with the dagger came back telling them to have located its weapon and they felt relieved.

The cloak figure reached the lake and bowed to the golden spirit who blessed it with words. You also died in a sacrifice, but you still stay with good people, why is that? the activist's ghost asked him as the figure shook his cloak in peace rather than such anxiety. I died for you. A great honour to protect your treasure. I haven't forgotten my duties, rest assured, I will prove handy, he said, flicking a few beads from his pocket so they could land safely in the lake. good job, I will keep your memory safe, the other ghost responded with a whole candle lit now as the night was dark.

Your pearly aura is too much to behold, it's a decent sight, the honourable spirit said to the cloaked figure. We must not stay long as the morning may come soon, but would you be able to protect the others? he asked with a ghost of a smile on his dead face. I am there to rescue, no worries. I can't handle two places at one time though, that's the only thing. He too had a ghost of a smile on his empty face. They both bowed to each other with cloak figures bending low towards the invisible feet and then he had turned away, it was a happy hour for the good spirit for sure.

It was early morning as Upendera lifted his stick to go on to the walk. Astitva saw him being awakened early but didn't disturb him as he knew the habit from the past. See you soon once she wakes up to prepare the potion, Upendera spoke quietly and he nodded as the stick could be heard on the stairs. The old man looked for any chimneys active before going as there was not much to find and he had turned away. He walked carefully, thinking of the moment when he may be alone again. For some time he has been wondering about where humans' souls are taken when they die and he walked away with such thoughts in his head.

You don't see souls being laid off on the street even when people carry the idea, he whispered to himself as he crossed the lane towards the forest. He simply started to go a bit fast as the lake approached his vision and settled on the old stone pillar feeling thankful to the spirit. It depends on your deed. The good ones are taken to heaven and the bad ones to hell. Those who remain in between flutter as ghosts staying on earth, a voice whispered in his ears as he saw the golden spirit present there. It may have read his thoughts and made him feel blissful.

Humans are always determined by the way they live in their realms which can be disturbed easily. However, for ghosts, they have their crossing path in the ultimate world which they don't want anyone to interfere with. The spirit let Upendera find the way life dictates as he has been a prominent member before his death willing to help those who have struggled. The old man remembered the end of his son long back and he could never come out of it, saving the ghost of the last moment. the activist understood it, maybe he knew how it had happened at the time it. In some way or another, the hearts are connected and he is trying to show the old man better ways to live life.

Across the bank of the lake, Upendera could see some fishes coming out with smaller creatures dead as they were crushed in their mouths to satisfy their hunger. He looked to the other side and saw a bird flying up with a fish in its beak flying high. He saw the bird tumble onto a tree and fall straight, dying just when it had celebrated the joy of catching the fat fish in its beak. all around the circle was blooming to its fold. Should they all come back as ghosts or would they be taken off for good? he asked but the golden spirit shook his head pointing to the other side with a different scene.

Few cloak figures were tussling with strange

identities, they flicked the light, and the other strength was tormented by such blaze holding the false figures in its scale. The voices could hardly matter as the visuals say it all in the backdrop for the old man who understood. It was a lesson of life Upendera had somehow come to find and he felt grateful to see the strength accompanied by it as he bid farewell to the omen power who had the ghost of a smile on his empty face again watching him go away.

Nastika was still asleep, Astitva had a temptation to call her and he finally took on calling her Excuse me, I am from Hollywood, we have sent you an invite to be part of our films, would you like to? he said changing his voice but the daughter disconnected the phone as she knew it was her father. The daughter stood up from her bed and texted back. We are from the ghost world, come and find us to lead your destiny be it alive or dead, the father laughed in the outer room hardly as Upendera climbed the stairs. The potion was ready as Upendera'swife offered it to both of them and they saw Nastika coming out from his room to wish morning to everyone.

There was a sudden call on her phone again. A voice spoke this time but not so familiar as she ran back to pick it up. We want a Turing guide. services shall be highly appreciated, it said as she tried to find who may have called this early. Charges are the same as read on the digital cover of a magazine? She asked and an agreement sounded from the other side simply. Let me know when to join, I shall come, she said, coming back to find his father and uncle just finished with potions and children climbing up to fill their hunger in the morning.

A new task, is it? We won't be worried now he is back, Upendera said, watching her come out again. Yeah, I am thankful for her care in my absence here, Astitva replied with glee on his face watching them over. He knows how troublesome these tours can be but he still appreciates his daughter for being part of them. Let's get cracking. I want to hear more about hunting birds. It is real as far as I can deduce now. The father said, leading Nastika back to her room and taking out a print from his pocket which he had saved to explore further with his daughter and he had been waiting for his chance.

Carnivora. Flightless in nature. It is known to have sharp claws. That's how it is known, the daughter spoke to him simply. This is not the only fact. Records suggest it is more found in places that are haunting or slippery in hill forests. the father told her as she promised to keep a close watch on it in the future. Maybe we might have to encounter it in our mission papa. I'll update you if I get to know more about it somehow, she smiled, taking the note and saving it in her bag for further follow-ups in quest to find those who don't want the treasure's safety.

The fear of place is not what affects us, He whispered so only Nastika could hear. It is what lies in the fear that makes us feel worried as we become weaker by the element, she nodded as children gathered up outside the room. We are the spies, we can hear everything. Come out now with your treasures before they are gone, it didn't affect Astitva as his daughter smiled and pushed them back towards the table and came out. Now onto the table or there won't be any fritters left for us, is it? they all laughed and it looked much better to fill in as all of them had been living with peace.

After the brunch, the children had gone to school and Nastika turned to her father, taking the permission to go which he did happily. You go, I will handle the beast of this world, he said looking towards the window with the view outside becoming clearer to see. She trudged away with her bag and a better smile than usual as the vehicle suddenly loomed in sight. Hi, My name is Prashant, I am the leader of this tour and I called you, a man in his early 30s wearing an official dress stepped out shaking her hand. I am more than elated to join, shall we? she asked and looked at 3 girls and boys in their mid 20s seated in the back seat of the vehicle with true excitement for what lay ahead.

They all welcomed her and their bumping tour began with a turn of the vehicle as 2 other cars passed close to them and out of sight in speed. Nastika asked where they wanted to go and told the driver to turn 3 times for the main road if they were interested in visiting the temple first. They all agreed as they spent an hour around it admiring the beauty and enjoying clicks. \They were not in a hurry for this day so the guide told them to have a stroll on foot round the outer corridor where the great statue of the golden spirit had been fondly created. They looked at it with true joy and then turned away, spending limited time with it.

They say he walks with us at night protecting the city from harm, a local camera person said as Nastika shrugged it off. Is it true? Did he do a lot to help the city grow? one of the girls with a smaller face asked as the gang started to go back towards the vehicle. They wanted to find more so Nastika decided to take them towards the place that has more pillars with names inscribed in them vividly. A few of them started to wonder why it was so rich, so Nastika said the city had many greats who made it filled with joy and pride. They were curious, hoping they wouldn't be followed by ghosts, and had proper laughter to make the mood warmer.

Let's go to the lower city, We haven't seen those stone carvings. the boy who was the most senior said to the others. Do you have any problems going there? Prashant asked the guide and she shook her head asking them to follow the lead. Let's find some more history of the glorious place, shall we? she told them, walking alongside all of them who simply marched inside a place that felt cooler at first vision but had a pure excitement to take into account for the visitors.

A mist rose from nowhere as they all went inside. It spreads like dust of gold and covers other people who have come to see it. They used to say that the place contains the secret of treasure. Only those who survive or can stay here don't think of it with any wish to claim its royalty. The People who have a false wish to claim it get strained as they start to cough and Nastika could feel the fact coming true soon. Why are they coughing so hard? Prashant asked her but she shook her head as the light of the treasure became more glowing undaunting to face by outsiders.

Three men who had been coughing hard went outside and she felt that they may have been captured by treasury security as they don't belong here anymore. Let's not get too deep. The darkness here pinches our dashing eyes, the girls started to complain as they walked past a statue, a trophy room, and finally close to the gate of gold which was carved. We can't let you in further. We must protect the innocent, it said and Prashant didn't ask why. They simply turned and started to walk close to the trophy room planning their return.

A figure appeared in front of their eyes suddenly. It was smoke-like, with hands, a tongue, and eyes creeping in the dark. No worries, I won't torment you. Have been checking the guards. Did you cough? Nastika shook her head again as it leaped in the air and then turned away leaving a scatter of dust behind. A nasty experience to count. it was asking questions, Prashant replied as they turned away from the fear and the dark spread in this place to calm their mind and pumping heartbeats as they circled in a closely located area for a hot coffee.

It is nothing new for us. We have faced it a lot of times, they are creepy moments, you can't even dream of Nastika told them carefully checking for her lighter inside her pocket and not found by anyone as it's her privacy to hold. It may not be good to roam at night even in the city, would it? the leader asked and she shook hands willing to go back. We wonder if you could join us the next day? We are looking to climb up for an experience, she nodded and simply asked to drop her off at the place where they had picked her up in the afternoon so they told the driver to drop her off safely.

Back at her home, his papa was still awake as it had been a bit later than usual due to a traffic jam in the local area. Astitva sat there writing on his notepad, occasionally coughing due to flashes of light outside and finally rose from his chair to welcome his daughter. She went upside down without the children noticing her and started to tell her papa about the things that had happened. He wasn't surprised by the golden mist. Instead, he felt relief as he had been warned of a breakout in the place. Finally, the night had circled so they both went to bed for a proper sleep and the day coming to close.

A phone rings in early hours of morning but it was not from Prashant or gang members but a guard from police. Bad news, we have sent ordered to shut down the turing process for 2 days, we are sorry to inform you, For a moment it gave Nastika chill but she ask din quiet voice. Why, hopefully no tragedy to my gang I was leading, The guard explained that due to the warning of heavy showers and the impact on the bridge due to its striking force. For time being , they have sent touring parties back home with their amount settled before the warning issued for not taking the risk to cross the area.

She felt annoyed by this but early charges had already been cleared and now she understood why she received them late at night as the next phone call came this time from Prashant. We are sorry we couldn't complete our tour, it was an absolute pleasure, let me know if the exact charge was accommodated for your services, she said yes simply and also felt gratified for them. However the leader continued speaking more quietly, We also had one personal tragedy. Nt here, obviously, he said as she gasped wondering what next could be waiting. One of the girls lost her grandma, she was old, but it's a sad loss so we have left simply. Thanks for help, she smiled and disconnected the phone.

Astitva saw her seated in a corner, texting to the girl with consolation after taking number from Prashant by a text earlier. He watched her lift the bag of find for a few case studies and wondered what she might be doing. With her mood not in the right way as it is, he let her do the work as she noticed him watching from the corner and sip juice happily. The noise was not much as children had a school fair so they had gone early today. Everything was calm except a machine coming from close by repairing quarters and it was under control for now.

She turned away finally, came to sit next to her father and explained the effect created by the ghost. the way they are causing panic, trying uproot bridges or disturb movement would surely cause mayhem soon. he agreed showing her a diagram of an old building, torn and broken now which she took with interest. he explained that this was the first headquarters of safely kept treasure but now its changed by the golden spirit. The father told her to keep it safe till the time came and, agreeing to it, she went back inside the room feeling miserable due to not having any chances on offer openly.

She kept reading the forward for the next edition of her magazine which had come by an anonymous person. It speaks about the tale of the forest, creatures who become strange to see and then they become a real part of the story line which depends on the level of research done for them. She checked for the description and was able to find the name of the bird which had done damage in the forest so she showed it to his papa who declined his head not wondering much on the subject. She turned back, continued her reading and had said 'ok' in a message to the person who sent a smiling gesture as the day started to close out with all of them still being together in the house.

7
WHEN THE SKY BURNS

Rain was coming thick in the woods, it was silent but strange as only its downpour could be heard by people from their roofs or balconies. Across the bridge, a few splinters come across as the cloud strikes in the sky above. The howling of wolves came back to the jungle, showered with more rain across the place. Everyone was waiting, to let it burst, to make it stop and get back to their work as it was not safe to roam in this weather around with it lashing hard.

Few locals were still out as they were daily wagers and needed to act for their earnings. Few lower-city people had hung out as they could be seen asking for noodles, sipping tea at a closely settled stall and all was somehow connected as more rain came to pierce the evening. Back at home, the children were seriously making a noise as their school had been closed due to rain and they wanted proper fun chasing the eldest for a hood they had found but it was knocked away by Nastika running upstairs holding it in hands.

What's all this? Why are you chasing her badly? The aunt tried to stop Abhi and Aisha from going inside the room. Find her, she took away our playing hood. We were frightening each other with it, Abhi said as Nastika turned out, went past them, and back into the lower floors with those little pranksters chasing her to get it. 'These kids, what got into them? Astitva smiled watching them run away in the best spirit. they need to have their hands on the hood but won't get it even after their best efforts from the eldest.

NO more ghost shows. Enough of this total fun, Nastika said in a sing-song voice irritating Dushyant who jumped into the air but she simply took her hand out. I am the fastest, let me try now to catch it, Vidyut came from behind trying to latch but could only reach her shoulder as she turned the hood into the other hand. Alright, alright. Let's be friends again, she said out of breath due to running as the rain continued to sound harder. They all sat together finally as Nastika herself wrapped the hood on her face and she started to play pranks with them feeling joyous with them.

The hooded person caught Aisha from behind and lifted her but she knew it was the eldest so she didn't frighten much but simply tried to take her hood off. After that, it lunged towards Vidyut and Dushant who ran into the cupboard shouting We have the ghost save us, save us. to the laughter of others. Abhi tried to go past her legs but she caught it too and whispered. I am the ghost, and will take you off, they all were having so much fun that they didn't realise what may be going on upstairs.

An official had come suddenly and he had passed the noise below made by children with rain in the backdrop. He stepped up gently, his boots hardly making a sound and now was talking to Upendera on the matter of safety in the city with concern in the eyes. Astitva has joined the talk further with the latest on how few people have died being stuck in the city after heavy rain. They considered it important and thought it may be a chance for outer powers to bring the skill to murder with more effect using camouflage.

Nastika felt the mood changing as she could hear a few voices finally which made her quiet the children who wanted more fun. Coming, no one will come up, it's urgent, she said in a more strict voice and all went silent below. She slowly stepped, lifted her hood off, and went to find the source of the voices. She knew the official who had come, he belonged to the order and had helped them during the days of Social activists. She touched his feet and he obliged, handing her a paper. She looked carefully at the news on 'deaths' in the rain by unseen elements that made her scared a bit.

We don't have any backup? The force won't work against humanless form and their resources, she said to the official in a heavy voice. 'We do have candle warriors but they may not be affected in the rain as water can repel them, he answered with a gesture of polite interest to her. We need venom force. Their smog can counter the false trails, I am sure it will do, Astitva replied, looking firmly at the official who nodded to them. Let us update you on the process, we will try to help if possible, they all agreed as Upendera listened to them with just mere interest but not speaking much and the official had gone with a wave.

Nastika sat close to her father with a grim expression on her face. She couldn't think much about how the threat may loom. It is all fine. You need to only face the fear when it gets dark, her father said and she shook her head. Upendera stood up from his chair, went to the room where he kept the golden coin, and brought something to show them with glee. It was an inscription written in gold and Astitva knew what it meant as he handed it to the niece with pride.

The light that burns the sky only appears when all the gold is kept safe, obliging the owning of the cultural glory to people , it read as she watched it closely. It gave her some sort of hint about the past which was not clear but those who knew golden spirits did know that it had the power to burn all the fears and transform it into a truly golden delight. Why did it have to go away if he had such power to burn the sky and destroy evil? The daughter asked Astitva who shook and thought it had been clear to them that they don't speak of the end as the golden spirit keeps a watch on them.

On the other side, a car stopped outside a cafe as three men came out. They asked for three cups of tea and retreated behind a sitting place as they opened food they had brought from home to enjoy. Nothing better than to have a campout and enjoy it truly, they said as the stall owner handed 3 teas to each of them. They started to share parathas amongst them with pickles and enjoyed the tea. Once they had paid, they went inside the car and decided to go back.

They drove through the main lane, into the famous watching spot, and turned away before the place where bridges cross and separate it. The front person saw the sign board on not to cross and decided to switch away from it. We should not cross the rules of the officials, shall we? he asked the men seated in the back seat who agreed. They turned away towards the lower city, crossed the great pillar, and reached closer to the statue. One by one they came out, touched the mental feet, and had a blissful experience to cherish the glory it aspired to as they took clicks and went back with the car driven away.

OY, stop here, a police guard came holding an umbrella. Who permitted you to drive on these rainy days? Show me the ticket, he demanded with a glee of trying to bargain with the outsiders. We haven't been requested to show with, I did get it signed, Please we may go? The front person who had been driving the guard asked him to come outside and show his driver's licence which he did. Fine, not a big deal. Pay 500 and I will let you go, he sneered as they had no choice so they did and drove away as he smiled with triumph at cheating tourists.

I thought he may ask for more money. My last tour was somehow the same you know, the driver said as they decided to leave the place not looking to stay. His mood has turned and it has affected his other friends with the incident too. They stopped outside one more place to buy some food for the journey and then drove out. It was a kind of bad experience as most of the place has been closed, people were in huddles or not politely talking and it has somehow affected those who were coming back after the closure of rain.

A flash happened as he took back the note handed to him by the tourist leaving away from the place. There was a spark very close and someone had hit him brutally on the cheek without a warning or hint of attack. Who's there? I demand you to show yourself, He ordered by firing a shot into the sky with his gun loaded. There was a crack, a snort of laughter and his gun had been broken into pieces in front of his eyes with shrew emotion for it. The next moment he was lifted into the air and crushed down heavily onto the floor with enormous strength that he couldn't imagine to face even in dreams.

The ghost of the order, the voice said in the air as the man struggled to take a breath being pinned down on the floor easily by the power who was looking disgusted. This is how we treat the people? Asking them to pay for their collapse in the hills? he looked in true rage wanting to crush the man. The guard started to excuse or present arguments that they must have been approved like they said but the ghost didn't listen and gave him a serious smash, thumping him on the floor with the person in true pain due to the way he was struck.

You have allowed innocent lives to face the surge of anger and lust, the voice said, making a deep slash on his other cheek. I am not responsible, I work for the place. Please let me go. the guard started to cry as the ghost hurt him more brutally with more slashes. If they die in the weather, it is you who should be blamed, Not they. , another crash and a gash came to his injured neck. goodbye, you loathed people, I am happy to finish you, it said as the guard's neck was broken and he was dead and dropped onto the floor.

There was a 'whee' as he died. The ghosts from the other side had come to follow suit as they could feel a death coming in some course. No more meals for you too. I was waiting for this mistake to come The security ghost who had crushed the guard told them with a flick of an electric shock. He knew fire won't work so he took advantage of the rain. The ghosts felt paralysed and were trying to run out of sight watching the spark of electricity rise sharply. He caught them with a prison bottle, flicked his ghostly thumb and they all created a huge gurgle before being stunned and destroyed by the shock inside it.

A better way to deal in this weather, you know, The golden spirit told him as he bowed his head in gratitude with further plans to execute. Sending word to Astitva and the members on how to deal with the weatherly effects, the figure said to the spirit who waved his ghostly hand in thanks. The figure took out a shadow ink, a tormented cloth, and flicked his fingers. writing came into it stating: 'Light and fire, according to the condition. use thunder to counter rain or water power. and the cloth disappeared with the figure too leaving everything to be calm except the sound of water.

A whistle was heard very close to the cave area as a vehicle passed at speed trying to go in. The person who was driving felt like someone had stopped them. No more tours around caves, please. It's Closed till the water gets clear, a voice came and it arrived suddenly. The men in the car felt a bit worried but it didn't affect them. What can we do for you, sir? Any problems? the driving person asked, still angry from inside, the way they were stopped by a guard asking for money if they wished to tour.

You planned to leave, why are you still driving around the place? it's filled with scary bumps in the road, the voice said, still following as the driver turned away looking embarrassed. Yes, I am aware you have been thinking that you were allowed to travel after paying off with freedom, it made the driver angry and lost the steering grip. To his actual surprise, a flash took place and the car survived from falling deep into the valley or it would have been the end of all 3 people seated in it.

We have lost a lot by falling like this, the voice replied again, finally turning the steering wheel of its own.

There is not much good happening right now. I would advise you all to leave, the car turned off the exit road before the driver could complain and he was feeling dejected for it. 'how are you doing all this? I am the driver, smoke came from his windscreen and he was unable to see for some time. Once the smoke cleared they were out from the hilly area and they heard a huge stone fall behind them with a crunch closing the gateway for some time securing everyone from the water.

We shall open it the next day once all pour down subside, the other leading ghost told the security in charge. they flicked their ghostly hands and a light appeared on the stone marking it. Locals were not going away but wondering how they might get food and other necessary items the next day. 'It shall be open in the morning, don't worry. the milk carriage and other good loaded trucks will come easily, a police guard informed after Upendera called him and he felt relief as he didn't want any disturbance in his life

There were few complaints about closing the main road as the inner way had become crowded due to it. No fuss. they never care for the public, a local official could be heard shouting in the way as he tried to drive through after returning from work. Other people did seem to be bothered too but the rain water has slowly started to contain in natural bodies and it would soon allow them to recover and come out of this mess having a perfect life. However, the ghosts were not complaining, with more rain they had the advantage, hoping that more people would be lured into the mist and they could have one more deadly strike.

The dagger ghost lurked close to the tree stumps if someone came in search or somehow after they were drunk. The other ghosts appreciated the plan and separated themselves. A few of them also stayed back to make sure they were not confronted by strange spirits who could give them shocks. They have switched the plan, we need to be careful, one of the main ghosts hidden behind the woods said to others as they leered trying to tower on. It was still drizzling so nobody could be seen and they were waiting for their chance to hunt or pry out their victim.

Inside the home, people were cooking meals as it was certainly cold and the weather had changed everything. Nastika was complaining about how much she had asked to eat in a few hours. The children were laughing as they found the eldest is not on the top when it comes to food. In other homes, people were trying a few dishes with their best effort. They could hear the sound of a cooker from the repaired building simply, the laughter of people, and the cold breeze flying as it took away the smell of food cooked to entertain everyone around with the best of time to cherish it.

A cloth flew with wind on the topmost window as Astitva caught it before it could fly away. He had one look at it, thought it had been well-directed, and handed it to Nastika. She smiled with a word in exchange for strikes, handed it back to her father, and started to munch on the porridge put in front of her. Good plan, they are thinking minds, she smiled as her father replied. Upendera saw the cloth with shadow ink and he understood that it was certainly well arranged to counter the fears presented by hidden tricksters.

Fear was gripping more people as a few slip and fall had taken place. A man in his late 20s had suddenly toppled down after he went at speed to deliver the package to his owner and be safe in the shop. Be careful now, are you fine dear? the owner asked as the person felt dumbfounded on the way he had the fall. he shook his head, turned away gingerly, and felt pain in his right arm after reaching the upper floor as the owner shouted, This is not the day for us, Let me check who delivered it, he slammed the package as it was not what he had wanted from dealer.

On the other lane, a lady lost her cool after she slipped while trying to drive off in her scooter and getting late. What the hell, it's not raining now, why is it happening? she scoffed with her helmet dropping away from her hand. She managed to stand back with her costly slippers diced in mud, felt angry, and then started her scooter. For 10 minutes she kept fuming as it didn't start either but after checking the time she felt relief as it was not 9 yet and she had managed to drive away finally just in time so she wouldn't get late.

A few junior players have got injuries in places that you don't expect as they were trying to reach on time, play the best shot, or were in arguments. One of them had a gash on their upper eye, the other had his ankle twisted, and three of the players were out of the next match in the local place due to broken jaws and it was looking more critical as the chaos kept spreading off. nobody could understand what it all meant as more news came with pain and sadness, and Nastika felt she couldn't help it as she kept watching it online, on TV, and messages flashing onto her phone.

There had been news of broken poles and clashes in public and it was getting worse in the city. Not a single person could feel why it had been such a fast turn of events. it could be heard with quarrels in the air, rasping of sad faces, and a lot of complaints as they fought. The guards were kept busy as they were summoned to control gatherings, to make sure social activities don't get affected and it has been an absolute mess. People were getting out of bount to do things that didn't connect to them and get into fights damaging each other badly in fights.

Upendera didn't feel the mood to be perfect, whether it was the effect or the moon. Nobody could hardly say but it had become grim. He wasn't going towards the lake, the golden spirit couldn't connect to him and it was strange. One morning when Astitva was also asleep, he decided to go across and finally managed to do it with stick tapping and the golden spirit kindly waiting to see him. It took some time to digest the calmness, the quiet and pleasant weather, and everything to stay for a while.

What disturbs you? The world hasn't ended, you know. There is a lot of light left to grasp, to fight out or pass through, the spirit made him show the gleaming energy of light at the tip of the lake. It is not humans that disturb me. it's the mood in the air, the palpable strength and its influence that makes me worried, Upendera simply spoke back in a calm voice talking to him. The golden spirit took a watch out of his ghostly hands, flicked it, and told Upedra to look at it with curiosity. It is of huge importance to us, the spirit said so he could come to know why he did so.

A star was visible in the watch so it had no numbers with strange elements. A hand was pointing towards the lake as the old man found how to click the maps in it by the spirit. The lake was shown in bright light with people around it. A time was flashing onto the top with creatures moving with few white dots circling. The whites and other colours matched together and started to create mayhem with so many noises coming. In response, the watch showed a lot of lighting as it was streaming a documentary and with burst, those who were the enemies had been destroyed by the light. Strangely, Upender felt he had seen this somewhere before and he handed the watch back.

Well, has it happened before? Your face says it all, the spirit asked not to confirm but to rejuvenate the mind. Yes, it was the night when you left. It's never been so much of a fight. the best show for us, the spirit nodded but had more to say before he turned away. There is someone in your city who belongs to me, the day he shall return to its identity, this will happen again, so one for the records if you like to, he flicked in the air and a carved inscription fell to Upendera's hand. you may leave keep it safe, they were happy to exchange few words before he went away smiling once more.

Few people have come to see an ancient site as the tours have started again for those who are known as tourists. They didn't have a guide but they hardly needed to as they had already come here before. No chance to get symbols on it? Are there? the youngest boy asked, looking at the lower city marbles with joy on the shining statue standing tall. The main leader shook his head as the party spread around the place and decided to find their way back.

They walked back with a few packets in hand as they had done shopping. While returning to their vehicle, they passed through a dark corner and a shadow loomed, leering somehow. For a moment the leader thought it may just be his imagination but then a voice came shivering all of them. Very early in your tour. Be careful there is a lot of water after the rain. , The leader nodded without a word as his throat had gone dry and they turned fast toward their vehicle with an evening on the verge of simply falling upon.

A horn made some noise, muffled the voices of a few students and they had turned away. The tourists weren't happy with the limited time they are given by authorities nowadays but they have no choice except to follow it. The leader spat out from inside the window pane and felt he had a vision of something on the glass. It didn't shatter as the shadow passed through for which he felt gratified. They were moving easily due to the stone of blockage removed but it has not been easy to drive. The speed has gone slow, rules are imposed and it has made things look better for all.

There was a sound of leaves falling in the woods. Someone was collecting it for a cultural ceremony without much fear in their heart. As it started to cross dusk, the person counted the leaves and moved away as a voice spoke from behind him. How come? The time is over to do the process, go away you thief' and the person who belongs to the order simply turned away. It is not good to talk with spirits in the evening or when it gets dark, they can capture your brain and force you to be taken towards the dead here.

A word has been spread by the humans of the order that a relative power to the golden spirit may come to exist in their world soon. It may not be wise to do any kind of mantras but they have been told to collect leaves like it is for welcome in the city. Not a word to anyone, understood? the main leaders of the group have said. It was tough to accept it but once the word was spread, the lower members started to form the pack and collectives in the evening time they do it before dusk or when the moon hasn't appeared so things can stay in far better motion.

The night was looming with fear with the shadows forcing everyone to go back home simply. A stream was falling closer to the woods which carved its hunger in it. The strange fishes were bouncing onto it with a man following the trail with his fork in the water. It looked like this man would be around 40 years old due to the way he was able to move and see with his short but perfect body to catch river creatures. Yes, that will be enough for the night. I am hungry, to be honest, he said simply, watching with his light in the dark to get habitual.

A ghost had appeared from the forest as he sliced the head of a fish and put it in a heavy copper pan to cook. Before the ghost could say anything, the person struck a match, created a fire enough to cover it, and the fish was cooked for his liking. He sat there with a light of fire to save his stomach as a few wild creatures came across to find out the source of food with its strong smell. The man put out his pan in water, filled it, and toppled it upside down so the fire could vanish. He used to cook the dead fish.

He turned right, moved with a candle burning in his hand from the fire which he had struck and he was gone. The creatures and the ghost turned too thinking he may come again with their chance to get him on guard soon but one more light has come broader than the first one. Someone came lashing toward the ghosts who were waiting and pulverised them with a bright stream of joy. A word to all of you, I knew you would fall into a trap, the figure spoke, trapping a few ghosts and sending them off with their end into the fire easily. We do the process of sacrifice, well worth it to catch you off guard, it laughed with their noise getting low in the light.

The figure looked for his pocket and threw a few stones on the place to mark it so next time when humans come, it would be helpful. The light was rising above marking the stones with a sign and the ghosts feared it. The symbol was the counter to the sign of horns as it was the sign of blaze which ghosts must worry about in the future to cross out. The figure smiled broadly speaking to the forest now, You have the right to protect, but you do not have the law to take into your guard, it threw a few more beads onto the place where stones are marked and simply vanished, going out of sight after it.

I saw it. Mark my words, a person rumbled the next morning. He was the same man who had caught the fish but he had no trust in what he saw in the dark. It could have been the vision, you have been fed with such a fat fish, you must have dozed off, the friends taunted him in the lower city. It was true that other people were not going to believe him but he had become a member who was going to remember what he saw. The forest is filled with fears and he had come to find out why it was not allowed to go there at night or you would be slayed off.

Calm down, the night is over. I have brought hot milk for you, his wife had come from behind and he felt surprised. The fear of what he had to encounter hadn't gone away as it kept looming in his mind. The thought made him worried from inside, some kind of illusion that may come back or interrupt his peaceful life with no other purpose. Leave me alone for an hour or so, Yes, hot my water so I can have a bath that will give me ease and take me out of my pressure simply, he requested as he was taken by his wife back home.

Thanks for saving him, the spirit whispered to an order member, who had made the mark. I am afraid your stones may be removed by greedy humans but your contribution is valiant for them, the other person nodded. they could see the stone till resting a mark but the figure who had put them knew they shall be taken for good by humans rather than the spirit. the prominent figure smiled, took out a map, and handed it to the other. A work for you. It shall be private, if you like, he nodded and took the map interestingly to find what lay ahead in an unknown haunted place for him.

We do fear the dead, but more we fear for those who are not, the figure said, going away. He has been part of the order, just like the other protector, he too had died in the process of protecting an honourable place. They were trying to stop ghosts at all costs but deaths were still taking place and ghosts were not the only thing that made them happen. The figure looked in the sky with everything in order due to sunrise, raised one hand in salute, and left as the sun spread its great blissful aura all around with happiness to everyone living in peace.

Upendera was looking at the inscription, It recalls a moment in his life one that is a certain connection and he walks quietly after closing the room locking it from inside so no one else can know. I can swap my position. I must keep the word of the golden spirit, he whispered to himself. a figure has appeared in the closed room. I am here to guide you, it said, the figure was identical and looked to be the ghost of the son as everyone predicted it to be staying with his father. What is left to fight? We lost it years back, Upendera said in a voice filled with sadness but the ghost shook its head.

It will never end. We didn't lose honestly. the time will come when you get the chance, it echoed but just to

Upendera shaking him who had put the inscription onto a secret box and looking up. It said you will return to the world, how is it possible? The father looked confused, like the tragedy may turn into some miracle and give him some hope to recover from the past. No matter, I am with you in this form, I shall stay here simply, he smiled thinking about the past and all that had happened.

A knock appeared on the door accompanied by Astitva who was looking edgy. I want a word, sir, Tomorrow I will be leaving so it's urgent, Upendera saved the inscription, opened it, and came out with a smile. Yes, the honour to protect you dear charm, is it? he said with a glaze that had mischief hidden in it behind. Yes, I may have to leave the treasure with you, keep it safe, will you please? He looked with patience as Nastika sat next to him with a certain hope of a positive remark as her uncle sat there quietly observing the mood.

We won't stop her from going out or having any tour, If you ask me, they are her best ventures, Upendera's wife said before he could say anything, she is the daughter of her sister so rightfully she had a better word to say on her behalf. Although it is necessary not to take risks in tough stages of challenges, they only make life worse. you know better than her, Upendera added, looking calm but with a touch to his voice as he gave a sharp glow towards Nastika. the father shook hands with his daughter requesting her to follow in her room so he could have a word.

It is prudent that we don't trust everyone but it's also crucial that we stay in different places, she nodded as he took out some currency and handed it to her. Not for you, but for the children. They like you, it's your duty to protect them from any fears looming, will you? he had a lot of hope in his lit eyes and she simply bowed her head in agreement with a smile. I hope mom would not bother you much to run for her duties, should she? The father shook his head and turned back to the seat where Upendera was now drinking tea and offered it to Astitva.

Thanks, I must be packing soon. It was good to stay here. ever since I came back, he thanked both of them who said it was nothing. Upendera's wife asked him to visit again if it would be possible for him. Astitva hasn't told them that he is only in this location for 3 months after which he may have to go back to the cave mission to complete the task and finish the horror once and for all. he hasn't revealed this even to Nastika and they thought he may continue to come here making a perfect mood for everyone by his presence.

Lot to do, I shall see when I may get time to come out of it, the daughter raised her eyebrows like he was hiding something but he had no intention of telling her to and the father left to a lower room to collect his things and pack them up as he got surrounded with children. Nice time, I may come back soon with lots of cookies, shouldn't I do that? They cheered for him and asked him to promise to bring cookies that are designed like creatures for which he laughed and picked his thing back upstairs with a smile.

A video was running onto the daughter's phone as a person was showing the recent number of deaths. A glimpse of the end of the forest was shown, the marking stones were brought into focus and the mark that kept popping was also discussed. She couldn't understand why certain powers were heading on each other like swords raised to conquer a place. She saw one more video that highlighted the rise of water levels, new streams emerging and deaths also taking place closer to such eventful water bodies. She guessed this time that was why it had been happening as signs of horns do like to transform and she would have to guess what may loom ahead.

Silence in the woods. People locking themselves. Losses of lives. it all means they want to go for a huge attack, she whispered as Astitva came back to her room handing her some handwritten notes to help. For the future, we all can't deny it. Your uncle may not like to explain but this will do, she thanked him as he went past and gestured to call aunt to make juice for the children looking at her watch. Nastika came out to help and took the juice down and the father felt that she had grown indeed as there was more noise from downstairs.

There were no hard noises, the breeze was coming quietly with very few ghosts left after the carnage of the light in them. Every life was calm, sleeping or in peace as the weather became perfect after the water had cleared up from the main corridor. This was one of those nights which was static and there was hardly a movement in it. The moon was shining bright like an orb hung in the sky, creatures were hidden in forests with some kind of word of exchange in them and the time had stuck on the moment where it would finally become intense with certain activity as everyone would grapple with fear of uncertainty and joy after the resolution.

8
THE GHOSTLY CONFLICT

A voice of a horn had come, Astitva stood up to leave the place, shook his daughter's hand, and said calmly, Be well, catch you soon, as she was also half asleep and said 'yes' watching him leave simply. he stood up, touched the feet of Upendera, and smiled as he left with most of the people still asleep downstairs. The vehicle had come on the other side so he crossed the road, looked towards the sky, and with a thank you to the heavens, he had settled and gone from the place with the vehicle trudging away in the early morning from the place.

It was somehow familiar as he went to the tea stall which was a bit empty in the early hours with only 4 people sitting there. Welcome sir, retreat time, isn't it, so early? The tea vendor asked and he agreed, handing him some money to buy sweets for his wife. He knew the kind of dessert she liked the most so he was happy to spend extra money to cover it. Your wife likes a heavier toast, doesn't she? the person nodded, took the heavy cotton bag, and went out towards the bus station to take the bus home as he sat inside waiting for it to start.

A message flashed onto his phone. Rival powers may clash tonight. Reach by 5 in the evening to be safe, it was his daughter and he replied with calm guessing what may come, Already aware of it, I shall see what I can do to fix the matter, he texted her back with no hurry on the way that a clash may happen. People were behind the diamond coin and it is safe, till no one knows where it is, there is no benefit to having any such as it may only create mayhem rather than achieve it.

I am coming back, will reach by 4, He said, calling his wife. Good for me, It has been an uproar with legal practice and trying to manage the home on the other side, he smiled as she complained about things she may have asked her locals to manage in his absence so they can be adapted easily. You lawyers always have a statement for things you don't do priorly, it made her laugh as the bus started and he left with it going away from the place with the sound of dust and petrol in the air as the bus moved around.

Back in the forest, a ghost was lurking close to the place where locals had been trying to collect leaves. It has been a plan to surprise people from behind but it hasn't worked till now as the protection of the humans has been strong. Whenever they tried to snatch, another ghost from the protecting team had come to counter and a kind of duel had started. Why are you so intent on protecting them? the dagger holder asked as the opposite side slammed his imprint onto the forest floor. Why are you so desperate to create mayhem? Duties sir, we all are bound by it, a cackle from the side which had knocked over others and the remaining ghosts had to vanish in the smoke filling around them making everything dark.

Keep a watch on them. It is a kind of feast they can't deny to hold, a figure spoke quietly appearing on the sideline with a flick of a candle burning quite strongly in his hands. It threw something into the air in the form of gas with the intent of setting a trap that caught some shapes which certainly got burnt by it. nasty plots, they are still lurking, when will they stop doing this around us, he threw it once more and other particles also were diminished. The figure walked around the stone markings, checked for signs of the blaze, and then stepped to go away with a salute to others.

I can wait till night, the dagger ghost whispered as it got out. We are with you, let's crack out humans who don't know our powers, they all had managed to circle in a tree's roots as the gas had come. They did have to lose a few of their members but the party was still enough to create horror and try to force an outsider into their trap. Let's get cracking, a man is coming this way, they had a ghost of a smile on their face watching a person simply lost in the forest with no clue on which way he should go from there.

Come with us, we will get you to the blazing sign, a voice whispered from behind him. The man did have some tricks as he heard the voice and flicked his lamp to burn with light. It revealed a pale face with a socket in place of eyes leering at him. The man must be skilled in chanting as he spoke a mantra to push the ghost away who felt a bit surprised by it. Fear of the dark, he said in his voice, I summon you, the strength of light to finish it, the ball of flames emerged and turned towards the spinning ghost that simply got destroyed by it once and for all.

A few more ghosts appeared as one got destroyed. The man had however reached the fork, the place where a blaze of signs lights the power. He bowed his head to the sign, said one more mantra, and went with the ghost chasing him from behind. It was truly frightening as the ghosts kept shouting harshly, Our meal, you can't light a fire every day, we will have you. It is enough to terrify anyone in a dream but if it happens to you in life, then it is surely going to affect you with fear.

The man reached his place, took out a jug of water, and practised with a few sips of mouth full throwing the water out. it is believed in the city that if you do a tribute in memory of positive spirits, your encounter with the ghosts would go away or be removed from your mind easily. he felt quiet after facing it and trying to get relax. he checked his hand where a cut had been sharp enough to reawaken the memory. he went inside and filled it with old sand lotion to get the heel. Now it's fine, I may survive, Thank you golden spirit, it whispered, flicking the light off in his room which he had left open before going and raising a blanket to his arms he had fallen asleep.

Nastika was checking her watch, it had almost struck late night. A loud noise took place from the building which was in repair. With light coming on from inside, three men burst from nowhere. They held guns in their hands with beads shining on their chess to tolerate the opposite ghost party. Get him, now? It's an order, you understand? the first one said, followed by the other two who came out and vanished in sight. A plane figure burst suddenly coming out from behind the footprints that had been left. It whispered a word like Begin, and the noise of the blast could be heard from the lowest room.

Astitva had managed to safely arrive at his place with no problems at the root. The noise was also coming from the nearby quarters that had been ordered to repair and it couldn't have been more like a coincidence to find it happening in the same way. He had managed to clean the upper floor, make tea twice for his wife and they had been watching TV. After getting bored of the glimpses of unknown people at a certain place, she got bored and decided to close the TV out as it was getting dark.

Back in the upper city, a few men circled a figure in an urge to catch it. You belong to the order, I will do my best to destroy you, the man in the lead spoke to the figure, shouting the words. Try it, this time it's not going to be easy, the figure flicked his hand, turned the man's revolver and fired 3 bullets, making him fall on the already broken floor. A roar took place petrifying a few of the people as figures had come from the sky. They swirled bat-like, hitting everyone but the figure had managed to burst a light of strikes making them all disappear with his absolute strength.

I was not that powerful when I was a human, you know, the figure said, lifting two men and destroying their bodies with a crunch. I also have power, I will show you, the other man shrieked, taking out a stone and conjuring more figures. they don't count, it's the last day for all of them, the figure taunted collecting them in one single light and crushing them all. he had a ghost of a smile and the last thing he had to do was to show his face which he did lifting the hood and letting humans run as those who were attacking felt backward by force.

The rival strike hasn't ended in the city. Masks were running in shirts and trying to throw everything down. They climbed the lower staircase, tore the hangings, and wanted to put their belongings that wouldn't fit. They ran towards the forest, breaking the new seating bench and crushing everything at their speed. Not so fast, it's not the end you know, one figure has come like the previous one. He lifted a few men and threw them over the wreck of the broken bench. One more strike and that will do, it said, raising a lamp and striking his fingers so the light became 5 separate images and it all struck the men trying to fight and killing them on the floor with no mercy.

Chaos ran all around as guards could be heard firing from their guns to keep things in order, everyone was in true fear as Nastika sat down in the lower room watching the TV. her worst fear was the children, if anything happened to them, it would be the worst jolt to her heart. Schools were still in control of the strong security established by the security ghosts as their pearly white figures kept moving in shadows or hidden in dark classrooms with voices coming to make children laugh and asking them to stay calm in tough weather around as they hadn't been sent back home early due to threats.

Besides, on the main road, traffic has been causing chaos more than anything as more crowds filled in making noise. A few cars crashed into each other with a bumper broken and a fuel tank destroyed. No more mess, a figure said, conjuring a strange bag as the leaked oil filled it and he flicked the bag to vanish out of sight. It was somehow a rage that had to settle and it has finally crossed the mark that

Upendera too came to notice. Children? Will they be safe? the aunt said. Come down and watch it on TV too. Nastika shook her head strangely with no clue on how to bring them back.

The noise of the bus, are they coming now? she said after a while as more figures could be seen fighting with strange shapes or creatures gathered around. I shall bring them today, Upendera said, lifting his stick and the female didn't say no. He stepped down towards the lower stairs and crossed the threshold. He could feel a ghost lingering in the backdrop as most of them came out to protect their lives. thanks for your bidding, they are safe, Upendera whispered to the bus and it inclined the pearly head as all 4 naughty ones started to go towards the quarters in his wake.

They all looked shaken though not frightened of what they had to face in school. Big shades of power, true giants, I never thought it would be true, Aisha was still in fear as her nightmare had come to become real. I would have never seen a teddy so powerful, true muscle, Vidyut replied as they settled in. No more noise, get calm. We shall find out soon, Nastika had come down and helped them as they all had a lot of things to tell her that night with all the details in their sharp brains with excitement.

In the other city, a gate has been broken, and a few ghosts have run through a machine and now imitate the sounds of creatures for their joy. A Duck started to quack with the voice of a ghost speaking loudly, Bring us more food, we are hungry as we are not residents of your city so let us go home, it made the people passing frightened as more sounds of guns came and blasts appeared so it had become an absolute outrage. The three figures had come with masks as people shouted going away. They took down the humans trying to create chaos and simply crushed their necks, sending them to the nether world by descent strike against the active powers.

It was easy for them, now they are free of their lives to protect as they crushed the opposition who had been working with them. One of the figures threw a pale white powder into the sky which brought calm and had fixed the energy of the rivals to be under control. Massive, like the last time, No matter, I will finish this one, it said throwing more gas and splashes of water bombs into the air conjuring them out of the pocket and the mood was soon cleared the potions and fears of the ghost so he decided to go back upside simply vanishing from the location to help others as it was urgent.

A ghost was standing at the entry point scaring the stalls, vendors, and other tourists with leering mouths open to kill anyone who dared to go past. the end of your reign, the figure said, striking it with a sound of thunder. It gave a strange tickle like a laugh and vanished from sight. He turned towards the tall golden statue and saw a few men and ghosts trying to claim it. Not so quick, here we go, the figure said, a burst of sparks and the men collided due to the force of fake treasure crushing them. The figure caught ghosts around, burnt them into the air and it was all clear now after most of them had decided to retreat from the place.

What's happening there? Astitva was on the call as Nastika had come upstairs to fill in for her aunt about how the children did get help. Not much to see through. The ghosts are good but also few are bad, that's what we have come to know, she responded by handing the napkins with boxes of the children to Aunt. Be careful till the moon is not in the sky. they may try to summon the ancient powers, he said as the daughter agreed and the phone got disconnected as more noise could be heard close by with moonlight coming back soon.

More mess, they will never understand the secret, from the balcony Upendera saw a figure covering all 5 men struggling to keep it on bay as it came to them at speed. The figure clenched them in his glove, flicks and they all crashed with a strange sound of no mercy in the air. Good bloke must be from order. Whatever it is, they won't get the coin, he proudly whispered to him, turning back and away to find both her niece and wife talking about the fear circling in the chaos.

A person has decided to turn towards the quarters. He had a gun in his ghostly hand as he wanted to do some damage to Upendera's house. A movement happened in the old man's face as a strange voice came. I will handle it, this is my chance, was the voice of his dead son and its ghost popped out separating itself from Upendera's head and simply faded away. As the ghost started to approach, it was clasped by hand from behind. the son's ghost simply tossed it up, flicking something from his white gash beneath the empty chin becoming bright.

A fire emerged from nowhere as the ghost shouted and walloped in the air for cover but couldn't escape the light. The other fighter crossed the mark and threw it away with the sound of metal so it crushed onto the lower side. The father watched with elation as the son, even in ghost form, was equally up to the mark. He gestured to his forehead and the ghost agreed to come back, restored to its safety both in Upendera's memories of the past and the true belief in him in his mind.

Our bond shall prevail, no matter what the conditions are, the son's ghost said, only visible and heard to his prominent father. It looks like you had long since abandoned to have fun with ammunition, A strange smile came to Upendera's face like he was pleased with what he had seen. They whispered something together, The order remains complete with us like they used to do back in days after destroying the enemy and the ghost had found its exact place in his father's secret as the time had witnessed them getting reunited again.

The curfew was suddenly lifted as the noises started

to get low. The police guards were collecting the wreckage, the broken canisters, and the bodies that had fallen on the ground. Both sides had few casualties but the enemies had been thwarted as 12 guards had lost their lives despite the best efforts of the ghost of security forces. Besides more than 50 opposite gang leaders have been hunted which has been a huge success. The moon had come out. Upendera could see a van passing in the road or it could be an ambulance. The voices were on high announcing the fear to have been passed but requesting people to stay inside due to the effects.

The ghosts had a huge loss in the requisite damage as they had led it but couldn't succeed. The figures bloomed with candles around smiling but not completely as their side had lost a few humans too and the rival force had finally stopped with no sign of the further onslaught. Upendera too felt peace as Nastika took dinner down by herself. She looked at the children who were not looking well and had no jokes to crack. She felt the mood and decided to set a contest on who may have the most chapatis so things could come back to normal and it felt better in the gang as her phone rang upstairs.

All is under control, one more father spoke, this time it was Nastika who was looking into the screen as the video call was happening and he saw no scratches to her with relief. Your mom should be more worried than I have to, honestly, he said, watching her smile. He lifted a framed design in his other hand to show her the exact damage done as the prophecy had come to fruition. The inscription was carved in it speaking of the night after a few days of full moon and watching it in her phone realise why it all happened in one single day.

On the other side of the repaired building a noise was coming, it felt like someone was calling for help but it was a trap. A car passed very close to the broken stone and the tired felt slippery as it drove away. The voice kept coming asking for help until a wounded person in their late 30s opened it and went inside it. Quiet, no more help, it said and the voice vanished. He was one of the rivals who had done most of the damage and had survived both the ghosts and men of the security forces. He went two steps below, opened a chamber, and vanished out of sight with a strange light held in his palms.

He had a strange glow in his eyes like he had been facing this conditional strike for a long time. The man knew how to open and close secret passages, to go inside and he had watched things moving around. Every year he waits for the full moon ceremony to happen and this leads to chaos. One for my ownership, I was the best but they dismissed me, he would be heard howling with pain on the night of the full moon, totally ready for revenge and it has become a routine for him. The convincing power was so much in him that he could control, to create false influences, and he was responsible for mass murders happening in the city with ease as he kept rounding the dead for a flaming activity.

Terrible! I can't forget what happened in the night, a guard was yelling to his son after returning home. Did you see? this is what ghosts look like, totally evil, the son agreed but he couldn't let go of the dream to follow in the guard's footsteps. It is better to die while serving rather than by their own hands after cheating the public you have to serve, his father has said to him once when he asked about true duty. This day had certainly been an upsurge as most of the houses were talking but they all felt elated to see their children had been left somehow without any certain damage inflicted to make them feel peaceful for it.

Everyone was closing their doors early with fear of the ghost still on the subway. Upendera however kept watching from his balcony as the moon had spread its emotions all over now. he didn't talk to his niece, hardly spoke during the dinner, and calmly walked around the quarters. he has got strong company to follow, it had always been there but the trust in its presence gives him more courage now it has revealed the ultimate strength. he didn't cross the line to get overconfident and try outside but came soon as he saw Nastika closing her room and planning to sleep with no more noise.

In the other quarters, the rival power was striking a few matches with a strange expression on his face. His cheeks have been burnt or have a few terrible scars but he puts lotion on them so they can heal soon. One of his eyes looked strangely blurry but the strength in him was too much appreciated by those who followed him. Usually, he looks for people who complain about money or riches and simply brings them in under the pretence of recruiting into an agency. They agree to it so the rival keeps a close watch on their activity and feels disgust and disgrace in their life. It ultimately leads to the decision to commit and better die than live such a horrible life for which the leader trains them so they can bring chaos in the chosen night.

It was getting dark as ghosts had to face terrible revulsion due to such a huge loss. I kept you here and It proved worth it, didn't it? an old ghost was whispering to one with the dagger. Before the rival's strike broke out, it was said to the dagger holder not to come from the forest. Few figures had bloomed with light towards the place in search but they have held nerves protecting the dangerous spirit and the dagger held in its ghost like hand looked more gleaming than before. We surpassed the test, now it shall be my time to do the honour, It leered sticking its lashing tongue out and it smelt something. A smell of human, trudging in the night and it can't help to follow the trail and hunt it down.

All the ghosts kept a back seat as they had been trapped twice and they didn't want to make any mistake. the ghost with a dagger transformed into smoke and had secretly hidden in the bush behind the man. As the person started to walk, the smoke started to travel with the wind inside the grass. The person was not happy with his leader, one who had been the rival. it had just run away after an argument and how the leader had been responsible for the deaths and loss of a ghost party in such numbers. The irony was that the ghosts were looking to put one of their men for dinner as the feeling started to stretch. In its presence the dagger holder ignored it as they hadn't tasted humans for a long time so they wanted to taste blood feeling hungry.

Come now, this is the time to go big with you human, it created a voice so it spread around the bushes. Alright then, I surrender. I am the one who cares for you but the night is just a disgrace for all of us, the human replied by flicking a bullet that hit him on the floor. That's the trick, how nice, you had fallen yourself, the ghost started to emerge from behind as the face that had fallen was hidden with a mask. They started to tear the muscle portions and the man hardly shouted as he had welcomed death being rejected by his master who was the true person responsible for all this mayhem done publicly in all corners.

The man died on the floor inviting the jungle creatures as the ghost left shouting in true joy, still not aware they had killed one of their gardening persons as they flew high into the trees. Yes, yes, yes, revenge, How sweet it is, the dagger holder spoke with his lips still drenched in the blood of the dead. They scattered a bit distance from the sign of the blaze and started to do a ghost dance in celebration. The body was still on the floor with half of it being crushed and the creatures had only left the skeleton killing it brutally leaving it separated as the morning would be approaching soon to pry others off.

The rival was fuming with lotion all over his face at the main place. He was sitting on a chair with a glass of hot milk served to him by his assistant with grace. Don't worry sir, He will be served well on revoking us, he nodded with something as an update. Find him in the morning before the guards do, we will be in trouble otherwise, he said in a deep voice as the assistant agreed. They had been talking about the map and how to cause more trouble but they didn't have many ghosts so the plan seemed empty.

It struck 4 in the morning and the alarm rang in Upendera's room. He had already been awake and turned it off before anyone could wake up. Now that Astitva has gone, there is hardly anyone who might be awake this early. He went in to get fresh, took up his stick, and decided to go for the morning walk. He had a lot of questions, especially about the secret of the coin to ask the golden spirit. He watched as some unknown faces passed away running who he did not know. One of them tried to trip him but got off balance in the process so they all ran away in a certain hurry.

With very little time for the sunrise and the pink glow all around, Upendera kept walking with his secret weapon in reserve; the old man reached the lake easily. The golden spirit appeared from behind and gave the wind a kind of royal shiver. good to see you here again. I can't tell you the truth as it's not time, he said looking straight like he had once again read the concern. Why? I can only own it but not know what it is for with its past so rich? the old spirit waved a hand in a hint that there was still a lot of time left before they came to unveil the secret.

The old man shook his head but he was bound by the culture so he didn't say anything further. The spirit was talking however not on the coin but for the inscription. Your son is not returning, that inscription is certainly made for him but not his body, Upendera came out of his thoughts looking beyond the mist of the spirit. Yes, you indeed have longing but that dream is different. You have to serve and the ghost is for your cover, it said and Upendera now understood. You are looking for someone who can be powerful like my son, ready to die or kill, is it? the spirit agreed with one more wave of hand as the water rose up and down with a gurgling sound in the lake.

Time to go, it's almost sunrise, Upendera spoke further with the glow fading and the voice of spirit going away too. he had one final look at the fishes emerging onto the surface with dead creatures. he didn't look in the sky, or on the other bank. he tapped his stick, turned, and started to march past the place. The guards have started to come back now talking of the last night being darkest and the fears with it. they can proudly say that they had survived the crisis and now they would make their own stories to fill in others.

Nastika had woken up early. She was talking to her papa as Upendera approached and could hear the voice closely from her room. Urgency in her now, good to see, he smiled and his wife came handing him the potion. Any movements you have found lately in the woods? she asked, being one of those rare instances as Upendera did raise his head but then decided to tell things later. He kept looking outside towards the window and was hoping to get some news for the other side of the place active in control of wrong powers with their strange motives.

The niece came out checking her phone as she did so. I have been offered a tour, can I go? she asked her aunt who agreed. It's been chaotic everywhere, are you sure it's good to go? Upendera raised his hand as his wife stopped to continue. I think it's a certain call. I have decided after talking to Papa, she said quietly rather than being ready to argue. It felt a bit strange but her aunt sensed the moment so she didn't ask much as the niece went inside the washroom to get a shower and be prepared for the coming tour.

Half an hour later, just when the children had gone to school, Nastika had also been lifting her bag to go and find the mess herself. Don't argue with your uncle or aunt, they may find out later why it's important, her father told her and she stepped into the bright sunlight which is not tolerable for ghosts or shadows. She had taken a tablecloth for safety if she may have to send a message in her bag and she marched in the sun going away. Two members came from the repaired building but they were holding an offer letter to the next-door shop and Nastika simply went away.

She waited close to a tree as a blue car came and stopped close to her. Guide services are needed, aren't we? a lady in her early 40s asked as she nodded and the front seat door opened letting her in. Nice to see you here. I am Kranti, she said, allowing Nastika to feel comfortable. Where do you want to go in this beautiful city? I presume you are the only member to have help? The guide obliged as the car turned right, into the main lane and out of sight lifting the filtered sand to fly in the hot air as it did so.

Kranti told her that she used to live here in the past. She had an accident in which she lost her husband and it is time that she may try to look for him. I presume there may be a chance that I can go closer to him or his ghost? she said while driving towards the inner lane. this may not be here when you used to recite in the city Nastika obliged, talking through the inner lane area with shops and a wide range of food. They stopped at a stall, asked for two buttered buns with coffee, and went back to the car inside to munch along. it was a certain ride she had been looking for and it had worked.

A shadow crept in as they drove through late afternoon. It was following the car with its trail and finally, when the vehicle stopped, it had covered the front window pane lurking above. Good on you, I have been waiting, it had the voice of an aged man rasping towards Kranti. It took you a long time to feel that I can come back for you, is it? Nastika felt a bit uneasy as she talked to the ghost of her late dead husband who simply smoked through the window and out of sight. Wait, I can't follow you in the woods, there there, she said and turned the car back before it would stop working in the woods due to sand and water.

Scary, do you come every year? It's good to spend some time, the guide said, telling her to turn right just in time as a scooty passed across trundling in speed. Dare me, one more test. lucky to survive it, Kranti said whenever she turns away from the ghost, she has to encounter a bump, tire burst, or such sort of close escape. Nastika smiled as this was one more person who had the habit of facing challenges. She felt like meeting with her again soon and the car had come back closer to the tree from where Kranti had picked her.

the tourist asked to pay but this was one of those times when Nastika denied her. I will charge when you plan a complete tour. Next season, she waved her back as Kranti went back, started the engine, and drove away. The niece felt better as she climbed the stairs, found the children hooting on a subject, and went up. She had come early the night before, in fact, it was just evening and she was in the mood to meet a perfect person to plan the future out of simply being fond of her.

A call came suddenly as she changed into her night clothes. Yes, Papa? She did help to show me new roots, she said, picking it up. I should say she was a calm lady, Losing her husband at a young age does twinge a bit, doesn't it? a few of her words came to Upendera's ears as he was just passing as the call had started. The daughter told her father about the views, how the ghost surrounded them, and the way things worked closer to the forest which didn't surprise him but he felt there was more to it. Keep searching the new angles, I want more news on how the massacre was planned in the city, he said as the phone got disconnected as Nastika agreed to find the clues.

The night was on top again, a few of the young age people had made the mistake of going towards the stream due to the popularity of fat fish. They promised to catch the best one and it seemed to be a perfect chance. The ghost with the dagger saw two of them being late and he threw the dagger hitting one who was in pain as he was collapsing onto the forest grass. As the other one tried to help, a ghost flicked the person's fork by which he had been trying to catch fish. it turned and hit him back as one more person fell to the floor in absolute pain after being hurt.

Yes, this is it. We are on for a better course to serve the night, They started to tower one after another as both guys felt their throats seeing as they couldn't do much and no noise came. They were in pain due to the scar getting worse and lights popping out in front of their blurry eyes with death coming soon. They were dead in the forest, killed by rasping voices and they were happy being on song and having a perfect meal after a while. They started to crush the human skin as the ghost with a dagger raised it like a salute to others and joined in the party to feed its lashing mouth and finished it.

Everything was quiet as the forest had become silent with the morning in close sight. the positive energy coming from the sun shall appear soon between the trees being bright. The dead bodies were left as empty corpses which the police guards may have to come and pick again as duty. Upendera was thinking of resting today as he does not feel well enough to go on a walk. He looked for a pot and let the water boil so he could calm his painful throat with heat as it had been hurting him. it felt strange as he had woken with his throat feeling thirsty after such a long time.

Everything was silent with hardly anything moving in the vicinity. the other buildings had no movement, possibly no flicker of light, and the old man struck a match from his hand to light a candle so he could feel calm which did help and he has settled on thinking it may not be worth this morning to go to lake or cross the woods so he has finally abandoned it for the day rather than to test himself and he finished drinking hot water.

9
BENEATH THE WAVES

It was a warm day, people were swimming in and out close to the pond with challenges to each other. California hasn't looked much duller than it does as people have known what it is like to be here and have gotten bored with the same sort of activities happening on routine at homes. It is much fun at the beach or the areas where people surf diving in and out from swimming boards as their faces shine with glee.

However, in local customs, there is still a tradition to wear for the rising sun and to differentiate for swimming purposes when it comes to using clothes. Most of the divers could be seen wearing shorts with swimming suits and stylish goggles in their eyes as they splashed the waves going down. . they threw their bodies in with speed and tried to rise above with their body crunching the sea waves as most of them laughed in joy. Some of them were warned not to dive deep, shouts were getting louder with more splashes and it was truly fun to be there to celebrate the time.

Children are not allowed in deep waters even in these families. It is strongly urged not to allow them as they can slip off, fall, or even drown in shallow waters. They have the luxury of having swimming pools at home where they are told to practise before they can unleash their strength. Richer families make strongly built swimming pools; they describe their lounges as feeling more extravagant with it. Simply, they like to have a dive board, to let things pass and submerge in water for the pure fun of it.

One cold evening a servant could be heard shouting to a child of 12 years as he was trying to nick off his father's swimsuit and plan to go to the beach for a proper swim out. You are not prepared, it's the first time you practise here, the servant said, holding him back as he took off the suit from his younger hands. Let me go, I have seen something in my pool. it can only prove right if I can find the same on the beach, he said splashing the water of the pool loudly as he jumped in water to have some fun.

Come out, your little prank-making machine, now, the servant said, closing the main source so the water was not much to swim in and it can help to reflect something apart from the little child. At first glance the servant was not convinced as the child went deep in the pool. After trying to find where he had gone swimming in, he opened the lights of the pool and a strange sight met his eyes as he tried to have a look.

To his fear he saw something like a shadow that was following the child and the naughty one came out, being in absolute fatigue. what's there? Are you sure it's a shadow or a creature? he tried to reason with the child in pain. Two other servants came running in with an ointment and a massage with body lifters. No need to bring that much. He will be alright, the prior servant obliged, taking it to help the child urgently. I want to know what you saw in the pool, It can't be that close, he turned to him, helping him come out of the pain.

In one more house, a maid was questioning a girl child. it may have been around the evening that she has been able to locate her inside a tub. The child had been unconscious for an hour and it was not sure why she had been in such a condition in the first place. The maid had told her not to open the main water source but it looked like the child hadn't been able to control the urge to do it for herself. the ghosts do lurk in shadows if you throw light or fire, they would vanish simply, her mother must have told her once and she is a child might not be able to look over the wish to fight them off

Wake up, the fear is gone. You are safe, the maid said

as two other working persons came in bringing the towel and an ointment to treat the child. The maid saw a cut close to her chin, some blood stains and she was frightened for a moment. With much care she put on the ointment, it let the child open her eyes and all were smiling now. You were fine, see. the ghosts are not here, they all spoke, opening the light and making it look more dazzling than her dream as all circled to make her happy.

I fell off in pursuit of the ghost, she said in her girlish voice as they all got a bit scared. It was reflected in the water as I tried to open the lights out and I couldn't carry the strength, the maid walked away holding her close to the pool, and in the reflection, she could see more than one shadow but she couldn't be sure whether they were ghosts. We will find it. your mom is going to come back soon, alright? The girl nodded, asking to bring her milk and the cook of the home came holding it in a small glass to let her feel better after the fear of what had just happened.

You sure? It can't be her dream or imagination for a start? The cook obliged with a smile as the maid wrapped the child in warm clothes so the cool water effects could go off. 'She is tormented, surely something must have hurt her. We are not able to deduce the presence of any dangerous beast of living power, the other servants agreed as they were asked to dive into the pool and find if anything lurked in there. The only thing they reported was a strange sound like a coin falling on the floor and coming out without any personal injuries to them.

It has been a strange sight in these homes now that they can't connect easily with living strength or find why the children are directly targeted. All they can deduce is that they were left close to water, drenched or with cuts and have been crying or out of breath which gives true fear to them. The problem has spread and it is becoming larger by time as more homes complain of the same cases.

Certain cases were coming in such places where the children were tormented by sudden vision and they were found injured with damages happening mostly in the lower part of their faces or chins. The caretakers were under huge pressure as a few of them had been fired by their masters for not taking care. The deeper the wound may be, the more trouble it causes for the caretaking parties. They were either punished with no salary for 3 months, asked to leave the place if they didn't have relatives for a similar duration, and fired if they were only members of the home working to help the family.

It had become a kind of outrage in a developed world how these incidents had become so hugely famous with time as secret cops kept trying to find the involvement of any trickster or regional gang in them, the numbers had gone up very soon. I shall be talking to him. He is the person who can handle it, an English cop could be heard speaking to the agency official with hope to get some help. Are you sure he can do it? The cop nodded and gave a salute as he left the place looking to get an appointment soon.

Mahendra was an Indian-born American who had been living here for a decade now. He had faced a serious loss due to his wife dying after suffering from cancer. He tried his best, and brought doctors to treat her but nothing could work for her. They say she had been possessed by a soul so powerful that not even local tendencies couldn't favour her to survive. After such a critical loss, he had gone away angry with his brothers over their practices or ritual turmoil so he left his 4 children to care for his elder brother and simply left India to completely settle in California after he felt dejected to see his wife dying.

He is fond of beaches but has also been known to do such practices by which he can easily control ghosts or spirits if it is required. After all my family is known to do this cool stuff, he could be heard speaking to locals whenever they called him. Due to living here for a long time, he has been known to balance out the growth as he is much better versed now. He easily communicates with people and has their trust due to which he is renowned. It seemed the right time for officials so the English cop had now thought to meet him to get help or discuss the whole matter.

A voice sounded in the outer gate as the cop tried to get in. He raised his hand to go through the security and simply passed it. The guard apologised to test him but the cop waved his hand in gratitude. He silently walked towards the reception corner where a woman of round 35 was seated with a smoking pipe in her lips. Yes, what can I do for you? She said, a bit surprised to be facing a cop in the area. I need to meet Mahendra sir, it's a bit urgent you know, the cop said with his tongue sticking the chewing gum out and she agreed for an appointment to arrange.

The lady told him to wait for 10 minutes so she could bring the approval and the cop sat outside with a cup of coffee offered to him by the assistant of the reception to get warm. What brings you here? the male assistant asked as he felt grateful for the service offered. What else, ghosts, pranks, or tricks of the city force me to get in touch with the specialist, He obliged, looking straight into his eyes. The other person nodded, taking back the cup and the lady had come out holding the approval pass so he could go in for a talk but it couldn't go further than 30 minutes.

That will do, he said, taking the pass and going through a covering of a small lane as he crossed the front door. The mood changed suddenly as he crossed and it felt like being in an old cemetery, a place of honour or to be very close to nature in the city. The cop felt a bit excited as he turned the final door and Mahendra stood there holding a pot of water in his hands. Sit down sir, he said in his low but strong voice as the cop removed his shoes and let him do the honours to clean his feet. Mahendra checked for his heart pulse, felt it normal, and decided it was fine to talk with him.

Water is one of the most potent sources, you know sir? the Indo-American started as the cop settled onto the comfortable chair. You know why I am here, don't you? Children are in threat of injuries and if it continues!, he op got silent as a candle was burnt by the resident and he smiled looking back. Fear of the dark is more powerful than the fear itself, the cop agreed as he was handed a document to let him read. It was a file missing from the main investigating office which contained a list of people dying in low age as they turn from children to adults.

The cop struck his forehead with his right palm as he held the file in his left hand thinking about it with a bad memory connected to it. His own nephew has died after he was strangled under water just after celebrating his 16th birthday in pure joy. It's an uproar that he has to remember it all but now he can get some portion of it coming back as a memory of fear and disgust only making him cry with the sound of longing for him.

Coming to the matter, Mahendra said, opening a book and turning on a table lamp at the same time. This picture was taken by your department 1 year ago, right? he said, gesturing to a shadow rider on a beach. True, it is correct. It was a kind of fear that loomed on the beach, the cop said, speaking how the fear of the ghost kept bothering them until they banned the arrival of boats in the certain beach. It's time you find out why boats were drowning there, the resident said, taking out a paper from the desk with some details for the cop to understand that will prove handy later.

I shall be in touch with you after I find more on the last death, the visitor said as it turned 25 minutes and only 5 minutes were left. Be safe, Now you know the reason. It may be possible that shadows might try to attack you, the resident said, expressing his goodwill and safety. I shall keep you updated regularly, thanks for your help, it was more than worth it, he saluted going out with a wave to people at the reception as Mahendra came out to ask for his evening meals at the right time or it may have gotten cold.

A phone rings in an official building. A man in an official suit comes to receive it. Yeah, he is available, wait, he said, turning to call someone to talk on the phone. Yes, how is everything? a voice came from the other side. Upendera has finally managed to connect to the other brother in the US. It's been a long time. You have finally been able to connect with me, Mahendra said from the other side. they had always been comfortable to talk to, forget the children alone, and try to find something peaceful in the weather.

More news of the chaos, Mahendra continued on the phone as people must have shared it on social media. These days it's easier to find out about each other even if we are abroad, Upendera laughed from the other side saying the words in an undertone. I have no hand in it, honestly. they may have done it for fun or a political cause, Mahendra chuckled from the other side as they were the best ones to pull each other' leg whenever they talked on the phone.

What about our troubling niece? How is she doing? Mahendra touched on the core angle of their past discussion. Her father has handled her well after returning from the woods, the foreigner took a sigh of relief as he heard this. They talked about how the events folded, Mahendra informed them about the trouble of underwater shadows in the US and Upendera assured them that he was the best to handle them. If you can't, then who else mate? he said, closing the conversation in a hurry and the phone got disconnected at the right time.

It was not easy to swallow for people why the weather had changed suddenly in the upper planes. Water Bodies were playing tricks as the update of more people falling from stones at higher waterfalls started to come into the news. The rain accompanied the movement as more drownings happened and people were still trying to do more adventure even after being worn. They thought themselves capable of challenging human limits but were taken to cinders by ghosts or creatures they had never encountered before in life or the darkest hours that made life hell for them as they asked for help, died or were crushed by such forces.

Mahendra was worried, hoping it may not be similar to what happened in his native country, and offered prayers in a temple built close to his reciting area. With threats emerging so fast, it was not sure how the future may come. The water powers had been responsible and were getting more intent. No shore activity, tell them it's not safe, the higher authorities were heard shouting and they were out of clues on how to handle the upsurge. The weather started to get more grim, there was a loud lightning in the sky and trouble was soon going to become bigger with time.

California has truly changed, instead of people coming to have the best dive, they have started to get frightened due to the way ships have got wrecked, there was a wind of ghosts all around and people not allowing their children to have diving lessons or avoid requests to build new pools. It's been an absolute condition of tragic deaths, Mahendra commented as he read a newspaper in the evening after calling his brother back home being gratified. We can't solve it as easily as we thought, the receptionist said with him munching evening toast with some concern on her face.

They kept a close watch on the process, and the threats and it all shows that something is taking place that is not even in their true control. The best of the developed world was not able to fix it and they were somehow worried as Mahendra called on people of Indian origin living in the local area. Tell me how to trace the cause by your skills, alright? he said, talking to them and they did agree on presenting the report so they found something unusual so he could dig into the truth.

There was an alarm as reports suggested a cyclone was coming closer to the city soon. Everywhere there was panic, but Mahendra didn't have much to ponder. The wise man had already hinted at the power of water and now the cop recalled it mentioning it on the phone. I have seen the movement of strange shapes close to the sea, sir, he said, calling him 2 days before the cyclone came. the person was worried but Mahendra insured him that the cyclone was not intent and would pass without doing much damage to the outer area which made him express gratitude for these words

A figure was illuminated at the shore as the cyclone merged the rain with the wind blowing upwards. it has a strange appearance, a gash-like mouth to feed, savers coming from the lower lip, and a tongue to lash at human presence. it smelled its empty nose into the air, flicked its watery cloak, and the sky suddenly turned dark. Everywhere the voice to protect and help started to pinch in its ears which it liked. The ghost of the sea felt relieved on looking through the mayhem with more deaths to happen soon.

The thing it likes has finally come this far into the developed world and it was looking to taste fresh blood as soon as its supporting ghosts emerged from the water to dine out. Soon, we will take over as the cyclone may end, it said to others who splashed water making it tough for fishermen to come to the shore or to find those people who have lost. a lightboat was bobbing through and the sea ghost flicked its cloak making it fall deep in depths of water with a cackle of laughter as the other ghost knew the members in it would die by such a critical act.

A few helicopters flew past to search for the rescue as the ghost lurked hungrily wanting to kill more. It couldn't come closer as helicopters flew away at speed but the ghost cherished the death of those whom they have accomplished.

The sea ghost moved without much effort as it saw a few more boats passing by the shore. it wanted to let them all drown but have finally settled to choose the one which is the largest. Lot more than those pitiful small boats, it said laughing with its voice gurgling inside the boat, easily fearing the others. Let's have a proper meal, it whispered to its fellows who crackled with a measure so the boat had been toppled over with shrieks and shouts as people started to drown and submerge in waters being helpless.

More to our numbers as it is an injustice to finish them off, a ghost with a harpoon leered past the leader of ghosts in surprise as he was not expecting the party to come so early. I think you have enough food so no fight this time? the leader asked as the shadow of their head shook, ensuring that they had an equal meal to enjoy without any tussle on who shall have it first in deep waters.

It has been years since we got active in the seas to get our job done. I wish we had more to find sooner before they bring the light and finish us, the she ghost shookits shadow head this time on such words leering from behind as its ghostly hand raised one more wreck of a boat taking out human flesh which it flicked to fall in front of waiting ghosts who gestured a kind of cross into the air celebrating the moment together in glee as they had proper time to do the honours and make it stand worth.

Report the weather, it's urgent, Adriene the leader of marine cops told the juniors to march forward as he flew the helicopter in search. No mess, all has been cleared. We need an update from our marine guards, the response was quick as he flew away. The air was pure with no dust or rain in the vicinity, the cyclone had passed but the damage had been horrendous. Few people were crunched, the cafeteria was broken and there was chaos all over. The night was certainly going to be painful as howls of losing members kept coming from homes where the cyclone had hit.

Mahendra had no fear but he felt for those who had lost their lives in the calamity as he was still wondering the reason for it. The TV in his room was stating the cause of the cyclone in a scientific way denoting the level and pressure of air in recent times. However, it has no answer to why such pressure has come suddenly. It has certainly been the act of someone who likes chaos getting pleased. The watcher looked closely at the images shown by satellite footage by broadcasters and he could link the angles in which the drastic effects had been made. It was done with a plan by spiritual power and he could feel the group that was responsible for making it happen for certain leads.

Back in the sea, Three guards jumped out of a boat underwater as the ghost dived to catch the fresh humans. they flashed a light from their live jackets fending them off and had caught the skeletons of bodies with damage done hugely. For a moment the main leader felt disgusted at the damage but then his eyes turned into fierce anger. Get them, Now. I want to finish this, he spoke, making a blast in the sky as the ghosts towering above felt the smoke and then were easily taken into the nether world vanishing with the flames.

We will find out who created the cyclone and why, won't we, Damian? his junior said as he was still fuming for the shadows that lurked beneath to create mayhem for true evil. He was convinced of the ghosts and the damage done by them for fun so he wanted to take them off and fulfil the duty of revenge. We will do the honours, don't worry folks, he assured his working team and had gone back to the sea leaving the trail left by it with ghosts inside.

They collected the wrecks, the boats toppled and everything was brought under calm after Damian reported back to Adriene replying by a satellite call. Not a joke mate, I am on duty, the leader smiled as he told how they had to tackle spirits and ghosts. Your laziness on not letting them captive has made it worse, will you believe it one day? he said angrily as Adriene kept laughing and the phone was dismissed. The marine guards follow Damian while the calamity operations are held by Adriene as a leader to report to the authorities. They both were capable of handling the condition but Adriene doesn't believe in ghosts or spirits and have hardly accepted the fact that they were involved in this chaos.

The night was quite close to the lighthouse. A silent stream was passing through into the sea as it met and the wave splintered the shore once it erupted into a huge fall. The silence suddenly changed its voice as it accompanied the noise of ghosts, trapped in a certain boat and wanting to hunt people out. They slipped, fell in, and simply dropped into the sea with their imprint only visible. The night had become chill as the ghost appeared and they had decided to spread all along the place lurking quietly.

They twiddle their thumbs, shriek into the night, and out of sight at the top of the island so they can find places that can help to hunt in a better way. Ah, I wish a human would do. It was really cold in the boat, they had been trapped in ice and were now free to join the sea brigade. There it is. A human walking with a torch. Should I pursue it? the ghost whispered as a few more shapes emerged egging it on. the ghost swooped past the ear of the man who was surprised and looked at his shining watch. the imprint just tickled close to the chest making him feel a cold shiver.

The sky was clear with no clouds but the man felt something woosh pass his other ear fastly. Three or more ghosts had come, making it a tight place to corner a human on the island. they whispered into the air, Come, We will take you to the sea. It's the place of romance and love, the man shook his head as the first ghost turned his hand away, making the light in hand fall below. A voice came from a distance into his ears which hardly had to do with life and the man fell onto the floor. The other three ghosts swooped on it, crunching him hard so his neck was broken and he was dead with pure silence spreading on to the sea.

What a joy! I was really hungry, the ghost exchanged the parts of the skin and took one toe of the dead man lifting it above with their skill Our joy is not over. We can take this as a memory so those who dare to come to us shall remember us, they cackled with glees taking few parts and leaving a terrible body on the island floor with creatures spreading around to munch the left portions with noises all over with contest on who may get how many parts of it.

What's all this mess? I haven't seen them gather this fast, a scientist appeared holding a cold shimmering light in his hands. He looked for the noise and saw the body on the floor. Ghosts were coming back as they saw one more human moving around. I see, you have been freed. Not good for us, the scientist said holding the colder light that made the ghost a true chill. He pressed a button on a device from where the light was brimming and it hit 2 ghosts paralysing them on the spot.

More for me to capture as memory. it shall be best if I finish them all soon, the expert said, flicking his hands with more devices being turned on and the sounds started to come loud as the ghosts were once more trapped. Another human appeared, this time a female, she looked at the light in the scientist's hand and smiled. Let's take them back to the wreck. they don't look good here, she lingered on the body of the dead person and covered it with a cloth mourning it. Together they used a strange purple light to put all the collective items and throw them into the wreck of a boat from where they had come back to hunt humans.

The next morning Damian called the cop who visited Mahendra. They had a serious chat about searching and tracing the ghosts. Are you sure, the power of the sea's mouth is open again? The cop asked Damian, who had proof. I can't send you images as you know they get burnt, he obliged but explained how the lashing spirits chased them to which the cop agreed. The person who was called Scamiar replied in a quiet voice, I will have a word with him on this. Hope he will explain, both sides started to plan and after the talk of 1 hour the phone got disconnected

The sun appeared on all sides as it was spreading the beautiful light on all corners with ease. The sea was making a strange noise but the surface was plain and quiet. The ghosts lurked inside, in the dark corners and they moved with creatures lashing on the weaker ones whenever they got a chance to kill. The voices were not heard by those who were not at sea and it made them vulnerable when they had to face the waves. The leader of the ghost was surely planning a fate for them and the city resident must be ready for it.

Calm down. they will be back, A few of the local marine guards were asuring fishermen as they were still not allowed. We have no choice. there is no proper food, the sea is closed and how will we survive? the mayor of the city had announced funds and rations for all people but they were not reaching on time so a few locals died too. The helicopter kept flying as Adriene threw down packages and people who were in need launched themselves to grasp it out. The balance of the distribution was not working anyhow as there were many loopholes in it.

I assure you, we will catch them on guard if anything happens to your members, make no mistake, the family was not convinced as it wouldn't bring the dead back from the other world and they may priorly become ghosts if they were not saved in the right time that fears the family most. No, they won't. Jesus will take them away, the guards said as a few of them expressed the fear. They shook their heads as the noises of helicopters came and this time official guards were stepping out with proper food packages for the remaining people who got affected due to hostile weather problems around.

A phone rang again at Mahendra's office. The receiver asked him to be ready to talk now and he agreed. Hello brother, how is this all happening now?, Upenra was on the other side willing to talk on the matter of disaster. it's the act of one who wants the coin, Mahendra said without much of an explanation. It didn't affect Upendera who smiled wanting to talk about other conditions. In India a bridge has collapsed, 30 people have died and a hotel was taken into fire. Both felt that things were connected but they couldn't find ways to stop them.

If you know the location of the coin, you should keep it a secret, the foreigner said, talking on the matter. Alright if you ask, does your current country know about the coin? There was no response from Mahendra. No they don't, a pause after which he said so low that even Upendera couldn't hear clearly but he guessed what he wanted to say. After a joke about being a nationalist on which Mahendra took a jibe at spending money on foreign offices, the phone disconnected with words on taking care.

A light came into the place as Mahendra stood up. the guards at reception sensed it but let it pass. They were confident that the master would defend it without much trouble. About time, I have been waiting, the leader said, looking at it and flicking its lamp to conjure it. Sir, the light has shifted through, can it be so powerful? one of the assistants came running in fast. Mahendra refused him to cross past the wake of light and he turned back.

The aura of my family, he whispered to no one, opening the main cupboard and taking an inscription out Hello, Can you hear me? he said into the inscription and a figure appeared in a female ghost form. 'Yes, I can hear, what's the matter? You always bore me with the past, don't you? the ghost of his dead wife appeared with not much of a change as he looked into her with benign interest.

It is happening now. the thing you said while being alive, Mahendra exchanged the light that had come and the ghost swallowed it with no problem. It had the power to inhale the prior strength as it had died a normal death rather than a tortured one or by the hands of someone. good! I will wait. I want to see you Americans beg for mercy, a soft cackle came from the hostess's mouth as Mahendra took the inscription back and sent it back inside it. Great jibe, I won't bother, he said and transpired the light fuming on her final words still livid in ears.

Everything was looking dull as Mahendra was also sad after talking to his wife's ghost. He asked for a cold coffee, told no one to disturb him and finally, he decided to plan a tour around other places. the fear of the sea won't be away from him so Mahendra thought to digest the fact that ghosts would follow the trail left behind. he had asked his brother not to reveal the secret of the coin and he would stay firm on it, he thought as he drank the coffee so he felt better after it as he stood up and looked for luggage to leave the place to spend some good time in the hills.

The next morning a cab had come with a true send off by the staff. The lady at reception ensured everything was in control when he would come back. This was then not the first time he was going but he cared for the inscription he had checked last night taking it in his bag for safety in a new place. Ghosts can only be repelled either by light or their counterpart, Mahendra knows it very well and he took it safely. A place has been arranged for him in a higher level of mountain away from the sea and he thanked his team for letting him go as the cab turned taking him away from grandeur.

10
THE DEATHLY CUT

It was a warm afternoon as people were heading down to a city in urgent need to help someone. Locals had no clue on what had happened but few of them were out of sweat due to the demand of the hospital as they served as volunteers. Cases are rising as they can see more young lads found either dead or brutally injured by a strange sharp cut which has made the whole process more critical.

Bring them in. I want to examine the body, a nurse said in a cool inner hospital area as more helpers were sworn in ready to lift the bodies. The helpers ran in with wait in their arms to carry them through, put them in the cold inner area, and left without a word as hospital personnel started to take out devices and check for the cause. Same cut. it keeps appearing, I wonder why? the nurse said, looking at the upper part of their neck brutally hurt.

The main doctor started to do another test of the body for confirmation. There was one factor that has been more concerning in these bodies. Either they were dehydrated or had not been fed well which meant they had already been weaker souls. I tried to find why they are in the range of the target, the nurse who was called Gelda said to the doctor who shook his head handing over the report. they were sure it hadn't been the work of a certain gang as stronger powers were involved in it.

Any news of the missing coin? I want to find more on it, the doctor said as the nurse raised her hand to keep the voice down. You think ghosts can't hear us, do they? he said passing through the place where dead bodies were kept with high security. a pale image passed through making Nurse release a sound of surprise but this time the doctor raised his hand. They all were aware of the mood in the place and it has been an absolute influence of those who have brought her after being dead for scrutiny.

A few of the hospital officials came in to handle the reports of dehydration and the scientific cause for it. The main doctor who goes by the name of Andrew didn't say much, watching it over in his hands. He called Gelda to do tests on the hearts and lungs of the unconscious bodies and she agreed. It was a busy area with people coming either to find out about their relatives or children or to take care of those whom the hospital couldn't treat anymore with its aid being limited.

A man called Ray appeared on the sidelines. He is a kind of medicine supplier and has just gone inside the cabin to talk. More deaths, soon it will be a huge pile if we don't take care, do we? he said, talking to Gelda as she did tests. This man had fancied the main nurse but she doesn't think much of him. The salary she gets is much higher than his business which she thinks is not fair to consider him and hardly talks properly at work. Your job is to bring medicine rather than count the bodies, she slammed as he put the box in a cabinet and went bowing to her while hardly talking.

Sir, we have tracked a man called Wimbleton, another nurse had appeared talking to the main doctor in the main ward. he confessed to passing the wrong medicine that forces people to get dehydrated and feel empty. it can also lead to suicide, she said smiling with a box that contained the same medicine. Send the evidence for scrutiny we shall see, he replied as more voices started to come from the room where dead bodies were kept.

Andrew sat quietly on his table, examining a small paper wait. He lifted it in his fingers and thought it could help him to give answers 'Why are we so desperate to get our hands on the coin? he thought not willing to use complete force to search for it. They say abroad that Indians are powerful, they can confuse, destroy, or even imitate your cause. The doctor looked at it as the message by Gelda flashed on his phone sending the same cause of fracture in blood vessels and he smiled while reading it. Let's get cracking. We shall find the cause, he put the paperweight back and stood up checking his boots.

At the outer station, a man was running in a hurry. He checked for his suitcase, had a rich watch on his wrist and he kept looking at it. I don't want to be caught this soon, he insisted as the car he was waiting for arrived. Two men stepped out in an official suit and before the man with the suitcase could turn, they had him handcuffed. Your order Sir. I am taking you to the station and to be locked, the main arranger of the vehicle said as the drug seller was dragged inside the car and had been taken into custody.

A victorious smile came onto the man's scarred face as the person caught started to struggle behind No more jokes. We have heard enough for your poor ones, Richard said, looking at peace with his work. We shall take the gang down by the river next, what do you say sir? The guard who had held the drug dealer said as he started to show signs of falling off Give him the taste of his own medicine, Richard said without looking back and an injection hit the victim as he fell asleep with the vehicle moving towards the police station.

Crystal looked equally greeting as the evening passed through. People in late teens could be seen enjoying food and filled with ice creams as the dates were in full swing. It was the month of February and they were loudly singing or throwing away empty papers. No more mess in public around, please, a recycling cart owner said as a few lads threw a bottle, an empty can, and torn paper outside a cafe. Take it away, we will pay you, they shouted and he lifted them getting aid for the service. It was an absolute mood of laughter.

People were somehow looking to visit pubs or get

together outside with new couples forging ties, making noises and soon it would be a true festival time for them, but something was going on. In the empty corners, more lads are getting affected, they are suffering from the fear of dying, the ghost of the city, and it will become true for all very soon. In the night the hospital kept rumbling with bodies which were brought and soon they all would rise together to hunt with their total might on display.

Ray could be seen on the outskirts of the city with a box in his waving hands The best drink, I assure you, he could be seen selling a few nutrition drinks to the young lads who were celebrating the season of love. they didn't say no as he sold them in smaller amounts. One for my darling, would she be ready to dance with me after drinking it? he said smiling as more couples started to ask for it and went away. He collected the notes and decided to buy something from a nearby jeweller's shop but he was denied. Pay us our past debt first then we will sell you something, he has taken gold from them so he can give it to Gelda the day they would marry at church being happy.

The trouble is that it has been too costly so the jewellers have stopped giving him any decent element. They also knew Ray belonged to the hospital searching for the diamond coin so they were after the trail. Get us in touch with your boss Andrew, one of the jewellers said, looking him up with a hand to shake with him. 'No chance, I don't work. I am just a medicine supplier, Ray said, going away with his mood going off as they had denied him the thing he liked the most.

Back at the hospital, something was moving, Gelda hadn't been ordered to do the night duties. It is Pomina who does it, an immigrant who has settled herself with the customs. She was in her official nurse dress as she checked for a pulse, tried to find more clues on people in pain, and turned the lights off. She sat in a corner and suddenly felt a strange movement in the hospital. Two shapes had come out from the room where dead bodies are kept. they said her name first and then vanished making her shiver with fear. the shapes loomed upwards, towered onto a staircase, and found a man standing there to guard the place which made them leer with pure joy.

There was the sound of a bulb crashing to the floor, a shout, and the man's throat was crushed with a horrible feeling and it let the alarm bell ring with noise. As the ghost leered, shaking everything that was in control the camera couldn't detect them moving from one place to another fastly. They swooped top upstairs, took the lid of a small baby who had lung problems, threw down the spectacles of a person who was partially not able to see, and finally went past the outer emergency room and out of sight. There was a flash of light in the room where dead bodies were kept, the ghost making mayhem felt it too and someone was coming back.

Andrew had come suddenly from nowhere holding a blue shimmering light and willing to finish off the problem. He flicked a button and all the devices started to emit the same light and finally, it found the ghost lurking on the staircase hidden in an empty box. The light connected and destroyed them with a sound of 'whee' ending their terror as everything was brought to normal. The baby was making a sound as it got the right treatment. The person was able to recognize Andrew and the emergency room was back to its active state with people connected to it deeply shaken by such a movement.

Report me, now, a phone rang as Andrew picked it up. It was from the supervisor of the dean's place who was a key person standing as chairman of the hospital watching all the proceedings. Yes sir, all is calm the light was effective this time, Andrew responded as the chairman agreed with 'yes' and disconnected the phone. Andrew sneers after the phone has been dismissed as he knows the chairman only cares about his status, the insult of the public and he can't ask much if anything happens to the place. The main doctor went to Pomina giving her instructions and went upstairs to find anything missing or not.

OY! Close the drain pipe, it's leaking, he said to a water management team member as people turned away. He saw Andrew, nodded his head, and turned away, closing the throttle down. I need you to arrange for extra cotton bags, you hear me? he said to another nurse who came following the voice and handed him. Andrew went closely to an inner cabinet, used his fingerprint to get entry, and found a body lying on the floor in true pain as he went close.

It is something which is a secret just kept to him and he covered it with more cotton pouches ensuring the wounds continue to thee well. I can't send you home, the ghosts are more in numbers as we speak now, he said looking on. A few weeks before Andrew had got a call while being busy at work. It was a strange noise speaking in his son's voice and warned of him getting injured if he didn't care. The man had been brave and didn't respond to anything as a few days later the news spread of his son being out of bounds when he found Logan, he had been wounded, not moving and he had somehow saved him by taking him to the hospital directly.

Not a word to anyone, he had said to Gelda and other nurses who agreed to try to help their boss. He is in such pain, what could be done to him? Pomina had asked as Andrew helped his son with medical aid. The boy's condition has become better but they have kept him in a glass cabinet with light surrounding the glass. They were afraid that ghosts could do mayhem or could crush him so strong safety was required. The main doctor had requested for a secret light device from the Dean's place and it has been approved which makes him feel gratified for it.

This night when the ghosts were in mood made him fear that they might come this far in search of his son, but with the boy safe and being treated, he is now relaxed. The mood started to change as he closed the cabinet and went back to his duties walking away with pain and a mist of sadness. He ordered morning potions from his staff as the night turned to dawn, sat in his room, and quietly started to think about how to make this place safer. It is not the question of his son but those who suffer due to ghosts and they want a solution to fix it or it may become an absolute uproar if he is not able to do it.

It was quite like it happens in the inner wings of the medical wards with the sound of people moving peacefully and taps of their boots. Voices were talking but in low nodes in each corner where new patients had come to get treatment. Andrew passed through checking for some strange movements and ensuring everything functioned well in his vigil as this was the morning and they must help everyone recover from the fear of night being fresh including the staff.

Outside a cafe, a car stopped, two henchmen came out holding guns and they robbed the cafe owner taking all his earnings away. In one more music studio, a strange gang has come taking all the mikes for fun, and has returned them after an hour. More news of chaos came in the city as it was quiet in the hospital. People were chasing after a person who had snatched a chain and he kept losing them as they were unable to trace them as he tormented them from behind in the shadows.

We are not able to find why he keeps doing this, they reported to the police who promised to have the thief in their hand. The rumours of a snatcher's ghost were also prominent in the place as these things kept happening in the shadows. In a beer bar, all the bottles were broken, the owner was on the floor unable to recognize anyone and it became like laughter for those who found him collapsed in such a manner. A few guards walked in trying to find the problem but he was not able to tell him which made it absurd.

To make this all more strange, a couple had been found dead close to the woods turning the mood to go more grim. They were told to be young. It was not clear whether they were married or not as the police couldn't identify them at first. After checking their identity, the guards considered them not to marry as they both belonged to different places. it may be possible that they had taken the chance of Valentine as an impulse and had come here camping Sir, I have found the report of missing by their parents separately, a guard called as the leader of the pack Richard tried to find more by taking clicks.

Good, send the photos of reports, I will find out myself, he said and the phone was disconnected as the gang lurked in bushes to find more traces. Sir, I have got the phone. it's here, but it's broken, one of the guards shouted coming back. Scatter now, all of you, we will get the thing, After 2 hours of hard search they found a boot in blood, a framed photo, and a few drugs which made Richards feel disgusted as they collected all the evidence to send to the lab on further investigation.

There was a noise in the silent woods as the gang was coming back. Humans can be punished, not us, you hear me? it made them feel chill as the voice passed through and made Richard stop. What's that? Trying to hide in the bushes to give the fright? He opened his flashlight to see a figure emerging with a strange face, a gash on its face, and moving in smoke. Richard was a conservative who believed strongly in old rituals. He took a strange ash from his pocket and threw it and the ghost made a sound of cough as it ran away with the guards following the leaders moving away too.

Thanks goodness. We are safe today, he said as more calls came asking for help in the local area. A few of the old people had fallen off the top stairs in their own house. An old lady had gone missing without a trace of her being lost and this all had been happening without an alarm or any certain concern which makes it worse. Everywhere the nightmare was becoming more horrible and it needed a reason to explain why it had been so fast or who may have been involved in it.

Richard called Scamier in America in the evening and it was finally going to be something to stand for. He told how things had gone wrong in a weather of love and joy. The murder at church, bodies in the woods, strange cuts, and hospitals filled with people made his throat dry as he talked through. The fellow who knew Richard well or his investigation ensured that there would be a way and if it did not, then he would put him in touch with Mahendra, an Indo-American who can help to fix the whole pursuit by his skill.

I am going to the western basin. the river is getting intent. I hope that it won't bring bad news, Richard spoke clearly as Scamier wished him luck. Be careful, water is powerful at this moment. I pray for your better luck, mate, the British agreed, taking the final words and stepping out. A car had come to take him as he stepped in the evening with lights still blazing. He looked for the sky and there was not a single cloud, it was clear somehow. He smiled, checked his watch, and promised to come back after 9 and he was off from the place.

It was almost 11 and there was no sign of the investigator and no one could easily trace him. The only thing his juniors knew was that he stepped out of the car after reaching the western basin and had walked away towards the river. They were getting worried as no calls were received, his phone was off and the only thing they could find was his boots close to the sand area. He was not dead however, Richard was chasing after a drug gang, one famous for using them as a drink of love, and inside the water he was fighting with them so intense that ripples were coming out from the water outside.

The expert got hold of a few people but 3 of them somehow escaped from his hand and he was swimming now to find their trace. I will get you. ghosts of the river, he said as a few strange shapes bloomed after the drug powder was thrown by the running away members. 'It seems you are so weak, honestly, Richard blasted a water cannon and everything was clear like the surface of the river. the running men shouted but now he had no wish to play with them. He took out his raft gun, loaded it, and made three fires hitting all of them on the chest as they collapsed in water that got drenched red with the blood of dead ones.

A few hands clasped the leader as he tried to come out. We won't drown you. There are ghosts in the water indeed, they said, giving him a guard of honour for his strike. You can enjoy the meal, I am off. shall I? he retorted, firing one more bullet to light the surface and it made a huge ripple as the guard finally traced him at the end bringing the protective gloves to drag him and let him safely recover. About time, I am happy to finish the gang, he said coming from the river bank.

Answer me, why did you go there? a man had come looking fiercely at Richard. he had been the chairman of the hospital which had a lot of investment in river banks, No damage to your sand, it is protected. I am sure ghosts are involved in the mess, he added, looking directly at the chairman who shook. Nothing pleases me more than the stories of ghosts, he made a jibe handing a letter of transfer to Richard and he smiled accepting it as the guards demanded it too and they were thrown and dismissed by the chairman being helped to the leader.

Scamier made a call to his friend the night after coming online. I am removed like the last time, the painful voice came from the other side. Scamier gave him inputs on the location of the coin and he shrugged. No chance. It can't leave India, can it? Richard laughed listening to the false trail of it and dismissed it. He promised to be in touch once he is relocated and Scamier felt miserable for him as it may not be worth it for people to find out why ghosts were so active in the place once he is removed as the call got disconnected with certain words of consolation by both men.

Another problem has struck in the hospital however as a gas pipe has leaked. Andrew reported it asking for help but he couldn't do much. Luckily it didn't affect anyone as a patient but it may have sparked the flame that the ghosts wanted. The gas spread right at the entrance and let pass through the corridor spreading towards the morg. The ghosts were lurking inside and were not prepared and a few of them got seriously damaged. Not all of us are vulnerable to smells, one of them said, hailing the gas and becoming large. it is time we take over the party and celebrate our reunion, the other 2 squealed coming from inside the lock and with a click the room opened from behind to get out of traps.

It was located at the exit point of the hospital for covering the dead bodies and the ghost fled away right into the forest leading the trail of their distant vigil in the dark. Find them, Humans. I want to crush them right now, the giant ghost said as it was fuming due to pressure and memories of the past. They could see someone coming close to the trees at night. They waited quietly and then there was a sound of 'haha' from behind frightening a man of late 30 with glee. Two ghosts caught it in the air, smashed him down onto the floor, and hit him. That made his breath come in slow motion, panicking.

One of the ghosts hit him with a strange weapon and the man felt paralysed after getting such damage. it struggled onto the floor and after a gap of fifteen minutes, it died. Yes, the first blood, here we go, the giant said leering with its tongue lashing out. All of them had launched themselves onto the blood coming and had made the body become an absolute wreck. Let the police come. We will hunt out a few of them too, the giant fumed, its anger still not controlled and the ghost caused a strange sound into the air making the environment absurd by such crime.

The next morning the morg was opened to check by the medical officials. They were sure something had been missing. A draped cloth was gone, a few injections were missing and there was a huge hole close to the lock. They couldn't find how it was opened from behind as there were no footmarks. Check the spirits, are they here? the head of the investigating team said, spreading a mist into the room with a device in his hands. Few burnt imprints could be seen in the backdrop but few empty holes could also be seen. it means the ghosts have fled. We missed them out, tell Andrew they are not here, he said, closing the devices and asking them all to come out of the room to guess where they had gone.

Richard safely landed in Portsmouth, he checked his suitcase, and all police devices and thanked the officials for dropping him off. We are sorry you have to face pressure from seniors, Sir!, one of the supporting guards said as all of them stepped out following him from the other car. You don't want to miss the fun out do you? Richard said, flicking one of the devices and its flash lit the close by quarter. Search them, he said without even going in as 2 of the guards went for the trail and 3 others took his suitcase to the new place as things started to get dark

Out of sight sir, the guards said, retreating. Welcome to the city of ghosts, sir, they repeated their words, handing him a glass of water. The leader looked at all of them and after watching the time, he dismissed them for the day. He arranged all his items, checked for his famous tea kettle, took the pouch of milk, and started to make it. He was finally at ease as his wife had always been at her mother's place and he didn't complain much. he sipped the tea, kept looking at the window, and felt he had finally been home, away from ghosts and their promising rewards.

Back in India, new movements have been taking place. It was busy at the government quarters as Nastika hasn't taken up any tours recently. She has been so busy as her foreign friends kept sending her photos of terrible shapes, fierce ghosts, or other imprints that it has made her mood light up. In response, she has promised to print them for the next edition of her magazine and they have paid her in foreign currency which meant more money. The children had been excited as she spent time with them, taking them to parks, and having ice creams and it has been absolute fun.

People from the outer world wanted to hear the reason why it had been happening so quickly and Nastika didn't tell them the whole story. Any clue you have for the coin? they kept asking and she would simply say no as she hardly got to do what they meant. Upendera has been kind enough to answer her concern saying the order works by having the coin safe and that's all she knew about it marginally. People from abroad wanted to come but their government was posing restrictions with threats looming in the sky. Things were changing somehow and how far they would keep them frightened is only the time may tell better.

Mahendra has started to get fond of India now as he keeps calling back home with excitement. Any change in the weather? Unusual things? he asked about his trip in the mountains, making Upendera laugh. When did you start to get fond of the stones? You were closer to the waves, brother! laughter rang harder on both sides as they kept talking about how to make better plans and India being recognized by the global powers with darkness looming ahead. No rush, they will feel one day that without us they can't hold the strings together, Upendera told him and he disconnected the phone looking for his watch and the time to go for a walk.

Scamier has updated him regularly on the shapes like fishes emerging in the sea with dark shadows behind them. No worries, water is still on top. We may have to wait for the light, he responded as he told how three men who had gone to catch fish were lost and only their skeletons are being found This kind of brutal behaviour is not connected to life force. it is surely done by someone else, he said as Mahendra told him some spirits like to brutally destroy humans and he agreed as the phone disconnected once more with the expert reaching back home.

Back in England, the fear has crossed its boundaries. it is not only in Bristol and Liverpool but people of London also start to have blurry visions. People fear to let their doors open in the evening, either by opening lights or singing to keep the bad spirits away and it is becoming more like an onslaught. Members of the hospital asked Andrew about his progress and were not able to tell much as the chairman kept him quiet only talking with members. Not a word till we can catch the intruder, he would be heard speaking to the council members. Logan has been feeling better However he remains in pain as a result of the memory of the night, and the spirit attacking and he is not able to talk much.

River basins are getting filled faster as rain accompanies the fear and dust in the sky with its noise. Officials were transferred, taken into custody, or sent to another city due to the way things were folding sharply. There was no doubt humans were involved in a race to get rich, but ghosts have also been freed. They take advantage of the wind, the panic in the mood, and latch themselves to possess minds, to kill and have the taste of flesh. Pubs are getting closed earlier as February is turning into March with strange winds, people are talking but in hushed voices and strained sounds with so much to lose out as damage is heavy.

It feels like climate change has finally made its mark in the cultural realm. With the rain of August happening early months of the year, a car stopped outside and with a cold in the air asked for two beers and settled down to drink them. It's not as frightening as the media is talking about, the girl said to her partner as they looked around 25 and may have been married. It's our first tour as couples after the wedding. Shall I take you to the woods? The other person tempted her as they finished their drinks and drove away with laughter inside the car with more rain to follow.

Come to us we are waiting, a voice came as it reached the forest. There was a strange sound and the car's windscreen was smashed. the girl looks just in time as the ghost swooped or they would have died in the first attempt. No matter, I still have the next chance, it said leering on as the partner took out a lighter and burned something to throw it off guard. The ghost raised in the smoke and sneered, We know how to counter fire, it's not going to work. It started to leer as one more device came out this time in the girls' hands and the ghost was slammed and destroyed onto the screen by a spark from it. They turned away hoping to get the recovery of their vehicle from the owner and decided it was not safe to roam in the forest area.

More cases of newcomers were coming from the outskirts where nobody likes to travel when it comes to locals. People from other cities were trying new places but they had to encounter the fear of ghosts. The smell of dead bodies, layoffs, and open areas had become a strange sight that you don't associate with the developed world. Creatures with strange faces were making noise as they found the dead and lashed on at them in fury. There was noise to get help, doors closing early, and everywhere the panic was getting worse as ghosts took over their world and felt they couldn't be defeated, at least in this part of the world, by certain powers laughing with glee to gain higher rank.

A few new chambers had also got opened in mistake to search for intruders and more ghosts had come out who had been captured in the past making it an absolute uproar for the administration to bring control or try to bring peace. Come, we are waiting for you, the ghost kept speaking to the lost people and they fell into their trap. Few ghosts kill by forcing the outsiders to hang from twigs, others may screw, stop their breath or crush necks and some fancy using water streams luring people and throwing them down.

A sudden mist changed the mood in the air with the arrival of someone powerful. However, there was a flick, the woosh of something, and the ghost fell backward. NO mercy, if you can't, then I won't either, a strange ghost said, forming a cloaked figure. My relatives sent me word that you would make chaos, it said, flicking a light dancing in its gloves. The ghost shouted to leave them alone but he caught them pummelling like nobody had done in the past and he was looking brutal to finish them off with such strength.

They started to shiver, the light made them stick on and the figure kept striking with a lot of them being sent to the netherworld with such force. As now it was certainly he who was laughing with peace in the air setting things back to normal with such power. A paper fell onto the doormat as Richard was just coming out of the shower. it said in strange writing, I have fixed the case for some time, he thought it may be the ghost of the security guard who was his best pal in the past and he felt gratified as he wore official clothes to start the investigation for the day. The same paper fell also to Andrew's desk and he felt blessed to find out a positive word. All around, the laughter started to bloom as people got back to fun and it somehow felt like a kind of bliss to them.

Nobody knows how it has been resolved but people have started to light candles outside their doors in memory of one who has solved it. They gathered in ranks and took out bottles to drink and eat. It has been in balance somehow. The fear has not gone away however, police officials brought more bodies from the woods and they appealed in official statements to people not to leave cities without permission. They would never take it on their own, an old man could be heard taunting the officials Just thinking on fewer numbers they have to bear, his friend uttered as they trudged along coming back around 5 in the evening and closing the door out.

They all felt a bit calmer after the help and fewer ghosts in the fraternity but they all know it is just an effort from someone who cares for them. The scary moment has not gone and they would lurk sooner so people are at least on guard now Be safe till it's not completely clear, a man told his son as he thought about going out or planning for a foreign trip soon. Once this is all over you can do the honours to search for the coin, he said wishing him luck. The son threw a pipe for his father to smoke, turned his socks over, and lifted his boots. He had gone in search of better security plans that can help him to get his trip going.

The truth remains hidden, from everyone in the world that Upendera holds the key. His son's ghost keeps a strong watch when he is asleep so no one can attack him, or go inside the cabinet to try to find out the secret of the diamond coin or take it away. It is still not clear why it is so important and Upendera feels pleased that the golden spirit didn't tell him the complete secret either. For him, a peaceful life is more prudent than a life in chaos in war, and smoke feeling in nostrils all around. He is somehow in peace, thanking the spirit as life goes on without any trouble.

11
THE COIN'S CURSE

It was a cool morning when a car came and stopped close to the quarters to ask for guide services. Nastika was looking gorgeous in her new dress as she sat in the front seat with the driver trying to find out more about the touring party. The driving person was a lady, maybe in her 30s and her curls waved as she took her head out from the window to check for any barriers. The men from the repaired building were going away, some sort of bag in their hands, and with a start, the car went out taking the seated people away in it.

It's a nice call to start the tour, isn't it? I am Eva, we are foreigners, she said driving out in the hills with ease as Nastika looked more closely on to the Global card lying in the front car pocket. For some moment she didn't speak as the guide liked to explore people first on her own terms. The car got slow turning as she gestured with her hands and it made Eva and other members feel comfortable with her. You will take us on the tour, won't you? the other member asked from the back seat and she got cheerful, becoming familiar with them.

Yes, for sure. Good to find you here. I am hopeful that we will have a great tour, the guide said looking out of the window with a smile as people seated also smiled from behind. The car turned left, through the main lane and the guide gestured to turn towards the lower side so they could visit the main place first, starting a perfect way to proceed. The visitors stopped the car in front of a statue of an honourable spirit, all 7 of them came out, had photographs and they were back inside the car still moving on to explore more on the right places to visit.

The team had been sent by officials of a native Asian

country with the task of finding out more about India. We are offered to have a trip instead of trying it ourselves, you know, Eva told the guide as she smiled looking out at the view getting clear. They had been told to stay quiet about the coin's location, to try to find if they could get anything on hand and Eva didn't reveal why they had been sent in the first place. They kept driving towards the main lane in and out and wanted to have some natural ventures for their joy after it.

This is more calm than you think, Nastika asked to stop the car too close to a waterfall. The sound was melodious as the people stepped out I won't go close enough, Markos, a young lad, spoke to the driver as she tried to have a closer shot for the memory. They say water is a potent source. I better not test its power, he continued, making others laugh as they had to step back with water coming through a certain level of force downwards and splashing with speed on a perfect bounce.

Are there ghosts too? Eva asked as Nastika looked for shadows to follow around them. They do have romantic stories to guide us through, won't they, what do you think? Debra, a younger girl said looking towards the carved stone It's much more complicated as you know people die in our country at the hands of those who don't want to break the tradition, Debra nodded looking at the inscription and she felt someone trying to catch her from behind so she stood up suddenly.

What's the matter? I still have my juice left. Markos asked, looking at her with some fear or somewhat unsettled. I felt someone willing to grasp me, her words remained in her mouth as a shadow moved, coming out so fast that it made them scared. It turned into a watery shape and splashed onto the waterfall. What a taste. humans all around. Nothing better than this for a toast, it tried to lunge on at the foreigners as

Eva seemed to be prepared to face the clash with them. She took out a device, flicked it twice and a strange light came out from it hitting the shapes that vanished as they got the treatment for their mistake.

We better get out of here, Nastika said, asking them to get back to the car before they started to attack again. They ran before the ghosts multiplied and somehow managed to escape from the place heavily. Nature always hides some secrets My word, Debra said as the car started to go down but at a slow speed. the cave is closed you know Eva inclined her head towards the other members. They shook their heads, not interested in going, and soon the car turned around the main road going down at a slow speed.

A man appeared, wearing a complete cloak even in the sunshine. It towered at the main street as the car was passing smoothly. Oy! Show me your licence, now, he said, demanding the car to stop. Nastika felt strange about him like he was made of smoke. Eva didn't argue and simply agreed. Fine, Pay me 500 or else!He waved a thumb in a gesture that he could destroy everything. Nastika helped Eva to identify a note of 500 as she took the right one and it let the cloak vanish.

Was it a ghost? I can't be sure, Eva said driving through but a bit nervous as she couldn't shake off the feeling connected to the person. It may be possible. I have heard of someone dead here who used to trick others, Debra spoke looking towards Nastika to elaborate who shook her head. They started to talk about safety measures and it proved the right time to change the subject or it could become more scary. They laughed at a light coming from the opposite pathway but they didn't know why it had appeared as Eva drove away at top speed.

Two cloaks have also come following the trail of the prior figure who had demanded money. No learning yet? You still gag the outsiders, don't you brother? one of them said, flickering a strange light to catch the swooping figure bobbing. It won't be easy now as I am not human, it said, trying to fight back with a strange light. The two figures captured the light in a strange ornament, flicked and the light sent by the ghost of the guard trapped him instead as he had to struggle. Now it's the end of you mate, the second cloak said, tossing it into the air, and with the blast, the figure of the cheating guard finally had met its end with no more bargain to the people around.

The city has less trouble after the massive chaos as visitors are more comfortable after the restrictions were lifted in the city. The news of people vanishing has been a habitual one for locals now so they don't bother about it much. it was somehow closely related to the way unfair deaths take place equally the numbers. Ghosts have affected some touring places so few doors are closed with signs of ' Not allowed, highly risky in nature they read as visitors try to go through. Eva and her friends also met such sites to their disgust and they stayed outside with a natural view to have company and enjoy it perfectly.

Eva was looking happier as Nastika told her the right place to dine out. Markos and Debra were talking about how they could get the best drink for the team. The other members were not talking much and they had a smile. It was going to be a perfect evening unless there was a ghost lurking past by. To their horror, a sound was heard from the inner rooms of the hotel where they were sipping cold coffee together. The voice was summoning someone and Nastika stopped Eva from going in It would be dangerous to find or we can be tricked, She spoke in her firm guide voice and Eva had no wish to find out more about it further as they paid and got out of the place.

I am following you, my dears, a voice said from behind suddenly as they stepped out. A man had come wearing the hotel staff suit and to Nastika's surprise, it turned out to be her papa walking quietly in the city. You are following us? Oh my word, she said laughing but Astitva refused to take the offer to come with them and told them to keep a close eye on the night's movement happening soon. She felt a bit calm after seeing him and they were all having a laugh on romantic nights in the hills amongst best lovers and how they work to feel their best taste.

Presence of her father lets her settle down as he is able to give her tips and also find ways by which things can be fixed easily. He shall always be around you with help, her mother had said once when Nastika had a fight with her on the subject of ghosts and ways in which she interpreted them as a lawyer. She told me how to get help. After seeing him today in the hotel, it gave her the feeling that Astitva was looking for loopholes and may try to fix them before she reach home as fear was still looming in the city.

The guide looked for her phone as the car had turned back, stopping at the place they were all staying. Why don't you stay with us? A night of true joy around? Debra asked but she shook her head looking sharply at the messages. You met my papa, didn't you? He wants to touch on some concerns, so I will have to report to him, Thanks for the offer anyway, she said smiling as Eva promised her to drop back after half an hour of pleasure. they asked for more soft drinks as Nastika had very easily gotten familiar with the way they play pranks. The gang was pleased to have the company of the guide too as they laughed and kept pulling legs making it get more noisy.

Eva stopped the whole mess by lifting the plastic bottles and safely disposing them in the corner bin. Let's get this over, she said, asking them to bid farewell to the guide, hoping to meet the next day for one more trip. We shall wait for your arrival, Markos said, shaking hands with glee. Everyone was certainly in touch but Nastika didn't know the main cause as they had no queries on the coin and she would be paid well for the tour once it was over so she had no fuss to ask them. The car stopped at the entry gate with a sound as two men from the building tried to converge on them demanding to show the pass.

Astitva came from behind waiting for her due to the threats of the night. The guide thanked the driver and Eva let her go along with the horn of the car while stopping the men to say something about the arrival of the vehicle this late and she was gone before they could follow her. I am glad you are here to cover up, the daughter said as her papa tapped her on the shoulder watching the back gate in pretence to check the light and they had gone in. Your aunt and uncle are pleased today. You will find it soon, he said, leading her upstairs and it couldn't have been more pleasing for her than seeing him back here as a proper helper to cover out the main course of the sudden fear.

Lights were on upstairs as Nastika went and she could see her uncle talking to someone Who could be on the phone this late, it's almost night? she wondered as her aunt requested with a hand to sit on the chair. She agreed waiting as Upendera laughed at the response from the other side. We would let you feel at home, don't worry, he said, making Nastika smile with his nature. She knows how much hospital her uncle is in and Astitva came bringing a cup of juice for her to sip as she waited.

Is a global call. He is talking abroad, the father said as she looked questioningly towards him. It is sure that you are coming 2 days later or do you have an excuse for no flight again? :She could hear her uncle asking the foreigner on the call as she raised her eyebrows. The children were asleep below and Upendera didn't want to get them awake so he gave the excuse to the caller. With a final word on meeting soon, the uncle has come to approach Nastika willing to explain it finally after closing the call.

Any memories of your other uncle? he asked,

holding an envelope as she finished the juice. You are surely not talking about Mahendra uncle? she got excited as he nodded. I am in touch with him. The coin is becoming more than required to the opposite sanctum, he smiled touching his forehead. Nastika looked for a moment and then asked, Surely, he is not coming here to visit or is he? Astitva waved his hand in 'yes' and she felt a strange connection to the past which she has hardly forgotten. After the death of her aunt, he got absolutely angry and left home with a word about not coming till he recovers from the flashback.

He is requested to solve the case of shadows lingering in water, the father said, expressing his doubts on the case and wondering whether he is wanted here in this place. What brings him here apart from ghosts and shadows is the way to give answers to the Western world about our riches Upendera joined in trying to give a further hint. They were awake so late as movements were taking place from the other side in the repaired building and they couldn't overlook the fact that people were simply trying to follow their words.

Let's get it straight. We are not the only ones facing fear right now? Nastika finally started getting into the groove as they tried to explain it to her. She has seen many images in trend, news from abroad with more tourists from other countries coming and she does have a taste for suspense. You are still on the trail then? Yes, they are facing it too, Upendera said, taking over with his wife bringing some food for the niece who took it happily as their talk continued in the night. They were talking about how changes have taken place, why it is getting so messy and the core of it leading the trial for visitors to come to India. It was smart of Astitva that he refrained from taking the coin out as he had the idea that a few shadows may be lurking to find more on it and it could make things tricky with them.

You have to be smart while you talk with foreigners, the aunt said with a smile toward Nastika. I know what to do now. Have got a few tricks up my sleeve, the niece said, eating potato fries with chapati and feeling composed. they had made it very clear that ghosts and repelling powers must not find the trick to reach up to the coin. As long as he is with me, I am not scared, Upendera closed the talk gesturing to his forehead and they decided to go to bed leaving Nastika alone munching her dinner.

In the dark hours of the night, a lamp came to life. The leader of the rebel forces was walking without any fear into the inner camp as he tried to find who else might be asleep. Wake up, it's not the time to get a nap, you know, he said, smirking at his two best servants on guard. They fell asleep for a moment and then woke up as he thumped them onto the back to do the same thing. It's night, you know, let us sleep, don't you? they pretended as he asked them to come to the upper floor for a chat on future issues.

There were documents scattered on the table as they both came up not wanting to face anger at this brink of hour. What else has happened apart from them, look at it? one of the called servants smirked as the leader told them to sit and have a cup of night potion. They did agree reluctantly as he started to give hints on the talk. People are coming back from abroad. What could all men possibly do? he asked, lurking in the shadows with his injured face being fierce. It means they feel the riches are here, in India, doesn't it? the second servant said, making the leader smile finally.

They were not sure what may have happened but the talk couldn't be completed as there was a sound of a bullet struck below. It happened so suddenly that the leader was taken aback. Get them, who has found our quarters this late? he shouted running down where a ghost was standing quietly. In honour of your betrayal master, it said, firing two more bullets from the weapon of the leader, making him fall back. It looked for a cause to kill them all but it felt like a waste of time to it so the ghost lifted an empty box, pushed a few chairs, and took out a grenade which he threw on the other gate. They are sleeping there, you idiot, don't kill them, the leader growled as the blast took place taking more lives than he could think in the background of striking hard.

The rebel has got the lighter finally which he flicked making the ghost turn around in the air. Get him Get him. the leader said throwing smoke into the air with the hope that it would contain the strike. To his surprise, the ghost toppled him, letting the lighter slip from his hands and wounded him by his famous snarling blade. My revenge. I will surely come back, you understand sir? it said whispering only to the leader with fright in his eyes visible to the ghost that made him feel pleased. the power flickered something that sounded like a blast and both of the servants to the floor died by it.

It looked like it wanted to get a few ghosts who could help him to get revenge on the leader and he had succeeded in swooping with the rest of the weapons easily away. I will see to it that he is destroyed, the leader fumes both with anger and pain checking the pulse of the fallen servants. Dead, Can't believe it, he said with tears in his eyes. The leader turned the blast portions of the gate and went inside. There were still swirls of smoke as he counted 15 members dead with their devices still active, unable to accept face recognition and fingerprints as security measures. The leader took his blasting system out, flicked it, and with no hope of answer, he blasted all 15 devices in one shot clearing them all with no evidence remaining for investigation if anyone dares to have a raid secretly.

He pushed a button going upstairs and a strange water source emerged. He put his fingerprint to allow and the water source started to clear off the whole mess in the location inside the lower floor. With disgust, he took an identity card from the main member in 15 and took its photograph to remember the level of chaos. He promised to summon these ghosts to his advantage as the ghost who did the damage was not aware of the powers. I will settle this before causing the mayhem, he fumed, getting on to the trace. It was still night and he sent an online message to the group for more recruits and now he wants to form a plan to settle out of the course making it clear once and for all.

The next morning was calm as Eva came again driving towards the main gate for her. Nastika had already prepared herself as this was going to be their final day. We will be leaving on Sunday, our official says it's limited< she got the message early morning as she came out from the shower. Good, the search for the coin, I presume, she whispered to no one as Astitva let her through for the touring party. Now the car had arrived and she simply sat in the front seat with calm as Eva drove it away with excitement.

Markos is in shivers you know, she said pointing out the lad in the back seat. He had crouched low feeling dismal for something that may have happened earlier or maybe last night. What's the secret, anyway? the guide asked, looking them up from the windscreen. He faced a ghost in the cupboard as he was searching out his hidden chain which he locked before coming to the trip yesterday, Debra spoke from the backside as Markos finally resumed talking, explaining how it made him vulnerable after it.

It's a habitual treat to get you to know, Nastika said as not much of a shock. They looked her up from the backseat and thumbs up proceeded, making the mood light. We go towards the royal place today then? Eva asked, watching as they arrived at a location crowded with people pushing the ticket counter and the guard aside. No rush, I will let things be arranged, Nastika said, stepping away as the car stopped. She simply went across the crowd, showed her official pass, and 7 passes were handed back making her smile as she thanked the guard and came back holding them in her hands.

You know all of them very well, don't you? 'Young

the other lad commented as they changed the entry root and went in from the backside. it's not what I know, it's what counts, she replied trudging away. Follow me now Be careful, one wrong step and you'll be gone forever, she warned them about the tunnel path and the slope taking them down. They considered her words as they were taking care of their steps and all of them entered into a beautiful garden spread with nature blooming around. They walked past, waited for the pass to check on a stone bench and finally, they were all in for a real treat.

Let's start from this room, Nastika asked Eva to let others follow in the smaller lane one by one. They went with quiet fervour of the place as they watched idols of ancient origin very closely there. The photography was not allowed so they simply passed through with a strange feeling associated. They crossed towards the other lane where a small stream was floating alongside a statue which made them have total bliss. Markos had finally gotten over his fear as he felt closer to nature. Nastika smiled at all of them and they followed her as she led towards a main place with a smaller pond located with fishes rising in number on the surface drifting in its wake.

They were able to fight their inner pain here and they all felt perfectly elated as it was a treat to be so close to nature. I thought you may need to come out of your inner struggles Nastika obliged, asking them to have a glass of cold milk filled with dry fruits and pure richness. One by one they grasped the glass and simply cherished it with its effect. The feeling was absolute like it had been hidden here for long and she waved at them as Ea asked for the charges as she wanted them to understand how to face their worst fears.

it's all in your past, the service and experience of it, she said gesturing on when to pay her or to make it after the trip has ended. True essence. it's an absolute joy, a pearly figure rose as Eva turned back with a smile. I wonder how it feels to be so close to nature? Nastika was ready to strike but to their surprise, it didn't woosh, cackle, or sneer but simply bobbed close to the water watching the fishes come to the surface and go back. they felt it may be the positive spirit, the ghost that linger on and Nastika finally felt better in such a peaceful mood.

They went back from the same way they had come as Debra heard someone crying from the smaller stream. They didn't look to search for the voice as they knew it could be a trap. I can't make your lives better. I am trapped, they can hear a ghost rasping from the stream below and Nastika gestured to follow her rather than try to find the voices. More echoes came from the idol room, We are trapped Please help us to be free, please, they could hear the strange cries but the guide finally decided to help her team. She reached for a conch in the inner passage, lifted it, and played it loudly so all voices could get quiet and it made the visitors feel more peaceful as they came out safe in complete strength.

A group photo session took place with Nastika in the centre as they all felt comfortable in her presence. We shall come back, for sure if the agency allows us, Debra said smiling as Eva handed her the Indian currency in which the guide checked for her charges and returned the rest. for your outing, thanks for making me part of your tour, it was true fun, she said, turning away but Eva stopped her. The promise to drop her safely at her entrance was not going to be taken away. They all asked her to sit in the front seat with music and laughter amongst them and the car dropped the guide back at her place and turned away. Astitva came down to receive her and he felt peaceful with a perfect outing for his daughter.

They didn't succeed, did they? he said, leading her as she shook her head. A shadow came suddenly making Astitva surprised but Nastika knew the ghostess had been waiting for love to talk. Great job, You kept your word, she said with her voice clear in both ears and she nodded leading in the steps of her father without a word. Nastika has been hoping to find Mritanjaali's ghost soon but now she has heard her, she needs answers to a few questions. It's not safe to roam around at night or she could have found it right now so she will have to wait for her chance.

A cool breeze covered everything as it was night and Astitva kept his light on as they crossed. Why didn't they ask me about the coin? she asked quietly but he shook his head like this was not the place to talk. she glanced toward the other building and a few lights appeared too, like they were following the trail. It's you who should be handing them the curse so that's why, Astitva smiled looking at the men who had come to face them. They wanted to turn on them, to fight and to leer but Astitva had everything covered. He bowed politely and led his daughter in without a word, setting the mood back to normal in his presence.

You are on time today, dear, the aunt said, leading her in as noises came from the lower stairs. They have been told already? she asked looking at her aunt for confirmation and she agreed. They told him on arrival to take place the next day as Mahenndra was already travelling in flight. It would take some time for any of them to adjust according to the foreigner but the plans are made and Upendera feels calm to see him coming back after such a long gap and being part of the family.

It's time we return you the spending you had done, Aisha said running upstairs and handing her a chocolate ox with Abhi and Vidyut behind. Mahendra had sent some money to Upendera before coming and the children had requested their aunt to bring a chocolate box for Nastika which made her feel elated for them. Nice of you, it's very cute, she said looking at the cartoon designed outside the box. It looked like a bagpiper playing a kind of instrument but only flying with smoke. they had high fives and the children had got back into the room lower stairs.

She turned the TV to find something after chasing them below. An image was flashing on the screen with an ad for some strange type of costume. Suddenly the channel changed and News started to come on it. flights are at high risk in nearby air borders. People who come from abroad must take a vehicle instead of local flights to come to the actual destination, Upendera had already known this to come but Nastika felt surprised watching a strange image shown on Tv.

Our sources suggest that the local airport is under construction because the runway was destroyed by certain influences last night. All flights are changed to other routes. We shall let you up to date shortly, she felt a bit relieved as a sudden fear came to her heart. Astitva came down as the news was running and he smiled silently Your uncle is coming by a bus to the local area. He will arrive here safely soon, He smiled, updating her and it was further joy. The children were on their feet waiting but they were told to go to sleep as it may take until morning till he arrived and they finally agreed after a few scolding from the eldest.

Nastika couldn't shake off the fear as she felt there was something planned to stop their relatives from being together. She had a dazed glow as the night turned dark. It is not one of those hours when she can be out of bounds leaving everything to be in chaos It's all in your hands now, she could think of what her uncle had said years ago going away when he had turned to her last time. At that moment she was young so she hadn't been able to grasp it but now she understands the main element of his speech while he was leaving.

It was our single chance, we failed it, the men who had followed them said to each other in disgust. They were rubbing their palms like they wanted to take revenge for the past. That man was part of the full moon ceremony like the boss told, wasn't he? they asked but they intervened before they could open the door to go in. A shadow has moved in front, surprising them and their eyes couldn't recognise it. The ghost of Upendera's son had come without any disturbance and had caught them from behind, which made them struggle.

What's all this noise? Who are you? Let us go it's our place, they didn't even get the chance to speak as the ghost has covered them with its leer and is willing to destroy the body soon. After toasting the smell, it crushed them, making the death look so simple and benign as it laughed, making the noise be heard by the leader who came outside as the ghost vanished from sight. Killed them? they are not the products you buy in the shop to be broken like toys, he fumed looking towards the building on the other side.

A white glow was visible there as it flicked something for the leader to read, Timeless days are over. Your time to taste death is also coming soon, it made him angry but the glow was gone as he stood there totally in rage with himself. they will go the same way as you did, he spat, opening the door to go in as some voices came from inside to hear out. The good thing was that the ghost hadn't killed the people who were in and the leader breathed a sigh as his numbers had seriously gone down in recent times making him feel alone due to it.

Upendera woke up around 4, it was his time to go and get some advice from the legendary spirit. The power around him has started to gather forces and he needs certain calm to figure things out. He picked up his stick, tapped it, and came down from the building without Astitva noticing it as he was in the bathroom washing his face. Nice bloke. He goes by the standard, the old man muttered as he crossed the building easily. He could see lights on the other side, ew men wanted to come out watching him but they didn't dare as they were told of a ghost who accompanied Upendera and could be worse if they tried to fight with him.

He walked around the lane which had become large with time and things that had happened here. The old man quietly trudged past the streams, he touched the sign of the blaze, made 4 circular rounds around it, and had gone before any of the ghosts would sense his certain presence. After half an hour of walking, he felt approaching the lake and it made him feel pleasant. The spirit was on the other bank but as he saw the old man coming, it drifted towards the other side simply with a ghostly smile as a tribute.

Ah, here you are!, it said with light shimmering around it. Your troubles are more serious than in the past, are they? He obliged as Upendera sat on his old favourite bench looking up They are gathering, what shall we do? he said without any prior description of what bothered him. The spirit had a longing to request to hand his son over who can protect it but now he can't do that. Instead, the light started to become wider as Upendera saw it and a shadow of a figure came closer to the spirit who flicked its front finger to let it appear in front of the old man.

The answer to your fears, the spirit said as the figure bloomed into the sky around and started to walk towards Upendera with delight. I won't come with you. I will come to your place, the figure said as the spirit flicked once more and a watch came clinging to the cloak wrist but only visible partially to him. The time is limited, make sure you do it exactly well Praveen, the spirit said as the name struck hard to Upendera's mind with the memory of someone who knew from the past.

the son of your long lost working fellow, isn't it? the spirit said as the figure bowed to Upendera and vanished. How do you find ways to be the best of your concerns? the spirit just had a gesture of relief as Upendera felt his eyes go wet listening to that long-lost voice finally. Praveen had been sent to find the licence of the gun by which Upendera's son had died as it backfired. After 3 months of his efforts, Praveen was almost close to finding who may have made the weapon so deadly But all that came as news of his death and now it may be time to make it all get fixed by having the revenge.

I will certainly come back. there is a lot to talk about, the old man said ingratitude as he turned with sunrise happening with light all around and happiness to come soon. You still have to find ways to protect them all, don't you? the spirit said, its imprint going away and voice fading. The old man nodded with his hands raised to the sky as a few birds flew with fishes in their beak but none of them fell. Everything was somehow coming back to calm now as it became a clear view to see through and he had reached home with taps of his stick.

12
SPECTRAL SMILES

A scene of pure beauty met Mahendra's eyes as he walked across it. He didn't have the urge to go straight home as he knew somehow that children may be waiting for him. He took an inscription and flickered it. A ghost came out surely. It was of his wife as she held a ghost of a smile too. Back in this place, are we? they said with a strange soft voice which he could only hear. Mahendra walked for an hour or so as it was almost dawn and as it struck 5 in his watch, he was able to find a vehicle to drop him to the nearby bus station.

The conductor felt a kind of bliss coming but Mahendra didn't hesitate with money. He had managed to get hold of some Indian currency during his final plan to come here and he is also familiar as He talked with the ghost of his wife before he took the flight who was not pleased. 'It looks like you are just hungry for money, nothing else, it had taunted him as he came here. Luckily he survived as the plane diverted to another airport and now here he is going back in the early morning bus feeling joyous for it.

I will be going there after a long time, anything that has changed sir? he asked the driver who was checking his watch and told him it would be 15 minutes late. Not a big deal. You come to see the boards changed, new shops, and people filling in, he obliged and continued further, Yes few great men have been honoured so you may find statues, He gave a laugh that made Mahenda warm up with excitement as the bus started to move.

Scenes were starting to change as they appeared but the visitor did not have much problem with that as the bus kept moving awayThis is the thing which he likes the most in hills as the serene beauty of the outside world can make you mesmerise in the backdrop simply. Other people were too looking out of the window as the bus turned to true heights and Mahendra could see a few young ones complaining of their head spinning as the vehicle kept turning in and out in the bumping road ahead. Your ticket sir. I presume we will stop at the next food corner. you can get your water bottle there, the conductor said handing him the ticket as Mahendra was busy admiring the scene and took the ticket quietly. A sudden shape bloomed as the bus took another turn towards the hill. It looked familiar but made of smoke as Mahendra stared at the window keenly. It didn't say a word, it simply came in and swept away, making him feel surprised but it had nothing to do with it as it hardly brought fear to him.

People were in mood inside the vehicle as few of them were talking of a match, players injured in it and how frequent it has become. Mahendra is not much a fan of it as he has lost interest in sports ever since he lost his wife. She used to be one who would ask to go to the stadium and watch a match live with a lot of fun but now it looks empty like No one wishes him to accompany. More people started to fill in as bus stopped as certain outer stations dropping the local people out and pushing of people with more of them coming in

My mind, what else will make me think honestly? he said looking at the two passengers who stepped out as they reached their destination. At the next sight sir, the conductor spoke not to Mahendra but to the driver who drove away very politely. They stopped at a food corner last and the remaining people stepped out. Mahendra didn't feel like eating anything so he simply bought a water bottle and a packet of chips. He came back sitting back in his seat and started to munch a few chips.

It's been a long since you came back, is it? A voice whispered to him as he was quietly sitting alone and made him feel simply surprised but there was no sign of fear again in the voice. You keep popping when I am silent or alone, why is it so? Mahendra asked him without trying to feel brave or show overconfidence. A strange but soft laughter came in response which he felt to be heard before. You will find out soon, won't you? the voice said and went again as he finished out his packet and lifted his bottle to have water feeling a bit calm.

The bus had finally reached the main station. Back at home, Upendera checked his wall clock and felt that this may be the perfect time. Mahendra came out from the bus in the hope of seeing something great but he was quiet for a while after hearing the voice. Three men had come suddenly asking for a lift or dropping to the place as he was still in thought. The visitor told them about government quarters and one of them had agreed on the exact price as the driver took his luggage to pick on the backside and asked him to get comfort. He felt this could be a perfect ride to find more but thought he should be able to do it here later as the vehicle turned taking its passengers away in the early morning.

Hello, uncle. You were not scared were you? a voice said again as Mahendra came out from the local vehicle checking for his bags and had just paid the driver who went away. A shadow had come looming and it slowly touched the hands of the visitor who finally broke into a smile. You are such a brave son. I didn't know that your ghost still roams here. The rumour was true then? he said as a few men came out from the other building. The workers on the other side didn't get a chance as Upendera had come before they could speak any word so the other side neighbours could only growl behind their backs.

The distant brother hugged, there was a joke about getting late and the old man let the foreigner make him get used to the place and the higher level of stairs. My recent hill trips abroad do get me used to quickly, the visitor laughed as Upendera's wife touched his feet and he smiled back here.

They were looking quite calm as he had come like the family had got their jewel bak. There was laughter all around as Nastika came out, touched his feet and she was followed by Astitva making the mood truly cheerful in the vicinity.

Let's get cracking then. I will meet the children soon He said going to have a wash and feel refreshed. The upper tap has rapid flow so just tap it only once, Upendera told him in urgency and laughter came from inside. He hasn't changed in these years, has he? He wants to try things of his own, ' Upenra's wife said and he requested to make some special dish as a greeting to welcome the visitor. Nastika was still in her seat and looking at the top bag which had a shining glow.

Mahendra came out and told her that it was for shadow and she couldn't be more excited to find out more on how to make it work. He simply lifted the bag and started to detect as a kind of screen appeared in the thin protective layer easily. All clear. I can think of making my mess worse so it can trace naturally, Nastika understood what it does and requested him to try it later as his tea would get cold. They were joining him to be part of the light breakfast as Upendera felt it's been years since they sat like this and it couldn't be about time now.

A strange emotion touched on to him and he was feeling touched. Keep your cool father. these are testing times, a voice told him without much touch in it and he finally adjusted looking between Nastika and the visitor asking them to start. Should I call the children upstairs for tea? the aunt said but Mahendra shook his head and gestured that he had just come and he would meet them later. No excuse this time, foreigner, Upendera said as his wife brought the tray alongside a plate of cookies so they could munch a proper food with true taste.

Did you get worried when the closest airport was closed? the niece asked, looking in the mirror like wrappings on the bag. It does scare you if it's urgent. Not much, we're habitual in the US as more construction stints happen in local places, he smiled, accepting a glass of tea with a few local cookies. I brought it from abroad too. let's try them now, he said, opening a low bag and taking a package of cookies brought from the US and sharing them around as Nastika looked at the label which was familiar to her.

Is there something connected dear? the aunt asked as she read the name and felt where she had heard it before in her life. It's something which I know from my tours with those who like to come here, she said rather to his father than her aunt. yes. this cookie is famous for being sold by those who are true guardians of protecting the coin abroad but I don't trust them too, it made her realise where that came from and she felt a bit anxious reading the label as she crunched a few cookies.

As long as we stay vigilant, it's hard for them to find it, isn't it? Upendera said, just touching on the subject as Nastika looked up at what might come out of his mouth. I am glad to see the ghost of your son. He must be very strong surely, would he? Upendera shrugged, not willing to talk to him as they were in a good mood and should talk about other things. Like Mahendra doesn't like anyone to ask him how his wife died, similarly Upendera had no wish to talk about the night to everyone and how he lost his dear son.

The way his brave son left him forever is not an easy pill to digest for a man of his calibre. The people around him felt a chill coming from him and he is somehow calm to find words with the ghost that accompanies him. Astitva changed the matter by asking about plans to stay with the children. It is not their wish that brings me here, honestly. I will stay here for a week and will leave afterward. I guess you know why I have come back here, He simply raised an eyebrow towards Upendera with a smile who obliged.

Back in the US, it was a strange evening. A few cops

were following the trail of a missing person and they had landed in the vicinity of an area that was quiet. We have put you under a trap, some strange voices kept coming as three of the cops separated and they started to fire. A shriek came from the outer yard which meant they had hit someone. For a moment, the policeman raised with glee but the next moment he had to kneel as something came whooshing past him. Not that easily, you hear me? a cackle could be heard. Scamier was leading the charge and he couldn't have asked these people to be on the tight corner than this

Spread out. be it humans or ghosts. We want to apprehend them, he spoke in a clear voice as the sound of something breaking came. The men raced away just in time as the next moment the whole floor was spread with broken glass and metal on it. How can this be so fast? What kind of place is this? one of them asked but Scamier raised a finger not to speak and he obeyed following the trail. A blast took place from behind as a few men fell to the floor in its pressure. To Scamier's surprise, there were other agency experts too and a few of them had died in the bomb that had crudely exploded there ending their lives.

It's all for the day, one of the senior experts said, spreading their fingers on his moustache. He looked elderly with a lot of experience and Scamier wondered whether the order was for all or only his gang. You too. It's not safe to explore here at night. The ghosts are at bay, he said looking towards Scamier, and his doubt was cleared. Sir! he asked his men to retreat and they all turned with a salute which the man didn't consider worthy in any sense being a gesture of affection.

A shadow loomed in the dark as the gang reached the main station. it may have been waiting from the dust but now it could be seen to them more clearly. Oh the ghost of the safety, let us in, Scamier said to it and the main gate opened with the sound of a creek and the wind rising slowly. You are not late. the leader must have sent you in the right time, the shadow said, allowing them in as they took back the main component, Scamier picked a diary to write a few notes, and the job was done. No clue of the coin. I am ruthless you know he said to nobody and all of them decided to leave for the day with their task completed.

India was still busy with its market as Mahendra had taken the help of the best guide, his niece. You like to go through these descriptions, don't you? they asked as they walked past the statue and into the main lane. Let's go to the food stalls, they won't ask you much, she said, leading her foreign uncle. Mahendra does have a pale white glow on his face which helps local people recognise him as a foreigner and he has no problem appreciating it. Funny, how easily they are asking to pay high from me, he smiled as they came off the food stalls and turned towards the touring attractions to explore the city.

This is my favourite place, Nastika had come to a tree on the outskirts and they both stood there. Did you ever think about coming abroad or trying a course out? I can help you Mahendra asked her, smiling as she turned her face away. She is more comfortable with friendly ghosts and the company of children in this land rather than going or thinking to get her fame. money and moments. They are two integral sides of a coin. I have both, I don't need to search for them abroad, She spoke to him in a whisper and he felt strangely disconnected from her for a moment close to the woods.

A cackle could be heard as she said this and it was well thought out by her so she asked her uncle to leave rather than find out why it had decided to target them. Moves started to shift in the air as they were trying to go away from them. We are not in the middle of a trap, are we? she said, her voice an octave high but Mahendra was standing in calm. He was waiting for this moment to show his strength and it has come at a perfect time to prove how much power he possesses naturally to handle such a case.

Mind you. I am fond of such moments, Mahendra said as a few shapes emerged. He took out an electric device from his pocket. Here we go, let's have a duel, he urged his niece to follow the strength as he converged. There was a flash and one of the imprints was destroyed as its other fellow shouted in rage and followed them. Nastika threw something from her pocket and the smaller imprints started to vanish around them. together, ready? They said in unison raising their clasped hands, Oh the sad and interrupted imprints of such sol, we ask you to depart from this world to peace, the voices turned into echoes and the ghosts struggled as they latched on to the said words and their natural effect making them banish soon.

There was a flash of light, a blast, and smoke all around, they all were gone as both relatives felt pleased to do the honours and finished them easily. Let's do this once more before I go, Mahendra smiled, leading Nastika to the outer area and walking past the old tree with its nail stumps. They turned away before any spirits would come out of it, found their way, and simply walked towards the quarters in true joy but the adventure was not over as there was also some activity taking place with fierce battles happening around.

The ghost of Upendera's son was in the heat of battle as 30 men surrounded him, throwing all types of attacks they could. He would easily flicker them, would close downlights, or even disarm a few of them. Blood stains spread on the corridor as more people came trying to catch it. Go in. I will handle this, Mahendra ordered but Nastika didn't move an inch. She flicked her wrists too and a blade appeared striking 5 men together in one strike. One more twist of her wrist and there more men were on the floor. this is not your battle. I will deal with it, the ghost said but she shook her head wanting to help.

Mahendra released a bolt of lightning from a device which struck all 20 remaining of them and they collapsed onto the floor. Our boss won't leave you unturned, one of them said as the ghost lifted and broke his neck without much effort. The last laugh was surely going to be his as he created a bubble catching all the men who were alive and blasted them with the bubble going up and all of them vanished, not capable of coming back as hosts in the living realm as the beloved son had sent them packing. he requested the family members to go towards the stairs and rest assured.

Astitva came down running and felt warmer to see both of them well. We were watching from the open balcony, he panted letting them go in as everything was cleared and the son's ghost replaced the damages and bloodstains by clearing them up by splashing water. The ghost flew upwards towards his father as Nastika too started to climb stairs feeling tired after the conflict right at the opposite side of their building that happened in such intent or true impulse.

What's all the mess? You were not capable of fighting them off? The leader was fuming at the next building on those who didn't go to fight on as peace started to spread to this side. He had managed to find out what exactly happened despite the clearing by his son's ghost and he was not going to leave it unturned. This dawn, when the old man will come, you shall shoot him. agreed? he towered on a secret assistant with fury and spit flying from his rage. He shook his head as if he had to say 'yes' but he knew it was not possible and he went in to find bandages for him to help his scarred face from old wounds.

The leader sat there absolutely tormented by the fact that those who live in peace are stronger than those who create mayhem. He hit his palm on the documents at the table and he couldn't digest the feeling. Meanwhile, Aastitva is worried for his daughter now she has taken hands to duel with the other building. this was the fear we always have and now you are involved, what can I say, he said trying to explain to her how dangerous it could lead in future. she gestured it was nothing but just a consolation to her long lost brother that made Upendera smiled as he joined him

I am seeing you trying to be told off for the first time, what's the matter? he said to him as the father shook his head looking straight into his daughter's eyes in calmness. We will take care of each other, a voice came from Upedra's forehead with the ghost still residing but not looking at anyone. It did make Astitva shiver a bit but he knows who it belongs to. Upendera tapped him on the shoulder and asked him to join them for dinner and they all got assembled laughing at a trick of the children as the water was not coming exactly from a filtered thermos and they were out of joy laughing out loud at the mistake

The children were not going to miss the fun. They had planned something for their father as he had come after a long time and hardly talked. Come out, we have caught the thief, they said as Dushyant pulled a chain out from his father's pillow cover and tried to run away with it. Mahendra took it back easily but as he was doing so Aisha had caught up with things and had taken off his money. Now I can pretend to woosh from the window, she gestured, touching the window pane as Mahendra took his money back in exchange for a toffee packet.

You are still going like you used to do, he said, trying to offer them sweets but Abhi had completely brought the bag down with his father unable to get hold of it. It's not that easy papa, I think we do have the right to have fun with you, Vidyut demanded throwing the bag back as there was more noise upstairs even in the night. Upendera and Aastitva watched from far away rather than stop them as they knew it was a rare sight to see where Mahenra was running in and out of rooms shouting for his things and the children had true fun going away from him.

The ghost of the house, are we? Nastika said with surprise as Abhi ran back holding his papas\' belt with awe. Not with us tonight, you hooded ghost, Aisha said, taking it off to reveal the eldest and it made Mahendra and others laugh as she became part of the chase. a voice came from outside the window to make it quiet and they all suddenly stopped wondering what it may have been. The ghost of Upendera's son played the trick and his father smiled as things were brought back to calm by just a single node.

It was very nice of you, the father said to his son as everyone went to sleep, including the children. Astitva had gone in to get his stomach clear as he was not feeling up to it. The time for the full moon ceremony was not far and he may be gone from them for good. Mahendra's time was also coming to a close as he hardly had a few days left now to investigate the stages. The mood was changing in the air but for this night, they had enough action both outside the road and inside the building which had filled up for it.

An online call showed up on the foreigner's phone as he was sitting in the lobby room where he had been providing the entire area to do his research and live in peace. Yes, what's the matter? he said as the receptionist could be heard in panic from the other side. Scamier, he is in danger, badly wounded last night, the voice sounded frightened like it had taken place by the hands of some unknown force. IN 2 days I will be back. I want proper details on what happened alright? he said looking confused somehow and bemused about why things go out of hand when he is in India every time.

He looked for the latest trends in the western world and found a picture broadly flashing. It contained the man he knew very well who was shown robbing a jeweller who had thrown him out. For a moment Mahendra couldn't understand why Scamier might go in such a mood. He looked closely at more searches and was able to find a video updated recently. In this, the main jeweller was accused of using drugs in powder cases which are handed to dealers when they buy rare gems. Mahendra understood the trick behind the matter as a few ghosts were also reported by the media to make things complicated in such a concern.

However, in another country, strange things haven't stopped happening. Richar was deported to Portsmouth but these ghosts are still around. There was a sound like a cloth torn, a huge noise of people helping and it felt like something had been released in the air. After coughing more than 100 people, Andrew managed to take the gas issue down as it spread, making a few people paralyzed or have gashes in their faces due to it. Calm down calm down, he shouted looking for order, and threw another gas into the air so the crowd could disperse easily.

It helped to bring peace as that let them feel relief as he has been a specialist when it comes to handling it. Now who amongst you shall be the responsible party for this mess? he said his voice changed into pure rage. One of the standing men recently released from prison stepped out in front claiming it. I did the prank before being sent. I will do it again, you see, he challenged throwing another fume into the air making it all smell absolutely bad and going away without even having a chase on him by the hospital staff for crimes.

Andrew knew there would be such a mess so he had his pockets filled trying to bring things into balance. Before the man could go out of the hospital's main gate, he threw a pin and it hit him on the face, making it go blue and he fell in real pain. I may not call the police, Why should I? Andrew said without any kind of mercy. The man lay there asking for help but no one came forward. his blue face started to turn pink and then a complete shade of emptiness as he struggled and died on the floor as Andrew wrapped the case.

You can share with me his report if you like Nurse, the main doctor has become cruel in recent weeks. Logan has been treated and sent home but he did have to face a tragic case. His nephew Bernard was brought to the hospital last week with a severe condition. The nurses said that he had been hit by a venom pin so he must be declared critical. However, in the name of emergency, his case had to be registered first and as they tried to do formalities, the nephew started to go blue just like this current victim.

Andrew watched helplessly as he turned pink, felt weak or empty with no help and he finally died on the floor in the hospital. NO, No, you can't be, his voice went cold and quiet as all of them watched the main doctor throw file after file into a bin in anger, watching the dead boy be handed over and he had no answer to why he had died here. He was in such a mood that the topic of lost coin was of no further concern to him and Andrew slammed the chairman asking him to dismiss him from the post if he is not suited.

We shall see what to do in the future, the chairman replied, asking him to stay for a while. Ever since the main doctor finds anyone making pranks, or trying to trick him, Andrew has one simple goal to that person and he is destined to kill. Logan tried to reason with him at home about how Bernard had fallen in trouble with outsiders and he must have taken the wrong medicine as he was already suffering in the past. Nothing came to be worth so Andrew decided to get back to work and with this man coming to turn over back from the prison, he got his revenge

Back in India, the foreigner was planning to leave finally. He gave some money to his children and told them not to play pranks with Nastika and also to keep it nice to their aunt and uncle. You are just like a ghost papa. I know you won't come back again unless it is something important, Vidyut tricked him by taking his purse and then handing it back. Don't say this. He is loving too, Nastika told them and they got quiet as it was a strange mood. A vehicle came to take him away as it was time to go back from here with hardly anything gone in his favour.

He had booked his flight the day before and by touching Upendera's feet, he went into the vehicle, ensuring that he would call once he reached back to the US safely. Farewell sir. I will see you again, Astitva said as the vehicle started and Mahendra left the place. The children shouted too, watching from the window and then it had gone quiet. Nastika was having a headache as she sat around her father who told her to get a nap so it may come back to normal again. Foreigners don't understand what it is to have emotions of family and it was the same with the great man just driven away.

In the US, It was complete darkness as Scamier walked again, alone with no help for him or hardly any police backups. He had reached the diamond shop once again in the hope that he could find the coin. Is a total waste. You don't know how valliant it has been, Richard has said to him with a scold after his news went viral of having sneaked into a rich shop and taunting the owner. I will find out the way to grasp it in my palm, you wait, he said as he thought of it deeply in his mind and kept walking quietly in the night for the secret mission on hand.

With a sound of woosh, somebody caught him from behind and Scamier fell onto the floor. Nice meal. The richest night for me you know, the ghost said with a cackle as it summoned four more shapes looming in the dark. The cop had no fear to their surprise as he gazed into the figures shown by the light of his wristwatch. Have your say first, I will retaliate once you are done, they all latched on to him in total speed but he was better than the power trying to catch the human. it hit them with pale orange light floating above and all of them were sent to their end.

One for the honour of the diamond coin, he coughed quietly as some dust rose and he had the disgrace of not being able to find it. He would have to call his boss the next day with one more apology and he came out realising his nose was bleeding. He took out some ointment, rubbed it on, and had gone before the shop owner could wake or taunt him again. 'I told you, It's a total waste of time, 'Richard said the next morning as he told the cop in Britain in an online call about it. To some calm and happiness, Scamier got the news that Mahendra would be back and he felt relieved hearing it.

On a bright afternoon, A car stopped outside a royal mansion as the receptionist came to receive the arrival and all the staff felt pleased as Mahendra had finally reached his home. What's the news on the scamster? his name suits very well, doesn't it? he asked as he went in to check for his natural cover which was all well-kept by his team while he was away. Marun, you did well. it's perfectly preserved, he said as the lower servants brought water in a pot to clear his feet and he felt deeply gratified.

Bring me my hot coffee. I have to call my brother as you do that, they nodded leaving him alone with a lot of happiness spreading through. The attendant at the calling room gave him a salute and he called Upendera informing him that he had safely arrived. Few ghosts even at the airport as I took off Bro, he said in a hushed voice not bothering to bring the alarm in his team. they must give you a guard of honour as you have survived mate, Upendera chuckled from the other side telling that Aisha is crying a lot and she did want to see him again. Mahendra laughed in response, promising to bring her more sweets, and with gratitude the call ended as he would miss his beloved children here.

A bell sounds in a cafe as two men enter without a word. They were looking for Indian people who could help them with certain metals. It's true gold. You don't find it here in our country, they whispered to the cafe owner giving him a bribe who shook his head Go to the mansion, you won't need them, they were told as the cafe owner put down the shutter with a sign of closing for today. Nice way to treat us, we won't be that polite next time, they said, turning away for a certain place where they could find Indian people.

A person of Russian origin has stolen an audio recorder from an Indo-American band so they can chase him, helping in his quest to find Trai for something important from the past. hand us our devices, you understand? they shouted as finally the Russian stopped in a lane covered with cafes and had gone in the biggest one to let all get settled. 'What do you need? it's not a fuss to take away such expansive instruments' the girls from the band demanded as he raised his hand for quiet expressing help to find a lost Indian pass which was crucial.

Damian as in absolute fury as Adriene has denied me entry to certain beaches that were most crucial for search when it comes to ghosts. Sorry boss. I have been ordered by my superiors. I can't do much with this, he said looking at him fiercely as they both knew how things work and it had been a simple trick to clear off. Threats of shorelines had become less in recent times but Damian knew it hadn't been easy for them to counter and they couldn't blame him so they had rather stopped him from visiting such places instead of an order of being dismissed.

In England, cases related to cuts haven't been solved, instead, people have been requested not to go to the hospital if they face such cuts and take governmental guidelines with specified potions concocted that can be helpful. The results had been positive in a few cases but in others, there had been an outpour of pain and sorrow amongst people in local areas as they got boils or strange marks or rashes. The policy wasn't working well but they were bound by it. Most residents look for Indian-born people who know certain potions and locals request them to circulate so they can heal and find their worth as it remains their only hope of survival in tough times.

Dust and smoke had become common in developed

cities as people coughed, shouted, or kneeled in pain. It is the hardest matter of ghosts killing them or they are dragged to death by the hopelessness around them. the officials just round up the empty bodies, sockets with no eyes to test or give orders on completing the process. Both the US and Britain were getting in severe strain and it's hard to say which one may go down first in search of coins or be crushed by the pain of searching for treasure and glory.

We need the coin. It's the only way to be powerful or protect all of us, the chairman said to Andrew one night as he was walking in his corridor calmly. Let me get to the coin first a young lad said to his father who had stolen a pass to go to India from a Russian earlier as he was told the coin had magnetic powers and he wanted to test them. I want to be in touch with Mahendra sir, it's urgent, Scamier stumbled with pain as his wounds were still not recovered. People abroad were getting confused and willing to get their hands on the coin but they couldn't latch on to it.

However, Upendera is pleased in India where he walks quietly around his room as he knows very little about the coin but he has kept it safe smartly. The order had been clear to protect it till the time came and he waited patiently for that moment. someday the ghost of his son may feel content that his death didn't go to waste as things would get back to where they were before.

In the brimming light of the dawn, the golden spirit summoned a few figures for a word. They were talking of the fears that loom, the level to which ghosts can go, and repentance for the false gunshot that took the life of Upendera's son. it was so close to the right moment but the spirit didn't feel it to be the right time. Wait till that next full moon goes over. That will decide the fate of everyone, he said and the figure spread out one by one from where they had come ready to take their duties to the legend in hidden form.

13
SHADOWS OF THE FUTURE

It was a sad day around the area as Upma took off for her legal practice to the nearby court. She has somehow gotten used to the way people react at work and it doesn't disturb her in any way further when they talk about the mystery of life. She is so much touched on the subject of law that she hardly gets to talk with her daughter but their closeness is not a concern as Nastika stays away in her search to excavate more on Indian culture and she doesn't have any wish to find what she might be up to anymore as her court work is more prudent.

Are you worried about your family? I mean do you get enough time to give them proper moments? a senior lawyer had keenly asked her once after she had lost a case very nearly as the evidence turned the table. not to worry. These moments are to test how strong you are. I do get along very well, you see, she had said, taking the loss deeply to heart and turning away in her car in a grim mood. Astitva knows she only feels dejected when she gets lost so he tries to cheer her mood whenever he is around the home.

The performance of the case is the only thing which brings joy or sorrow to their home. Most of the time her husband remains in order to do his service and Upama holds herself back, not interested in his work. I will find out one day what he is up to, she would mutter whenever Astitva had been absent and it has become a kind of routine in their place with no proper family time, lack of togetherness and more than anything no proper care for the only child as both husband and wife keep things to themselves.

It's not that she has no interest in ghosts. She does get to turn to her husband in certain moments when she feels unnerved. 'I did get a glimpse of a certain image in my sleep. What should I do, honestly? she asked once in surprise to him. In another moment she has taken a tip from Nastika calling her when she was not expecting. I need your aid dear. How many times do I have to turn the pot clockwise when I have to water it outside? she asked her in urgency and the daughter obliged, explaining the process.

She knew the tactics, but for now it was a feeling of gratitude for the query thinking the right time might come someday with all in its fold. You will know my role at least one day, she whispered with a smile sent on phone to her mother and then came back as she knows she is not willing to talk much and Nastika had simply turned back to her work.

You are not as bad as I think, Upma had told Nastika after the return of her husband as the absence of Astitva pinches her the most. it may not be sure how she might behave when he has to go back to proceed with the full moon ceremony for everyone's aid. For now, everything is calm as she goes in, takes her cases, and strongly fights for legal turns that involve murder or charges on accused who are put into a trap. In such cases she does have to face the angle of ghosts sometimes which she has always detested. she doesn't give much concern when people say they had a vision in the witness box and she simply crosses them out

An error in judging the slipping stair, Was it? she said as one more case of such nature came with trial on the accused for murder. Your honour. My client had witnessed the shadow loom before he stumbled upon and that shadow killed the man, the defence lawyer said as Upama was on the other side of the argument process this time. She was cross-checking the person accused and felt certain pain as visions came back. How many times a shadow can kill a human, sir? she said looking towards the defence lawyer in a smile as he tilted his head in surprise at her words.

It is not one murder your client is charged with. yes,

the person has been guilty of causing damages, creating neck splits and now he is under the charge of murder if you think so, she spoke further looking towards the judge's bench where the evidence documents were spread through. The past crimes were dismissed If I shall remind you, the defence lawyer said to Upama who waved a hand behind shadow to surprise the people watching and laughed on imitating a ghost as the judge called for the order. I may be sure that this time he will again prove tough to question, shal he? She asked the judge for permission to inquire about the accused on certain grounds.

The accused brought to the court had been blamed for past crimes but he claims they were done by a ghost who belongs to his uncle. he keeps coming in my dreams the night before a crime takes place, he had spoken frightened in last hearing when he was accused for a neck split case where the victim had died brutally. How honest you are. We wonder what may be the dreams about them? Vishvanath, a prior lawyer for the case had commented but the judge had declared him unfit and to be hospitalised till he may be in proper condition to answer the questions of the lawyers as he had been proved very tough to handle for them.

Do you accept to be present at the place of murder? Upama asked, walking towards him as the accused agreed. Do you take the word that you know where the weapon was kept? she asked as the defence lawyer opened his mouth to speak. the accused shook his head in denial this time. Are you familiar with how to hold a British dining knife? she asked, checking the documents to confirm the exact name. the person agreed finally as she bravely asked him the last question. Is your uncle still coming in dreams to teach you how to do it? The accused shook his head and wanted to speak but felt quiet clearing his throat with a dead stair by the enquiring person.

My client had been put under pressure by Your

Honour, the defence person argued showing how the accused had been living rough. The problem with the court was that this accused had run away injuring a person when he was sent to hospital last time. it is not sure how much he can be protected. even the defence lawyer hadn't been able to keep him quiet when he consoled him on the losses and the way he was connected It's just a camouflage, if you ask me. he kills the person, simply runs off and asks you to defend him, Upama taunted trying to have a lead this time.

The judge took her word for an actual concern but told her the time had been off for today. We will have one more hearing. if he still stays with the preemption of ghosts involved, then we may have to think it otherwise, he told the defence person with a grim expression on his face. He took a hand on his head with a sigh and then turned away without talking to Upama. After a heated hour of debate, she felt quiet and had simply gone away hoping to see her husband soon as he had gone off to spend more time with family including a naughty but chilling daughter and the foreigner coming from the US amongst them for certain business.

Back at the government quarters, a few jokes were cracked on how Nastika may look when he or she gets married. Your tummy will come out, no smooth fitting, her aunt told her as she made faces on talk of the marriage. yeah, I am suited for a wed, am I? The ghost of my husband shall take me out, won't he be happy? she said, making her father laugh as Upendera saw her getting edgy on to it. The tour into the hills had again got simply closed due to a rock break in a certain road and the guards were clearing it as there were official signs of no entry till the road got fixed.

For further problems of the guards, a stream had opened up in a closer area where the rocks had broken and the water kept coming out faster than before. They couldn't understand how it happened until a guard broke his finger trying to push a narrow scuffling and he yelled hard in pain.

Ouch, Someone caught my hand, he shouted in true fatigue. The senior guards asked him to pull himself together and he somehow restrained his feelings as he wanted to say something about the presence of a ghost in the area.

A few more crashes had taken place on the opposite side of the road. A camping area was blown by strong wind and they could see the tent flying. Oy, catch that. We would be in true trouble if we don't do that, the most senior guard called and a few men ran behind the tent flying like a long loose cloak of someone in natural bounds. They didn't fear to chase it and finally got hold of it just before the entry point of the forest feeling relief. Are you there my darling? one of the guards heard a voice lurking but they had turned just saved by luck this time.

Narrow escape. We may have been having dinner if we hadn't turned, they said, telling the senior about it. We do have pain and joy in our task, he sighed looking closely at them as they were dismissed for the day. He took his phone and called, The missing tent is being recovered, Tell the German party to meet me tomorrow he looked excited as he said this, and the phone was disconnected as he sat there alone but with no fatigue. I will be the one who shall be handed over the money, he spoke to nobody and thought it may be his best chance to earn his reward from foreigners through it.

The next day a white bloke had come to meet him. Gluek, Reichtom, said in a German tongue and then switched back to English I feel elated to find the treasure of my life, the man looked around 50 with his pointed beard and brown hair. His eyes were pale blue and he wanted to get more into the subject of the tent. Any ghost I can pry off before I leave? he asked as the senior guard offered him a cup of coffee and he accepted with a peaceful smile taking out some money from his pocket to hand over to the Indian.

Es schmeckt mir, he said, willing to talk in German

but had urgently turned back to English. Tell me how much for the tent honestly? He was counting the foreign currency and the guard looked a bit hopeful. It's up to you sir. I may be happy with your settled amount, whatever you think it's worth, the German looked quietly sipping the coffee, and finally settled for a bill that may look decent giving 500 euros to the guard who looked delighted to get such an amount. He showed the money to his members and they didn't get why the foreigner paid him such high value but he has gone so they can't return it.

The night was absolute in a quarter where the German bloke had stayed. He was called Magalay and he was not alone there. Getting the tent at such a low cost was dear to him as the guards didn't know what it worked like. He was not alone as he summoned 3 more friends and they spoke sprengen in German and then to themselves in English in unison. they shouted, The night before the bombing as they laughed, cheering a toast with a glass of wine in their hands. They were over the moon to get their hands on the tent and now they were going to do what they liked the most with the panic of the ghosts in their favour.

Back in the city, a figure was moving fastly in the whole area. It was looking for a piece of cloth missing which it had kept alongside the tent. He took out a light and vanished, coming right onto the spot where the most senior guard laid out of fit after drinking much that night in joy. Oh, I see. More corrupted souls, he said, blasting off the door and being able to easily locate the cloth. Where's the tent mate? You have sold it, very well, he smelled guilt and loss of words in the guards and flicked his fingers, a blast took place and the guard was on the floor dead. The figure checked for his pocket and found out the foreign currency as he already suspected an outer hand in it.

The figure was so powerful that he sent something in a currency note. Magalay was also on the floor's mat as the note reached him. Return the tent or you will be wrapped in it with your throat crushed by it, it was a warning and the German blokes laughed reading it through in their posture. Knurren, they said to each other as a flash happened outside. The figure has found them and didn't talk or try a strike. He simply threw a light towards the tent and it got a clear light expanding on to the entire place. Before Magalay could act, the tent had opened, wrapping his friend and inching towards it at top speed to kill him.

The bloke shouted for help but the tent had wrapped all of them and there was a horrific sound of crunching inside as they were killed. India can be cheated, it can't be destroyed, the figure said, taking the tent away with pride as a few birds flew across the sky. He knew that the tent may be in the eyes of the outsiders so the figure had left it outside on purpose so he could trace them. It was the one that is used for the full moon ceremony to match the blue surface and he is now pleased that his plan had finally worked.

Back in the US, a man was running around the fish market. A strange circular object remained in his hand and he was claiming it to be the coin discovered in the United States itself. Scamier was running after it as the man turned left, went into the market, and vanished out of sight in hurry. Get him, folks. I want the man, the chasing person shouted as a few cars speedily went after him from behind honking in his wake. After a half hour of hard work, the chasing party finally caught him soaking wet totally in sweat and mud all over as the man kneeled to the floor in front.

This is not the coin we know, one of the guards said, looking at the round coin with disgust. I am sure it is the coin, I promise it, the man said, jumping up and down as the guards had certified it of no use. True folks, this is not what we are looking for. Who cheated you brother? he asked in a polite voice with a gun pinned to his ear. The man looked fierce as he kept claiming it to be the original one but the purpose for which the circular object has been sent has been achieved. It was a trap for a scamier to follow from the other country and now the location has been detected easily.

A look at the round coin made the boss suspect it as he could see the seal on it vividly. From Germany, is it? The return of the old food? he smiled as he took it from the man asking him to leave calmly. He should have locked him up for a false trap but instead, Scamier handed him a 50 dollar note as he went thanking him. What's this all going to do boss? one of his supporting members said as he looked at it closely. It connected to a memory, something that had happened in the past and it looks like he is still worried about remembering it due to its effect.

You know Jacques? he asked one of his older undercover cops who agreed on the word. scamier used to be part of a gang that worked undercover to trace a drug gang. They were so skilled that they were promoted and sent to the UK to find out more about that. It was this venture where he met Richard, and made good friends with him, and in their trace, they found that a hospital was involved in harassing young people while they profited heavily from it. The team was about to close the matter when Scamier was requested to leave the country as they were deported due to official orders as it could have exposed stronger powers in the process.

While leaving off the sharp cop managed to track Jacques and kill him, however leaving other of the drug gang members deeply wounded. Whatever the future may be, we will be friends mate, it is a promise of this cop, Richard had said the night they were deported shaking hands and clapping for his bravery. From that day Scamier never forgot what happened in Britain and hates people who try to play as double agents to him. The trouble was that this hospital was also in pursuit to get the diamond coin and this is why he is scared a bit now as the older undercover friends look to him for inspiration and pat him on the back.

We will not expose those who protect the coin. What do you say? he asked for advice as his idea was favoured from vote being 3 to 2 amongst his working fellows What shall we do then if we can't get our hands on it? one of them said as he wanted to find it badly. The leader told them the fact expressed by Richard and as long as he tried to dig deep his words were getting sharperYou sure the coin is not in the west? the first cop said and the boss nodded thinking hard. If Richard has been so certain there was no question on it and he is going on with his word even to the grave.

You say what we will do? the famous word in the US is to turn the gate to the wrong side, isn't it? they laughed as Scamier said this loudly thinking on his emotional words. We will turn away from the sea and shall be safe in the port you know, they said laughing further as the evening started to get dark and it was time to go back home. Someone was hearing them from a quiet distance and he wondered why they had turned against the office. He was a ghost, a member of the secret order and he somehow also felt calm that they might not try their hands now as they realised the truth to be much far.

That night a strange thing happened to Scamier as he was sitting at his reading table quietly. A shadow moved, the figure appeared and he was surprised to see it didn't attack. I want to talk with you, it's urgent, it said smiling and the reader obliged. The thing is that I am from the positive faction. You sure it's not very important to trace the coin? the ghost of the head inclined as it asked politely, wanting to hear it out from him. I know the coin can only be owned by the one who is destined for it. No chance of any else who can get it, he smiled and the ghost felt more calm with its light still visible. What if you may be sent to India? Would you like to go there? a strange feeling emerged on the reader's face but he shook his head in amazement.

The reader starts to talk with the ghost about his past.

The day he was selected, his skills as a swimmer, and how impressed everyone was by his effort. He talked about the day when Damian had recommended him for best swimming safety measures but Adrien denied him and Scamier left in disgust. His past seems to unfold in front of him and he starts to speak as it strikes 4 and the ghost has vanished leaving him alone in the reading room. he felt in the company of someone whom he can trust and he rubbed his eyes as it was Sunday and the only place he can visit was the church in the local area but before that, he needed some sleep so he went inside his bedroom to have a nap.

In a city away from this country, right in the middle of a harbour, someone was waiting. It could be a man but with the looks of his eyes, it is tempted to be a ghost rather than a living figure. He threw something from his cloak and two men appeared on the sideline. I have the code you idiot, he said as two more shadows loomed from the harbour's back dock. They did have an image through the coin sent to them and they can see the man very clearly. Our target resides there. What shall we do with him? the leader said as the voices said in equal measure, Shoot him sir He, agreed but they needed a plan and Scamier was certainly on the mark of the ghosts lurking abroad now as they plan to end his life sooner than a flight coming India

Prove you are worthy to take there, he said as two humans came and all four of them converged to strike out. this will not work. He is a top-level cop, you idiot, he said in a whisper that was like a taunt. Two of the ghosts went left while the other 2 went in the other direction. The human felt the movement and he had sent the ghost flying on both sides with a flick of the device that threw them out from the world with the effect of dazzling light. So weak, I don't need you either, the cloak said, flicking to the more figures coming from the inner harbour and they were all banished within the light by sheer force of the cloak's strength.

The main figure cackled not with joy but disgust as he turned around and caught a young child. The fear had gripped the child as he was going back and had been lost in the crowd close to the harbour with his mother running away. I want you to do my bidding, the figure said, not killing the child but offering him a bowl of filled chocolate pudding and training him in some arts. I shall know them by yourself? the child said with no hope to go back home and it looked like the figure had found a match for the opponents.

Scamier went to the church round 10 with his renowned boots that gave him a feeling of comfort. He looked at the empty light sphere, took a candle to light, and felt thankful to the god that he had still survived this long. Being a cop is not an easy job to do, especially when you are under the command of someone superior. He had made a lot of mistakes but Damian had always been with him trying to protect which made him feel well. The night's glory was still in his mind as he turned so one voice came out from inner speaking, Your hurdles remain with the place of the past you don't want to go, Amazed he turned but the voice had gone and he kept wondering the words as he walked back home thinking what may come next as fear.

Back in England, few people have been marching around the main road. They wanted the release of a person who had been convicted of sedition by the local police. No more shouts or you all will be locked too, he said as they tried to cross out of the jail willing to let him get released. The man had criticised the government telling them to be real ghosts who had been indulged in drug and human trafficking openly. His words have not been testimony but the way he had said has brought a huge uproar due to which he was arrested for inflicting emotional fervour with his voice and words in a crowd.

Bring him in, a senior police officer said as the crowd was dispersed by openly sending sparks into the air with certain weapons. The man was brought to face the charges as the police person looked at him. Last year you were charged with hitting a boy brutally, is that correct? he said looking cleanly in the records for details. You have been claimed to have been involved in sending a few men outside England without a permit? the person asked further for which the man shook his head. Ghosts may be involved or not, you are certainly messing with the law sir, aren't you? the official said, starting to taunt him with cold fury.

Fear won't do me sir. I have the crowd with me this time, he said as more noises could be heard from outside becoming very loud to face out. Another march was passing through demanding details of the couple dead in the woods and as the case was closed with no one found guilty, the police were baffled to see them come again in such numbers. I will get all of you to disturb the order. What do you say? the personnel said, taking out a pistol and dragging the man by the arm. Come with me sir, he said politely as he showed the man to the crowd in custody asking to be cleared away.

Clear away, all of you or this man shall be dead, you hear me? he said, shouting it clearly into the sky above. A figure had come from behind holding the policeman silently. The man who was in his capture felt surprised as the figure sliced one of the person's ears off with his pistol falling with a clunk onto the ground. Now you face the real taste of it. Force is never going to work with social bonds, the ghost said leering and pinning the inspector onto the floor as he gasped for his breath, was turned upside down, and with a cling, his neck was broken making the crowd roar in absolute disgust

The crowd kept running in, few of them burnt a police wagon for emerging loads inside. Some of them took off the ammunition and most of them wanted to break out. A horn came suddenly with a water cannon coming straight to the burning jail as the crowd kept leering asking for injustice done against them. More blasts of showering water cannons and it has been brought into calm by the supervision of good leaders. Now give me the details. Who killed Xavier here on the spot? The recently arrived chief of police said looking at the man scattered with the crowd. He looked at the gun, checked all bullets in place, and then glanced at the twisted breathing pipe which gave him a clear idea of the death and the way it was committed.

Clear off, all of you now, he said, coming to business. I shall talk with the mayor on how to help you if injustice was done to your families, the crowd didn't say much but few of them had retreated. I have no interest in hurting you. It's not the gang of enemies, he said in a calm voice and the leading man from the opposite side thanked him to quiet the situation down easily. he may have brought you by force or he won't be killed, the chief said shaking hands and the mess has finally been cleared as the police team tried to balance the wreck.

They dared to go inside the station, did you see that Andrew? The chairman had called a personal meeting to discuss the progress. Your man did enough damage to force a whole crowd in his favour, didn't he? the main doctor replied, sipping a potion with some meat in front. I don't say I was involved, it's never been a case honestly, a strange feeling came to the environment as they dined celebrating the cause. The mood had changed as the doctor felt it and he took out his night device which can trace a shadow looming close by trying to fetch something in the air.

I want the coin, Andrew. you know how blissful that feeling would be, the chairman said, eating more food. a voice said slowly in the chairman's ear. I like it too. I would help you, the chairman felt somebody may have played a prank so he stood up talking Andrew to be off who agreed. The doctor took his glasses, put them on, and left calmly. The chairman went into his royal bathroom to clear the mess and felt someone simply watching him from the mirror. Come to me. I am already in your dreams, the face said, making him turn with true fear as if it was a horrible dream coming true.

A few nights before this rich man who hardly feared anyone in the world had been sleeping calmly. For some moment he dreamt about his long-lost girlfriend with joy. Then the dream changed as a man came to face him holding a coin. The man said he has no right to claim it as the coin is the property of one who truly owns it. This thought made the chairman angry so he started to chase the man. Chaos met his eyes with blood scattered, bodies on the floor, and someone hanging from the trees. When he looked up, he was staring at his soul lifted in the trees and he had woken up in fear, panting from the vision of such a dream and in fits due to what he had seen.

I don't want to come with you, the chairman said in a strained whisper, becoming worried to see the same shadow. The ghost had a dead stare at him as it lurked in the creepy corner to quietly hit him with something. For a moment the chairman thought it may be his end but then the shadow had gone due to a sudden spark of light from the other side. His assistant had just opened the door to find where he had gone and the boss felt pleased for the first time to see him in years of his service as the ghost had retreated into the shadows.

Well done, I will honour you, the chairman said as he turned away, opening the light in his hand looking confused. The shadow hasn't gone however and it may come soon to take his life. Did you face a ghost right now sir? Perry asked as he served him night dessert. the chairman shook his head and didn't want to talk about it. A memory of a bad dream, that's all you know, he laughed trying to change the mood but frustration could be seen on his face vivid with panic.

The next morning Perry couldn't believe his eyes. He had been knocking for an hour but no answer was coming from inside. He rang the alarm and played the chairman's favourite music but there was no answer. After 50 minutes of shouting and noise, the assistant decided to break the door with a wood-crushing machine. After a crash that landed the door with a thud, he met a horrible sight inside. blood was soaking up onto the door handle with some portion of it also on the grand carpet visible clearly. The chairman was lying on the desk, his heart slashed to pieces and it was hardly a concern who may have done it.

Sir, what did I say last time? you had been thumped by a ghost, Perry cried as everything was close, no one was coming and the chairman was no more. Perry called Andrew telling him to be urgent. He was told to be in the surgery room and would arrive in an hour. Perry couldn't stop crying with disgust, Chairman is dead. Please come fast, It made Andrew leave his chair as he mostly excuses from joining meetings on the hidden coin but now it has been important as the main criminal has been dead by a secret shadow.

Any sightings of strange figures? the main doctor asked as it was tough to say anybody who had planned the murder on the spot. An investigation team was also called to see through but there was no sign of any break-in, plan, or plot to commit the crime. I may think you can leave. You can check for further clues later, Andrew said, walking to the bathroom and focusing on a strange smaller sight in the shadow. A figure was leering there, pleased to do it and Andrew tried to talk with it, reasoning with the figure on why he did that.

The wait for treasure is too much. You are a wise man and have committed fewer crimes so I can say you understand, the ghost said, taking out a fake coin from its pocket. One for the memory of it. your son will stay safe with this, he said with a hint of what may be coming ahead. Andrew gestured a sign of thanks as a strange light came from the figure and it had vanished. Perry saw Andrew coming and the doctor confirmed him with knowledge of how the assistant saved him during the last night. They didn't feel much for the chairman but the absence of a strong person was going to taunt them for some time with its pain.

The hospital was quiet as all of them had been informed of the death. Would you go to the funeral then? Gelda asked Ray politely as they had become good friends in recent times. I can't say whether I may or not. it decides the main doctor, he smiled, taking the lid of a box and removing a few medicines to give to Andrew upstairs. The mood had changed as there hadn't been as many cases to treat but the fear still looms as the ghosts of the dead in the past would certainly retreat.

It's not my order to take over, Andrew spoke to Ray as he handed the medicines You all are free to attend the funeral or if you wish you may not, It gave the supplier a hint that the main doctor could find ways to get information from different angles. I presume Gelda wanted to ask to go there so I asked, he said without a hint of getting together. Soon the doctor raised his eyebrows, turned the file and the supplier had gone without much further word to him about it.

Perry was lying on his bed, the death of his master had shaken him badly. Being an orphan and with nowhere else to go, he had been serving as the chairman for the last 10 years. Be it the bad days or happy ones, crime or celebration, they had been together and now he sobbed lying on the bed broken It's not good for you to go at this very moment sir, we were so close to tracing the coin, he said reading through an old file where the mention of India with a secret order being mentioned. Now he looks back at it, he feels to have been betrayed by the time and he can only rejoice the way he couldn't bring the coin for his master when he was alive.

News of the people dying was still coming from the woods as police horns could be heard louder in people's ears and they closed the door in front of them. The rules were getting tight and it was strictly denied for people to go abroad as only VIP pass holders could be approved to go and the murkier time had been coming faster than it could have simply. Andrew had brought his son back to the hospital, luckily without a threat this time as he had been vomiting badly. Gelda's aunt has passed away suddenly due to a heart stroke and she has taken leave for 10 days. Few hospital members had been infected by the few and the ghost kept lurking.

All people could do is to run away, ask for help, find their relatives die and remain helpless. People who belong to India tried to help them with mantras, potions or certain objects but the solution was not permanent. Besides, Indians were charged for performing rituals which made things critical as most people were not going to office or doing half work in fear of both the government and the ghost looming around in places. The toughest time was certainly spreading with more pressure and it would ultimately reach a breaking point.

14
SPECTRAL BONDS

A cool mist was flowing as Upendera walked back home with his stick taps heard clearly in the courtyard. A guard passed close to him and wanted to talk but then he had turned simply. The ghost of his son smiled with a whisper, Trickster wanting to loot people off in wish to find the money, the father looked up to see a movement just in time that few more men had come following the guard and his trail to trap Upendera by force as they scattered.

Leave them to me, I will know how to tackle them, the ghost said, covering the attacks in the air as a guard pelted Upendera with stones, making his morning a bit rude with swear words. Come and have a fight with us, You old man, we need to know why you always survive one of them said, blocking the entry to the main gate of the quarters with its gun pointing towards the ghost's father. There was a blast from behind as the bin exploded and the guard was on it dead.

The other guards turned to Upendera in rage to take revenge but were caught in midair to be dismissed easily. Leave us now idiot, who do you think you are playing with us like that? In order the sound of neck splits came louder than ever and most of them were killed by sheer skill of the son as Upendera knew his strength from past and the way he enjoys to be part of it. It was not over however as more folds of the plot started to open in wake of his strike when he broke the neck of a false guard.

Ghosts of the dead started to outnumber the only positive ghost but something started to move with a blissful light. Hello Satyarth, It's been ages since I saw you, the voice said as ghosts of the recently dead guards tried to pry off the fighting ghost. It was Praveen's ghost, one of his most trusted friends from the past and it has expanded the light as the opposite ghosts start to shiver in them. Together they flicked with it no mercy and all of them were sent to a banished world as Satyarth laughed in pure joy seeing his best mate again.

Upendera had a glowing look as he saw both of them join forces and it gave some hope that his dream may come to reality soon. Both ghosts started to play tricks on the wall chasing after each other to show how much they had missed company. They whispered trying to surprise each other, went past the wall and right onto the top floor where Upendera saw Satyarth with a ghost of laughter very vividly. It was a strange joy for them as they reunited again in the courtyard located on the rooftop and bounced down with no fear of death in them.

The old man walked upstairs like nothing had happened to find Astitva packing his bag to leave. 'You are going now? Is it urgent? The old man calmed himself with a few sips of mouth full of water, opening the inner basin's tap and feeling better by doing it simply. Yes, I think the moon will be big enough to ask me if it will come soon, the younger person said smiling as his daughter was still asleep but she would know it somehow from some source one day. Astitva wanted to keep it quiet but now he knows the owner of the main strength, so he does not doubt telling Upendera about it.

You have heard of the tent missing, yes? the old man asked in polite dignity. 'Nothing much to bother. it has been recovered from German thefts, the elder said looking firmly at his face to make him feel better. Aastitva took out a piece of paper from his bag, wrote something like 'the last resort, and with an image designed, he handed it to Upendera so he may recognize it. After the event, Ah yes, the elder said, waiting for something to woosh pass and showing it to the ghost who agreed for the right time to come soon.

It was a map of a certain place which the elder knew very well. The place had been a secret to the location where the coin used to be protected before the death of his son with heavy security. At an early age, Upendera used to visit it with the blessed wish that one day he would become the safety official and it looks like the spirit had made him the owner as he didn't want the riches but wished to protect it. Astitva joined him looking at the benign smile and told him that something else resides in the place where the coin used to be protected in the past as the elder looked up with interest.

How come? Something more precious than the coin itself? Upendera asked in a very quiet voice. The spirit has told you about the return of someone, one who may perish the enemies for us, hasn't he? Astitva said as he also knew a few secrets connected to the elder person who bowed his head. What does it have to do with the one who may help us get free? the elder asked and Astitva waved his hand like trying to say you may know as soon as he settled on to have a cup of boiling water with him feeling positive.

Wake up you Hollywood queen, the interview will be over otherwise, Astitva played the old trick of calling his daughter from the next room. You are leaving, isn't that so early? she said coming out to see all things in one place and order. Astitva gestured towards Upendera who agreed and she couldn't say as the eldest had spoken about the matter already. Give us a treat before you leave, she said, trying to turn towards the stairs as her aunt stopped her from going down as Aisha and Vidyut had been ill recently.

No words on them by your side, I was thinking why it's not so noisy there Nastika said as she was told about their current condition. Better go and check them by taking milk. they won't drink it but it's essential to get recovered, the aunt said, asking her niece to work and she obliged by taking the tray and the jug below in a rush. You will miss her or she shall try to connect you is a quest to unfold, Upendera said as the father saw his daughter going down and leaving out of sight in the below stairs with the echo of her footsteps.

There was a certain movement on the other side of the road as the building is operational now. The leader came out buying a few gifts for someone as it was a birthday time. He asked for 5 bookings for food service in the evening, turned away and soon went inside. my effort won't go to waste, he whispered to him, putting lotion on his face harshly. It's the birthday of someone who had died years ago at the hands of Satyarth while he was chasing a golden thief in the woods and the leader wants the ghost to come back as it can help in fighting the opposite group with strong intent.

In your honour dear, sorry it's not much, he said to Pradipta's ghost when they celebrated the ghost's birthday last time. Call me whenever you need me. it would be more worthwhile if you do it on the day I was born on this blissful earth, the person had great affection for nature and he stopped the golden group from opening the mining at all costs due to which they had declared him a thief in public and he was dead by hands of the best shooter. Now was the time to set the dice on the right move and the leader was going to do it exactly.

A strange mood circled the city as the pandit in the local area asked to arrange pooja so it could help to calm the nerves down. During the process, a strange wind started to blow making a disturbance in lighting the lamp but the Pandit's skill proved powerful to the effects and it was lit. Once he had done the process, the mood changed somehow as people started to feel better and it was going to affect them as the night of the full moon is not so far from the day and may linger upon all of them including Upendera's family.

Praveen had been delighted to find Satyarth as they flew across and struck the cords together to remove a few bad spirits in the city. They caught one lurking behind the old statue, some strange shapes coming out close to the waterfall and it did help people as those who were frightened by them had a clear vigil to enjoy the best tour. The duo went towards the cave, found it was blocked by a deadly power, and with the strength of the blue flair they had dismissed it making it a perfect venture for visitors in the future.

They looked at the slow stream falling into the tip of the cave and it reminded Praveen of the first time he made Satyarth run away from the creatures that lurked inside. We are not going in this time, Satyarth said with a ghost of a smile as he knew the prank was already becoming firm. yeah we can deal with them later. they will join the dark forces so we shall fight them soon, you know, Praveen had grown up now and the other friend felt blissful to feel the pressure easily removed by him.

They shook their hands right towards the entry point, spreading it with flowers and it became a fresh and perfect weather with a little bit of drizzle. They lifted their hidden figures in the air for a salute, turned around, and saw a figure watching him who smiled at them. sir! It's been a privilege watching you protect our city, Satyarth said, identifying the security ghost who smiled around with great cheer.

Your sacrifice won't go to waste either, sir, it was a true honour, the security ghost said with some delight and they were feeling better to join in as forces for the final strike coming soon with all positive energies gathering in the city. The two of them lingered on for the moments, transformed into blue swirls rising in the sky and had vanished back to their place to protect people.

Back at the opposite building, three men appeared holding an injured person in their hands with fright on their faces. What's the matter? One more injury, who did this? They were carrying the man who had been looking after the ghost of the cave and he had gotten injured while running away from the blue flare. I shall have my say later, fill in for now. it's Pradipta's birthday, you idiots, he dismissed the injured person who was taken for medicine in the below chamber and received proper treatment to get recovery.

all of them took on their hooded robes to join the night as the boss called them onto the top floor. There they gathered shouting the long lost person's name and to their surprise, it emerged like every time they had done this for him. Welcome my friends. I am waiting for this day, it said without an offer to speak from the leader. the ghost remarked on how the opposite powers had gone stronger and what they could do now. I shall not linger for few moments this time, but I shall oblige to help you boss, he said smiling and spreading its ghostly arm in the air with a torso visible the ghost had arrived on the fork of the night

The ghost swooped out from the top stair and straight down onto the bottom one with ease. It leered in the empty corner and had traced something hidden there. It started to fiercely engage in a battle with a ghost of the guard who had revoked the leader and had been killed in the forest. After a few strong glows in the night that rose against each other, Pradipta was able to manage to pin the ghost on the wall, and with a 'whee' it crashed it into the light closing down the reign that made its end as people came to rise from the central rooms as a gesture of delight on the end.

Well done sir, we can't thank you enough, a few of the humans said as the ghost looked for dead bodies and waved them to come closer to the corner quarter. I should calm them down. I know the trick, it said, summoning the ghosts of the bodies killed by the guard's ghost and asking them to do his bidding. We shall be under your guidance, we promise master, they said as more glee could be heard and the leader had come down. wonderful news. Now we can form a pack to go for the strike, Pradipta's ghost shook his head, wanting him to bring some more bodies and people dead here who should be together first so things can work better for balance.

Collect them together boss, it said finally rising again. Shalt do what you have ordered, for sure the leader spoke, taking a sip from his old drink and feeling a bit calm as the ghost of the rival guard had done too much damage to his place. He checked for devices active with people working and felt kind-hearted towards them for the first time. It was time for them to get their salaries on time and he disbursed the money checking it online which made them happy to find it had arrived. We shall be honoured further if that ghost keeps things at bay, one of the workers said and the leader laughed, calming them and feeling perfectly on the moon now. .

Praveen was watching it from the other side as the mood changed in both buildings sharply. Satyarth didn't want to interfere with the busy party as he knew they would come to them soon. It was Praadiptas' ghost who felt Praveen on the guard first and he vanished from top to bottom stair again. I want to find how strong you are, the rival ghost said, looking towards both of them. Satyarth didn't need an invite to fight but Praveen did the first strike. The bolt of white light hit Pradipta forcing him to turn, but he also sent a bolt of green light which made both of the other ghosts turn to the opposite side with a flicker of lights.

Another flash of blue lights and Pradipta was on to the wall turning back but Praveen had caught it before it could lash and gave a strange red spark which made it paralyse for a moment Much powerful than what I was being a human, a gunshot sounded inside the spark and Pradipta was not able to bare it now. Leave it, brother, he is not strong yet. I will do the last strike one more time, sSatyarth taunted Pradipta who sent a grey light easily stopped by Praveen and both ghosts sent it flying back to the building from where it had come to fight with them.

If we had failed to counter them, the boss would have sent us packing forever, a man said quietly watching from the stairs below as the others agreed. There was a grey light and the man forgot what he had seen as other talking went quiet too. Pradipta went back to the room where his birthday had been celebrated and started to think of some way to counter the powerful opponents as he felt weak. He always makes me feel I don't belong to the fighting group, the ghost taunted himself with the memory of Satyarth shooting him in the jungle after hitting him brutally in the past and he felt strangely empty despite being a ghost.

Astitva had gone waving goodbye to everyone in the evening to accomplish the task. He promised Nastika to come soon but she wouldn't be able to trace him easily this time. Why shouldn't I? Secret mission again? I will intrude you know, She laughed instead of having panic on his departure as he was leaving. He took out his currency purse, handed her some money and he had gone not listening to excuses from her side. As he stepped below, few men had tried to stop him but the friendly union of two old friends had stopped the men from converging on him.

He thanked both of them and had gone towards the woods as the evening started to turn into night. Why is he going again? Is there something important coming? Two of the blokes who had stopped saw the footsteps turning away. they guessed Moon may turn to become complete as this man only leaves to do ceremonies. 'Shall we tell the boss? I think he may need to know he has left, the other one shook his head as if trying to say that he may know it already and they had turned away to hold their bidding.

The assistants proved themselves true as the leader was not there. He came by the name of Jakathy, a foreigner who had been living in this place for years but used to serve a drug gang before. His hatred for the cultural realm can be seen clearly due to which he attacks the people who stay strongly with it. The wounds on his face help him look more like a lion but the way he crouches gives a feeling of a jungle leopard. He took out his pistol as a plan and slowly started to walk in the forest behind Astitva without a noise.

The moon is not complete but it may soon turn out to be and Jakathy wants his revenge which he couldn't succeed years before as he was tricked by a false coin by his foreign friends. Ah yes, how sweet it is to trick them, he thought as Astitva reached for a fork and bent down to touch the sign of blaze. Jacathy couldn't strike him on the spot though he did have a chance but the fire went past the sign and the bullet was destroyed easily. Fail attempt, we shall try more soon, he thought, moving quietly as Astitva got distracted by something that moved in the bushes very close.

There was a flash, a woop, and then a sound of something caught by a glove. What's that? Jacathy thought to say but he was on the floor before he could react. Meet your new opponent, I am certain you wanted to hunt him first, indeed, the figure said, turning the leader's pistol towards him and he fired two bullets as he fell onto the floor. I knew they would attack you so I tricked them, the figure said, now approaching Astitva and had caught a few imprints in his glove which were banished by his light coming from the neck and their shout were gone with the strike.

I haven't met you before, thanks for saving me, the moon warrior said as the figure asked him to follow him quietly with not much noise. they turned in the bushes, felt more ghosts lurking and the figure kept catching them hard either burning or giving them sparks harshly. They have also come to find ways to come back to earth, the figure had a ghost of a smile as Astitva walked without a word. |We swap positions as more options give a better edge to face the opponents. He spoke to Astitva this time asking him to enter the stairs which the visitor knows well to step down by now.

Back at the old building, Praveen was fighting some

guards with such a cool attitude that it made Satyarth laugh. You don't get affected by bullets, the sparks they fly, or the heavy artillery? the ghost asked another as a few bombs came flying which he had simply sent back on the opponent blasting them off. I don't have to do much as they are using it. Almost done, he said, blasting a few more men and an entire hole had appeared on the place where they were fighting which helped both send the dead bodies without much effort in it.

Our leader will take care of you, the ghost of the dead men shouted as they were repelled not by fire or light but by a splash of water. They struggled with the wait as it became heavy and their imprints started to drown with its impulse giving both friends a ghost of a smile in the darkness. I wish the leader would be dead too. He gave us a lot of pain last time around, Praveen said and his words would come true soon. Just when it was time to dawn, the police guards were honking at the jeep and they approached the constructed building with someone in their arms.

No, how did this happen? a strained voice shouted as the ghost of Pradipta had seen them coming. Master, what happened to you? This can't be true, two of the loyal servants came running but they were all made quiet by the guards raising their hands. He was found dead with his gun striking him. Any clues you can give? they asked to check the signs of blast and damage with the wreck below the stairs. The residents shook their heads as the body was taken inside and they were still in shock as there would be no moon treats for them anymore.

People had come out moving in numbers as they all tried to see it being a strained sight. their leader so brave with such horrible gashes had fallen by a simple trick and they couldn't bear the thought of it. I will take care of the ghost who may have done this, mark my words, Pradipta said looking it over and it was a kind of strange emotion they had got covered after such a mess in front of them as the guard kept asking questions and they said no in frustration or absence of knowing it.

We need to search more in the woods, shall we? the guard in the lead said and they had gone shortly. A man who had been part of guard duties in the past before he joined Jackathy thumped his hand on the table Show off, like they will get something to chew their necks in the woods, there was laughter from behind but it was hardly of any concern to the gang. Their leader has been sent packing and it is certainly a huge loss for them as they miss proper leadership which Jacathy was able to do in the past without much trouble.

Those who had been paid a few days back looked for their remains and decided to leave the place the next morning urgently. The security persons promised them it would still be safe to work but they didn't take it seriously. Only those who had seen or believed in the powers of Pradipta managed to stay back as they trusted him as a leader. The showdown had helped them recognize that things can change at any time but how they will earn now is a concern they had to figure out as the dawn changed into the sunlight and the sun rose shining bright and warming the opposite building with sun rays.

Abhi walked quietly to tip Aisha as she had felt well after last night's tomato soup as she had to drink it hot. He asked her about any horrific dreams and she raised herself asking him to be calm. Vidyut threw something from his pillow and to their surprise, it turned out to be a teddy bear. He had finally come out of his fear and fever as he felt refreshed and started to make noises of 'hoo' trying to scare them. What's all this? on to your old course then? Nastika said coming down with a tray and jug in her hands to let them have milk for energy.

Vidyut tossed a teddy bear and it hit Dushyant who got up to watch it and it was laughter all around due to them all being well and the excitement brimming in them. Oy, you were not that rude when you were not able to stand up, Abhi said, turning the teddy back and Nastika caught it. Yes, you have got lazy, pick those juice bottles up or you will show signs of weakness again, won't you? Aisha laughed as Dushyant and Vidyut turned them back with a smile and they were moving much better with all the weakness gone from the body now.

Nastika picked up the teddy and started to affectionately touch it to test Vidyut's fears. He gets more worried when you move the peace in front of his eyes. No fear came as a response so she felt better to see him. What made you come out of it? she asked to take the glasses back as they had finished the treat. It helped me to overcome the pain I was having in fever so it worked, he smiled, tossing the teddy in the air and catching it again. Aisha was now being pushed by strange ghostly noises by all 3 and it was getting a perfect match to have the eldest so she could quiet them off

It was a strange sight as Upendera was laughing upstairs as he was on the phone talking to someone. Mahendra called him telling him about a fake coin legacy and it made him go berserk with joy as he heard the news. What's the mess after all? If you can't get the real one, Mahendra said from the other side as Upendera managed back his laughter with a huge sound. Pity your cop friend hadn't got it first or he would have become famous, mark my words, there was more laughter, and somehow the panic they had felt gone for some moments with everyone being at peace due to less news of damage, deaths or crimes in woods.

The call got disconnected and Upendera sat back munching his toast with pure joy to have the treat. It's been long since he dipped his fingers into the honey jar and he let it happen to wrap in through sugar today. Nastika saw him filling the toast layer so she took it from him walking from behind and he didn't mind as she handed the peace back. Both children are out of fever, she reported to the aunt who also looked calm and there was no thump or crushing from the other side which gave a huge relief.

Back in the US, the guards were underwater again, Damian was leading the charge and he had called out all his men to search for a lifeboat that had been missing for 10 days. I need to report this to the superiors so I want complete control, you hear me? he said with his voice clear over the gurgling of the sea. Their boats passed a gash opening wide, few of the men who were chasing fell inside the mouth and the rest carried on as the seas were in danger due to these ghosts who laughed and Damian had to use flashes of light sending them to the nether world.

Come and get me, we are here. Your boat is with us, the sounds of the same creatures came with four arms sticking and 8 eyes which were watching them as the gang passed through. Another guard has been caught by the creature who tossed him up and the guard was dead before Damian could come to rescue him. Keep moving, it's a matter of pride, the main officer said as the remaining group kept searching for the lifeboat with more action happening under the water in absolute force.

There was a splinter of wood, a flash of light, and someone called upon Damian. Fair enough, You are my inspiration after all, The senior saw the man at complete speed as he pushed the lifeboat up. He did a flash and a few severe ghost-chasing toppled over as the boat was lifted. Scamier, you are here, what a surprise, the senior said, looking at him inside the sea as more flashes and bursts of fire caught a few more creatures, sending them to hell with pure strength.

The boat has no treasure. it was a false trail, you get it? the junior said, swimming with the help of a life jacket and throwing back the remains. The gold, this is it. the watery gold. I get it mate, Damian said looking over the shine that was fading as they kept tossing the lifeboat onto the surface. all of them had come out except those who had been taken over by the ghosts. Damian tapped the junior on the back and felt glad to finally see him help the naval target while considering the strength of the mission with its risk.

I am sorry sir but I can't help you anymore, he said, sipping a glass of beer as Damian brought a few remains of the lifeboat and examined them. It's true. You have already forfeited, I am aware already, the senior said gesturing to a figure which was bobbing on the surface but turned to greet them. He has been your informer then? the great lost bagpiper? the senior nodded as they had a few jokes, and the possible right to own the diamond coin was far from getting closer now as Damian had also decided not to trace it anymore and decided to be off.

I am retiring this Sunday Scamier, he said, sipping his drink and looking at him straight. I feel it's not been any good tour to be part of, honestly, the junior felt a bit sad for him as they all had been unable to do what they had sacrificed to attain a higher position in the past. You will be my admiral. Sir, the ghost said, playing a tune for 1 minute and then getting silent as the senior raised his hand in salute. It was a calm evening all around, Damian had already told Adriene that he wouldn't be anymore with the department and with a sigh the air operations chief had signed him off last day as he felt peaceful sitting with Scamier and having tales of life rather than failed adventures of the diamond coin.

The next day the junior visited an old house, one that was located in the farthest corner of the city and he was able to find someone there. Bad news. the boss is also getting retired, he said to an old person who liked him and then recognized who he had been. You went from the home years back fighting with us that your leader would be correct, didn't you? an old man said, which may be Scamier's father but the faces don't show the same glitter. The eyes were smaller but the linings of the faces may resemble them together. Your best friend has also been robbed. Someone took away his Indian pass as he was wandering in the city, the old man said as the son looked surprised at the news of Russian friend.

They sat there not talking much but there was some food as the son knew his father to be well connected with the local bakery priorly. he used to serve them before retiring as official caretaker so they take care of him now That's all I can offer you, dear, I am sorry, he said handing a loaf, a glass of coffee, and rich cream pastry for which Scamier felt gratified as the mood change from pulling each others leg to find more on the place.

Few men had died here as the son got the latest on what happened with more chain snatchers active and taking more gems from locals. He felt sad that he couldn't do anything about it as his father reminded him to be a police cop, not a local spy on duty. Finally, he started to think about his mother as they kept talking in low voices about recent headlines with more murders and what police could have done about it.

Where is my mother? she is not coming out being excited, the old man stayed quiet as the son asked again, totally desperate to meet her. For a moment there was no voice and then he asked the son to follow him on a short walk to tell him the truth. After 10 minutes of their stroll, the old man reached a place that was very silent with no exact noise to hear out. Why have you brought me here? it feels like the place to make a grave, he said to his father who raised a hand and asked him to walk on.

After another 2 minutes, Scamier came to face the reality, it was his mother's grave and tears trickled down his face watching the dead body. His eyes could believe it but his mind could hardly accept it. He stood up, not able to digest it anymore. He went back with his father with both of them hardly talking and he searched for things left here for one last time as some movement sounded from the bag lying close disturbing him silently.

The son started to search for things that were closest to him: His old mouth organ lying in the wall drawer, the lighter he had found in youth when he was not aware, the broken cricket bat of his school days, the old clothes and snow gloves of his past trips with his father and the wooden car he used to play with that had been safely protected with a lot of care. He packed all things and the son had left with his visit over the place being the final time.

It's strange. when she wanted you to come, you had an excuse for a job. Now you are here, she is no more, he said as it was not baring to him. I haven't gone, you know. He is a nice kid. I am proud of my son, a voice said as the ghost of his dead wife appeared from a bag Scamier was carrying during their visit to the walk towards the grave and it was strange that the son didn't notice it well.

I am happy you told him the truth, it would make him stay calm now, the ghost said looking past the windows with mist in his eyes. I can still trace him. After all he had taken the snow gloves with him, she said to make him feel cheerful and the man felt warmth after hearing the kind words as the night was strange and everything had changed in the city.

Damian was also packing, he had put his official suit out for the final party before he may retire. He was missing the staff very dearly who may be present there. for one last time, then we shall all be away, he said, taking out his popular fireworks which were famous even in his local area. He took out an old bottle, packed it carefully, took out a few boat guns and raft crackers and he was silent now lying on the floor waiting for Sunday to come and be removed from the pressure he had always felt while being at work.

Adriene had been sitting on the desk even at this hour of night. as he wrote a note in memory of the services of the naval boss and he felt some tears come out. I was under pressure not to accept your wishes Damian, he said, wiping his tears off and removing the paper, saving it for the farewell speech. People were going away everywhere, the jewellers had stopped selling heavy ornaments, few drug dealers had surrendered and it was somehow linked with the treasure. The wish to not go for the treasure connected to the diamond coin has changed the mood and there may soon be peace there.

15
A DOCTOR'S MYSTERIOUS TASK

A voice was coming from a drain that had been left open. Andrew couldn't understand what it meant at first as he got close enough to find the smell and felt disgusted. He closed it with a simple flick but the gutter had opened again like someone was trying to manage out. What do you want, the honourable ghost? he obliges, opening his device to strike if he is being caught from behind. I need your help. There is nothing much I wish to do against you the voice said as Andrew looked closely at the familiar figure.

Go to London tomorrow. My mother is ill, you know, the ghost said, raising out to stand close to the main doctor. You are surely the ghost of Bernard, one who died in this hospital? the figure nodded with its ghostly head in the air as he asked. Take my tip. Go to the capital, You will find something interesting, the ghost said, taking out a fake coin as it may be the only way to enter as a ticket so the ghost asked the doctor to keep it with him or he may feel troubled if he loses it.

Andrew didn't wait for advice from anyone in the family but he did make a few calls where he was told that without an entry coin, he may not be permitted to travel even being the head of a hospital. he smiled walking past the closed drain as the ghost had vanished and simply checked for his suitcase in the main room. Don't tell you where you are going. If somebody asks you, just tell them your nephew's ghost has been sighted and they will get calm, The doctor found it useful as a few of his staff had gone on strike suddenly for past dues that should have been cleared by the chairman or other staff members who look at accounts.

He ignored them, rose from his bench, and with his car ready outside the main gate, the doctor had gone in the wake of the night leaving the complaints behind. I will accompany you for the security cover, the ghost said flying invisible alongside the car as Andrew drove through the main city road, turned twice from the woods and the ghost kept a close watch on intruders as it was almost morning when they reached London with sounds of horns very clearly heard in the air.

What brings you here with me? Andrew asked as the ghost told him how to fix the entry coin, told him to turn in the direction of his car and the gate had opened. You will find why You are here soon, the ghost said, lurking quietly and it was absent for a while as Andrew sat in a chair, a jug of coffee in his front with glass and a few sandwiches offered to munch along as he waited patiently. A woman came out suddenly, dressed in a cultural dress and Andrew recognized her as Mafalda the mother of Bernard who welcomed him with a surprise in her voice.

Bernard brought you here, surely? she asked with a warm hug as the doctor couldn't understand why he had been called upon. She laughed at her being ill, told him about the selection of Danika for an international sports contest and they needed official documents for which he could have been the perfect man. I need to come that far driving in the cold to do just a test, isn't it? He scowled looking at the ghost which had a sneer in the air.

Andrew knew he couldn't fight with him so he tried to have a cover-up. Alright, I'll do it and shall be gone, ok dear. Would that do for you? he said, but the ghost waved a hand and a woollen sofa appeared in front of him Andrew felt tired due to driving in such motion. The ghost requested to have a drop in and with a gesture of the hands to cover the linen bed sheet and lights being turned off, he had been asleep with nothing but peace.

He has so much to bear recently, doesn't he? Mafalda whispered to someone as The doctor woke up. What is all this mess? he opened his mouth in pure awe. Logan, who brought you here, tell me? he asked, looking at the son in surprise who greeted his father equally. Bernard's ghost spoke to me. it told about a taxi booked and I am here you see, he laughed having a fight with Dannika on who shall be the best racer in future. it had suddenly turned into a positive mood as having a ghost amongst you does not always mean chaos, pain, or striking the enemy with fear in surprise.

It was like a year since the main doctor felt at home. He was obliged with his favourite cookies, tea, or coffee on time and the mood couldn't be better as it was time for celebrations in the home for all of them. mafalda had somehow recovered from the loss of her son that happened in the hospital but she didn't blame him for it. Those who were on stake must have taken the call so you can treat, she had said after hearing the news and it had pained Andrew at that time but now he has also overcome the thought of it.

They had helped Logan with lemon tea in his tough times with medical recommendations after the vomit hadn't stopped. They were not sure whether to try it or not but it worked. the doctor feels to be in the right place for some while and it looks like things are calm for now. I will take care of him till he recovers, Danika had said when Logan had been struggling badly and it may be the doctor's time now to return the favour or help done in the past.

The daughter of Mafelda had to pass a test of fitness before she could go to India and do her best in the individual round of athletics. You surely need a test to pass dear? Andrew joked on the dinner table as the ghost raised a knife in threat. Not so rude Bernard, please be a cheerful boy when you are here, the ghost's mother said as he put the knife down with a ghost of a smile but still glowering. Danika however took out an official letter from the sports ministry, handed it to Andrew and he understood why she needed to pass as time was not so great and panic was still in the air.

I will take you to the grounds in the backyard the next morning alright? The ghost felt pleased as the doctor agreed to do it in front of all present. He has heard from staff while being inside the rain as a ghost that Andrew doesn't get agreed so easily which made him raise a knife while he was trying to find an excuse. It had not been easy for his staff to get signatures on their holiday letter, celebration meals, and all other stuff that required permission. The ghost thought it may be prudent to get this done sooner before he tried to pry away from the request.

Mafalda called for the servants to arrange for the tour the next day and they agreed easily. The main park was 15 minutes away and Andrew said it was better for Danika to walk through to reach there and then have practice. It would show whether she is fit enough or not, Logan said before the ghost could have any further remarks on the doctor from behind. yes I will prove you wrong lad, she said sitting behind and they all were laughing at the joke of the ghost as it had reversed the cup with the spoon in its handle grip tossing it on the table.

In the night A strange feeling came to Andrew, like he was away from something and he may find it true when he comes back. People were not listening to aids at the hospital nor the nurses were doing their work. Even a few of the nurses had gone out with a board of 'not available' put on their working room simply. The assistants were not happy as they tried to call Andrew but his phone was off which his ghost nephew had planned. The troubles kept rising as the mood changed and people who brought patients also started to shout so Gelda had to come back and she had finally brought it to calm with her leadership skills for which she is known.

Not a shout anymore. Those who had brought people to the reception room needed to register first, she spoke harshly but in a calm manner. Those who have not received medicine call on the emergency no. I am here to help, she turned to the assistants. all of you who are not in the mood to work must listen that we are paid to serve the public and shall do, she had raised an official emergency group call online with same message of high alert as the other nurses had to return too who were thinking to skip off in absence of the main doctor from the hospital.

People started to get help as Gelda brought it back to order. The lids were fixed soon, blood tests were happening and the nurses were told that they would be fined 15 pounds for having an excuse which made the working staff put pressure. We are not paid by the authority, you know, some of them shouted as Gelda went into the financial corner allowed by Andrew to do in tough hours if he is absent to make things work and bring it back in order.

I am handing you the emergency coin to enter the room with my permit. If I am not present, you better have the lead to distribute the money amongst all members of the staff, he had said and this was not the first time she had done it as she had been asked to do by the chairman in the past. Once all the members paid and 15 pounds were taken as punishment for the miss out they all felt calm and the process was back to normal with money in their banks and their smile back too.

The next morning Andrew took Danika to the park to test her physical might. He asked her to sprint first, turn around and he gave the order to jump when she may not be expecting. Logan watched from a distance as his father commanded her to stretch, to take sharp and slow breaths, and finally checked her pulse with all the tests declaring her fit to participate. I can only hand you the certificate if your ghostly brother lets me go back to my hospital, you understand? she nodded as the ghost cackled in the shadow watching the process calmly from behind.

Mafalda had brought Andrew brunch as the exercise got over and asked him to have a dig in by offering a chair to sit easily. Danika was handed the fitness diet by her mother so she could keep her weight perfect for the contest to be held in India next month with a lot of people coming. All around the world, it is happening globally, she said talking with her uncle who had a desire to go to India but he thought it was not wise to ask and had a quiet session after munching the food outside.

Back in India, the cave had revealed its entry to Astitva as the figure tapped it with a flash of light. They had gone in without a word and the moon warrior started to walk freely. You don't get scared if somebody attacks? the figure asked, flashing light and clearing the ghost away. the warrior gestured a word of gratitude and said, 'You keep an eye open for the intruders. all of you, I am elated he said walking quietly into the blue and purple carpet like he did last time and he feels to be more connected to the world here.

Any idea why we're here now? The birthday will only come next year? The figure loomed the light once more as two figures had been creeping into the shadows. They cackled and then shouted for mercy as the figure clasped and destroyed them easily. Imposters everywhere around. it's a kind of time when something good may be happening, all bad things get active to stop it, the figure spoke not to Astitva but to another seal entry which he opened with flashing the blue flair like the earlier figure had done in the past.

I do know the cause. Someone is coming who may serve as guardian to the golden spirit, Astitva spoke so quietly that the figure could only hear it in the backdrop. He knew why these ghosts had been lurking so he had to keep things calm as the figure had a ghost of a smile. Yes, the ownership changed hands with time, the figure kept a close watch as he continued the walk. Finally, it had taken him longer to reach the place where the furnace was burnt and the figure had asked Astitva to sit down and have some food for his liking, and this time he was not that tired or weak being desperate to have it.

He did miss the furnace or the royal carpet to sit so he bent down and opened his leg to feel the comfort. The figure offered him a chocolate drink and royal nut dessert and it felt that the figure also knew what he actually wanted. The world is too big to fill in the hopes of everyone around. it takes time but people don't have such patience, Astitva said as he accepted the glass and they both started to cherish the moment. It's not their fault. the cultural stigma and lack of information is what does the trick, the figure said throwing smoke in the air as two shadows tried to converge and they were banished in its glow.

We may get going then. Lots of people are waiting for you, the figure said, removing the glow of the furnace and leading him on. One more flick and the final door had come in front which Astitva knew very well. He simply went in and had a huge joy seeing the old party back there. All of them had been waiting and they all clapped as he went in to take his seat as the old woman handed him a cup of soup to get into the mood. I have filled in already, thank you, this will do, he said, accepting one more glass and feeling perfectly in the right spot.

It may happen any moment. You are not late, sir, the figure who had brought him in the past touched his hands from the shadows with crucial details. Alright, I am equally excited, let me get my gem, he requested as the figure helped him to reach the box and he found his gem glittering with pride like it did last time. He felt more comfortable coming back, seated and all of them were now waiting with their eyes on a strange fiery glow visible onto the farthest table.

Back at home, things were getting a bit messy as Nastika had not been allowed to go alone outside or take a guide from home if she wanted to go. The people inside still feel that an old gang may have been active in the opposite building. You have heard the brother's ghost. He has told you that the leader had died, she complained, trying to go out. She hasn't missed the tours much as a lot of things have been happening abroad and people were sending images and money to get them covered in new editions of magazines so she is well kept busy with such tasks.

You won't miss it much now as you have that big coverage to do. Give us some money too, ok? the aunt had said and they were simply trying to keep her busy at home with some certain requests or tasks. She was asked to take the orders, give tuition to young ones, to check for updates on digital editions of previous magazines and she had been fed up after being so much on the inside. She needs company of nature so it must be a time soon to get out and feel fresh.

Upendera had been busy with calls. Now the time was coming closer. He had a call from a government official who wanted to visit him. After he had arrived, they both closed the door from inside and after 1 hour of talk that was too loud to disturb anyone the official had left hoping to get his help. He had gotten threats from abroad about having the right location of the coin and they wanted some help to figure it out. The old man is daring enough and keeps things quiet as Nastika could feel something that was boiling inside his heart. The ghost of his son keeps him calm with certain happy memories of the past so the mood is not very tense.

Mahendra is also asking questions these days on the call. They are not related to his children or coin, but to how the time will be negotiated. He has been sent a notice by the government to either accept the citizenship of the US or consider the process of dual citizenship from INdia which is certainly not possible at present. Upendera had explained to him to accept the offer and stay there as they could take care of his children in India. I am not bothered by them. My worries are known to you, he said a bit politely as Upendera laughed at the issue one evening.

They were talking about aspects of those who are coming to an event next month and Upendera had requested the foreigner to come if he wanted to as he has decent connections. It may not help to change who I am. Will it? I still have to report to the governor about my status. It made Upendera's wife curious as she was just passing by and heard what he was saying. You like to take risks, now it's your turn to find where they are easier to cross by, she replied as Upendera was helped with a glass of water that made him feel better. His pulse had suddenly gone up this time as he was talking which his wife had denoted so she was making fun of the global status now as Upendera got finished with drinking water and getting back to normal.

I can send Satyarth to kidnap you. They don't have any issues to find what happens in the physical world or the connected law do they? The Indian asked the foreigner with one more chuckle to himself. Mahendra thought it was much further than imagining things and started to talk about the law. I am familiar with what kind of laws are drafted in the US. You don't have to remind me that, Upendera kept laughing in frustration as the call got over and now he may somehow regret leaving the country at least as he used to be very proud of Americans and had called them the best in the past.

The foreigner can't take his words back as he still has a lot of pride. People in this country respect him, not to say the contribution he has made has any effect as he is still called upon. There had been some odd times like the case of shadows in the swimming pool which remained unsolved, but in most cases, he had been thinking first and had fixed the matter. At the point when his status is questioned or considered to be an upgrade he feels to take advice from higher ranks but it doesn't feel to consider going back as he had a recent tour to India and his investigation didn't prove any help there so the only way is to keep calling Upendera.

Nastika came out as Upendera lifted his jug to refresh his throat. She hasn't come to ask to go out but she has been trying to show him something but he hasn't been taking care of what she was wanting to say. Do you know this place? This is where Papa is right now, I can trace him, any leads should do for me, Upendera looked at it, he took out the paper Astitva had handed before going and the image matched making a smile come on Nastika's face as she was not worried for his absence anymore with him being traced through such map showing him on the screen.

Good, we can see what may be happening then, she smiled as the location's image was coming but it got blurred suddenly with a light popping out and covering it. Reveal yourself, it said and Nastika turned the phone's screen towards Upendera whose eyes became visible to the figure that had asked who bowed. IN honour of the family who guards, The new imprint will appear soon, it said and the cave's outer portion was only shown as the niece went inside handing the phone to her uncle with some anxiety.

I don't need to see the proceeding. This is just to confirm the daughter of the member present, Upendera said and the screen became blank for the moment She will get the message of new arrival when it happens sir, a text came in response and the phone restarted without any command and a sound came not surprising Upendera but making him smile easily with the strength of his presence.

Nastika came out with a glass of water for herself as she was thirsty, calmed her nerves, and took the phone away in silence with no further words to her uncle. She went back to her room, started to take clicks of some designs she had been sent by a post last night and now it felt like a perfect time to bring the best to the world. The hopes were high even this far as she too guessed what may be the cause of his father going away and she couldn't wait for something special to come soon.

It felt the same at the cave where people had gathered alongside the ghost. The defence of the firewall couldn't be breached as all ghosts waved their hands and sent a few new spirits packing as an extra security cover. Astitva also went on to take his step as he pressed the gem and a strange light came from it helping the figure to clear the intruders easily away. He was waiting with all the others as he could see a few of them looked tired, in fatigue and he could understand how much it meant to them now. All they can hope for is to have the right moment and the child may come to the earth after a long time.

The voices were coming from the closer circle as they kept watching with patience for the arrival. In the moment very close to dawn, a flame lifted everyone with surprise. There was a flash of light, a strange sound for a bird and then it turned into a cry of a baby echoing in the cave. For a moment everyone looked at the table, their hands clasped and eyes watching, then they started to shout in unison, celebrating the moment and the child had arrived to their pure joy.

People started to surround the child with ladies in front who were truly pleased to see him coming. We shall call him Agnivesh, a strange voice came and all of them stood up in salute as the golden spirit came looking the process over. it stopped to linger just for a moment as a map would be seen active in the background. He traced its position back to Upendera's home and the old man's face appeared on the device making the golden spirit feel elated to see him.

Congratulations everyone. Your presence and effort are absolutely of most importance the spirit said, looking at the child as he swapped hands, and one by one everyone made their blessing. The journey is not over yet. Now life has brought its seedlings, we shall have to be more prudent to protect it, the spirit said, making everyone smile instead of being worried about giving in more effort. they were all part of the journey and if they are asked to do more, then it only impresses a compliment on what they have done.

Now I shall ask you in the presence of the honourable spirit to carry forward the ritual if you please, a figure loomed from the shadows holding a huge bathtub, turmeric powder and a shining metal glass to be held by the child. They lifted the newborn inside hot water for a moment, let it feel comfortable and soon it felt like it was in this world as everyone circled him. May I request Sat Vahini to come forward and do the honours please, the figure asked the mother of the child to proceed who looked for the flames and was still over the moon on the way fire played its role to summon the wish.

She raised the son in her arms, simply gave a kiss on the cheek looking at him completely in the light, and let the process become complete by her touch. The mother waved a hand with a dance of flowers happening in the centre and all of them felt blessed. I will never be able to fulfil the efforts you all have made. I am deeply gratified, she said, waving her hand as a salute to the golden spirit who felt equally pleased by the process complete with its finishing touch by her hands as she obliged the son feeding it now herself.

This is the effort of your prayers, spiritual belief, and making the way forward referring to the fire, As the golden spirit said some coins started to bloom easily from all corners overtaking the noise made by the newborn as it tried to catch them in his small fist and they rolled away in top speed. We will organise an international event calling all the people as we have already planned, the spirit said, taking out a paper that expanded into multiple ones and they flew across, falling onto everyone's lap. this will be the best way to mark the arrival of a new owner, he said and with a final wave the spirit has gone.

Back abroad, Mahendra has not been feeling well as he has to face a lot of problems this morning suddenly and he couldn't think of a way out. It started with a letter by Scamier who said that he may not be in the US for 3 years as he had got a ticket to be part of an arctic visitors camp as an official. a true treasure indeed, You shall be going away then, the Indo American felt disgusted and turned off as a message flashed on to his phone. He kept reading the letter and finally decided to toss it away waiting for his coffee which came a bit later than usual.

He checked the message and it was from his receptionist who had sent an apology as she was going away too. I am sorry that I may not be available anymore. I felt great to be part of your system, sir, she sent the message with affection. Further things started to get edgy. Mahendra got a message from Marun who said that her father had died last night too. surprised firstly to find that he was in round 45 only, he further felt annoyed as she had sent a note on going off for a holiday.

As the evening came the coffee maker had also found an excuse to go out. I am sorry sir. My date is not happy with me, you know, he said with a whistle in his mouth so he wouldn't have to talk with his boss. With the night coming very fast, the cook finally also left burning the chapati or the whole meal with less salt made him fume with anger as she turned away with just a sorry closing the door as she left.

Mahendra checked for the flowers who have not received watering properly in the last few days due to no help to do it. Marun had gone quickly whenever she came, not caring for them and he did get some hints that the mood may be changing here. The drain had opened again and the plumber was not coming to fix it either. Mahendra had no response from the legal status of his citizenship and he thought it may be the right time. Things were folding fast and he kept looking at the clock as it came to be midnight and he had decided to leave the place as he had no choice left.

He expressed 'sorry' to officials for making them wait who understood his condition and let him have an official pass to go. It was initially required so they agreed to keep an eye on his status and with his name famous, they allocated VIP passes so he can easily go. He started to check for his bag, the things he may need the most and it was his final decision to go as the event approached in India too.

Back at the marine headquarters, a call had rung asking for a word with the retired officer being urgent. Damian was connected from the other side as the official status remains to be high when it comes to him. Yes, Oh it's Arvind, nice to hear from you. What can I do for you? The naval officer was told about an invite, and a ceremony to be held and Damian felt pleased to get the reception as he agreed to come once it starts the next month as he does wish to be in India and have the cultural joy.

I miss the fun with those blokes, they did give me true naughtiness, he said to nobody as a figure came out in the dark watching him become excited with what was coming for him in a foreign land. I want to go there, what do you say? it would be a true joy to find the lemon curry there, he said remembering how he was treated in the past. The figure hesitated to say that he was not an official anymore but Damian shrugged on the gesture hidden, took out a cold beer, and started to drink, recalling his work with the Indians with joy coming in the backdrop for all of them welcoming him.

Mahendra had sent a word to his brother the next morning that he may be coming to India as his status is still not clear. They were all in mood after the news had spread and the musical band had come out making it a perfect moment. It was absolute noise so he just read through the message and felt calm as he hardly had any words to say to Nastika. Everywhere the people were singing, on foot and it was a true carnival as people in the cave also danced and made the mood brighter by their performances as the child felt pleased to hear it too.

Upendera was pleased that the foreigner may understand why it is prudent to feel closer to India. The past may have been separated from the present, but the fact is that without India it is hard to feel stable as the world is huge and the contest is large. he thanked Mahendra for informing him, wrote he would be waiting for the update and that the foreigner would be coming back soon as he too had a word of apology for not taking his word seriously.

In England, there was also a better mood as Andrew came back from his exploits in London. A rally was passing with white shirts amongst the people as the whole staff had come out to celebrate What's all this? I am a simple bloke with my own choices, he said as a few of them started to shout his name. They had got word of his niece being selected and they needed a party as it was an international call so he guessed that a celebration order would come soon to pass which he was ready to do for them as a gesture of gratitude as they were closely connected to his life.

Gelda did well. She had to be strict when you were not here with the situation present Ray came to sit and told the doctor who obliged, signing the meal finally with cheers from the members. Yes, I feel she did well to control the chaos as I can find it out now he said showing a video saved for him to examine and why it had become a serious concern at that time for all of the working staff. The doctor didn't say much as Gelda replied, I came to know the use of our specific coin, Hope you did that too, she smiled like it was already a wind to her where he might be going and she may have guessed it right.

Your wish is not fulfilled even after all the mess, the ghost spoke from behind as Andrew sat in his office turning the files and checking the recent case covered by nurses. I have done your bidding now, what else can I do for you, Bernard? he said with an edge to his tone being abashed. the ghost flicked a paper in response and the doctor caught it seeing his photo in it. It was a letter from the Department of Family and Health and the ghost told him to go through it as there was a surprise for him quietly hidden in it.

Dear Andrew, We are glad to inform you that you have been selected in a panel of certain doctors who shall be sent to India alongside sports persons from England to participate in the global event happening there, his heart felt like a swelling balloon as he went through We shall be grateful for your renowned services if you agree to come, please send your answer online, the letter got finished and he raised a thumb in gratitude as he looked up with the ghost watching him intently.

Mom did it, I guess to see how Danika does when you are around as she won't be nervous at least. Funny for me, I can track you all even if you are abroad, mind you I don't need a permit to come, it crackles in soft emotional fervour being closely connected to him. The doctor felt calm to make his wish come true and he wanted to keep the moment with him for now as he asked the ghost not to tell it to others who laughed quietly. Yes we may be best to keep the secret Uncle, it said, going away as Andrew sat on his chair feeling relaxed after he had got the invite and he had sent 'yes' online on the official portal confirming his presence.

The hospital had also got calm as there was not much to hear like someone in pain and fewer cries were coming. Logan may be back where he wants to be in a hurry to chase his cousin and prove he may be the best. The ghost feels happier to be in his company and he doesn't ask Bernard to go away as it feels good. the doctor asked to bring his potion. everywhere the happiness was spreading and only time will tell how effective the arrival of a child may prove to the world as the days are progressing at a much better pace now.

Astitva also had to go back, he can see the movements and has played his part. They all have to get back to safety measures and there is a lot to tell Nastika who is showing the world how much India has grown. She is dancing outside a musical place, maybe taking photos or talking about her growth. Upendera didn't stop him as the other building crashed and there was not much threat. The happiness was certainly spreading at a fast pace as children were having fun in their food ceremonies and their contest of ice creams had come again, making all of them in one fold as laughter and joy spread around the corner.

The figures check for intruders at regular intervals as they can pose a threat to the child We are on alert, don't worry about it, the other ghost said, catching more shapes in their palms. The child had grown a few days as glory started to shape all around the world. Peace has come back with retreats of threats and people just have happiness to talk instead of the coin and how to find it. The treasure we can keep is to make everyone smile together, Damian said one evening after coming from the walk and his old folks laughed. They all were excited as everywhere things were back to normal and they would soon join the ceremony together where the coin would be finally handed over to the new owner.

16
THE RISING BLAZE

There was a strange wind that was blowing today, the forest in the city of honour had felt it too and the trees standing tall felt that the wind was trying to catch something as it was still almost close to dawn. What's all this mess, want to catch us now? the dagger holder said, looking out in the wind as it was rising in a strange welcome to someone the ghost couldn't see in the mist. The sign of the blaze rose as the wind passed and then it settled where it had been fixed as the ghost watched carefully looking closely in the backdrop.

A movement happened in a room upstairs, something popped out and Nastika woke up with the flap of her bag opening as the sign of the horns came out with the tongue side in front. It's time you are thrown once and for all, she said in her sleeping voice as she held it closely but not wanting to keep it. She slowly stood up, tiptoed close to the window, and with a soft thump, she had finally thrown away the thing that had tried to cause most problems in their life.

Back in the woods, a few imprints felt strange as they were hurt or had been turned over. The ghosts lurked in corners as a huddle to find what may be the cause of their pain but they couldn't understand what it meant. I can't feel to exist anymore, what kind of power is this? one of them said like a crying baby as their shape started to shrink faster than they could predict. Only the dagger holder and the old adviser remained safe as all of the other party members were destroyed by the impact. Nastika threw away a sign of the horns taking it off from this world and closing out its effects.

A few of the ghosts who were tumbling down wanted to say something to the dagger holder but they didn't get time to speak except a few words. Be well, that's the only thing he could hear as most of the ghosts were taken with severe toll by a strange power they didn't know to counter. How did we survive then? the advisor asked the dagger holder who showed that they hadn't been part of the massacre due to which their imprint remained safe but from now onwards they would have to be careful in the forest.

The effects were also felt in the opposite building as most of it had been crushed after the death of the leader, but few members were still living in the broken mess. Some of them felt a strange fatigue as the horn's sign was thrown. I can't bear it. Please leave me alone, the main security member said, feeling some kind of pain in his head and most of them were asleep due to it. Only Pradipta's ghost was able to feel stronger to resist the countering power and it kept a watch over as it knew guards could come anytime to make this wreck be destroyed and he must keep things together so the place remains safe for the coming duel.

They woke up after an hour as the effects were lifted and started to find their potions which had been preserved inside. I want to get the person who used this power, one of the working people said as he could feel someone had tried to trick them. it's not anyone who is doing it, pradipta said in a quiet measure showing the burn close to where mouth had been and it has turned into a strange tongue just like the sign had been. I hope we will still be able to resist them. For one last moment, all of them said and the shadow went back to the upper stairs feeling shocked by the influence of power.

All gone to plan then? a voice said, making Nastika push her hair back as she saw her father coming to give her a surprise below. What kind of habit is this? Are you a human or a ghost? she asked, poking her head from the window as he tried to climb up the stairs with a huge set of bags in his hands. Coming. Just wait, she said in a sleepy voice, and for 5 minutes she was down receiving him and taking the upper bag in her hands so the wait had gone less and easy to pick around upstairs she had a smile as Aastitva finally settled onto a chair.

Will you also take part? I can see you with a lot of actual potential, he asked without talking of the past as they had seen most things happening this time from their homes. Get settled first. Calm down your nerves, she scolded him sounding like her mother, and handed him a glass of water. He looked at her finally with the hope they could do well being a reporting person. I am asked to bring you to the event, what do you say? he asked again as the daughter took away all 4 bags into her room making him relaxed.

Upendera had been on a walk and he hadn't come back as Nastika kept looking outside thinking about what may have happened. The son's ghost kept trudging with him so there was not much to worry about. He had been talking with the golden spirit about the event, how many people may come, and what might be the main course. I am sure sports is the first thing you may like, the old man had asked and the golden spirit did oblige. I like to do athletics, weight lifting, and even group games If You want, the spirit had said in the presence of 4 organising figures who had been listening closely.

Satyarth had simply been resting itself on a tree nearby as they talked and he hardly had any interest in these things. Your most wanted sport, would it be displayed? the father asked, noticing him quiet. The ghost looked up, speaking firmly, Why not. The list talks about sharp shooting and point-blank shooting, It made the figures laugh and smile further as Satyarth continued in his sharp voice, Add horse riding and powerlifting too. It shall strike the spirit of the game, the organisers agreed with the way he thinks and this had been the reason why they wanted someone like him for the future to keep the city protected.

I shall think to be the guide or not later master, he said as the talk concluded where the spirit was asking him to nurture the skills of a newborn. It is his personal decision, sorry to interrupt legend, We may need to let him think, the figures said and the spirit agreed. You haven't talked of the coin sir, Upenra said, changing the subject as he turned to walk and he was stopped by the figures. they gestured something like coins and told the old man that these were the coins for now till the ceremony concluded to which he agreed keeping his word till the end

The room was filled with the smell of potion as Nastika's aunt had woken up and she was making the old drink for her husband. He is late today. Wonder what could be the matter? she looked at Nastika with some strange emotion in her eyes as she gazed back. there he is, coming with taps of stick, Astitva said as Upendera approached. he stopped to check the opposite side with any movement which was silent and then with a glance he had turned inside climbing the stairs. he noticed Astitva sat and shook hands as the younger touched his feet and it had become a much lighter mood for everyone.

I am going there but with my camera, the daughter said before her uncle could say anything. He was busy with the soft taste of potion arranged today so he didn't say much on the subject. Astitva just had a glance at Upendera and nodded to Nastika. I am thinking the same way. You can help in coverage and with your fan base abroad, it's no wonder how much we shall be greeted, he said, hoping to get a nice response for her clicks from every corner.

As the aunt had brought hot water for him and his daughter, Nastika started to fill in alongside Upendera who was still enjoying the potion with no word to anyone. The hot water had lifted their sleepy mood and gave them a refreshing feeling so they expressed gratitude for offering it. I wonder what is in the bags papa? The daughter asked as he gestured with a finger towards the empty plate lying in the corner. Food, oh yes for the kids, she laughed looking excited and he felt a bit tired as she spoke to him.

She told him to have a shower for a change that would make him comfortable from the trip after such a tough effort to cover the task and the aunt opened the heating tub. Turn off the sound, will you? It disturbs the kids below as they may be sleeping, Nastika said, stepping herself to close out the alarm that sounds once the water heats up. Let's plan for the event soon, shall we, Aastitva said, preparing to go to have a bath and get fresh but then stopped as there was some time left for the water to warm up in the tub.

You have just come. Get some time to spend as the celebrations would extend to a whole month, the aunt said, advising Astitva who didn't say much as he was thinking something. I will have to go home first honestly. There is a lot to explain to Upama you know, the daughter looked a bit surprised to hear him say her mother's name and she knows he only says the name when he has to convince her to come together for a treat or party and he must feel dejected if she says no this time as it was a true feast waiting.

Not an easy effort to ask a lawyer on an official date even if you are married, is it? The daughter laughed, pulling his leg as he walked off hoping to get a perfect shower to get things going. She will agree this time, the uncle spoke finally as Astitva turned and the elder gestured to him to carry through his process to be ready. I hope she will come, it may be the best way to show what our culture offers The niece tilted her head towards the wall.

After the potion had ended, the old man had stood up to discuss things with officials. There was a lot to do with a plan to execute for the committee that was organising the event and he couldn't stay with it. Now he feels like he is back as a government servant like he used to be in the past so the niece goes back to her room in search of some clues as her uncle also starts to plan inside his room thinking about how to balance the wait for the coin and things that may be missing.

Back at the opposite broken building, some people were coming out. They can be seen with red bands on their wrists as they wanted to create some problems in the public. Satyarth saw them as he took off and the ghost of Praveen followed him. This may be their best chance to take most of them so it was time to have some action. OY! You are so weak after your leader has gone, aren't you? Praveen commented as few of the members were trying to launch a bomb towards the city hoping it would explode close to the organisers.

One of them shouted a word and the bomb went into the sky with a sound of clinging like it had been defused by someone in the air. My turn now, Praveen said as he brought back a light with the defused weapon turning it into strike and it happened on to the building where the rest of the members were waiting for command from the guards below. With a furious sound, Pradipta came out as he saw Satyarth lift 5 men together and crunched them to be dismissed as they were dropped on the floor with a smash.

What the hell is all this? More terrible when you are a ghost now? Pradipta said, trying to throw off Praveen who had wrapped a strange banner around the smoky figure. Keep struggling, we will not wait, Satyarth said, lifting towards the broken portion and spreading a kind of acid that flickered into flames as he turned away with the sound of a woosh in the air. Stop that, you ruddy ghost, the people inside said as all of them started to get agony from the towering flames that licked both humans and ghosts before taking them all in their true fold.

Let's fight now Satyarth released Pradipta's ghost from the capture banner as he looked more furious than before ready to strike back. A flash of dark blue light and Praveen felt something burn close to the ear, feeling it white hot. One more warm and Pradipta was thrown backwards. A smash of glass happened tingling behind the ghost as Pradipta fled downwards where the acid flame was spreading out. Three ghosts tried to swoop past but Pradipta made them aside as they all were crunched by the fire in his backdrop.

A bolt of blue light from the resident ghost hit Praveen right on the ghostly chest, he felt paralysed but he had turned the odds as he hit the opposite ghost with a red spark so both shadows started to shimmer in the backdrop. There was a splash from Satyarth as Pradipta was caught in it and Praveen was released from the bolt. The resident ghost tried to hit Satyarth with the shadow flame coming from the splash but got tangled in it as Praveen finally charged again with red sparks covering the whole stone floor in his fury.

3. 2. 1. . .They counted all three and with a huge boom, the building collapsed with crunches and noises from upstairs. The mass felt like a wreck as all was dust, smoke, and fire in the vicinity. All the ghosts had come out of it as most of the people inside were trapped and dying gradually. There was one more explosion as the central hall of record keeping was blasted like a bin by them, a gas was struck by Satyarth and all the specific rooms inside got into pieces as all the ghosts started to move away in fear as they would be destroyed by it.

What's all the noise coming from there sir? the aunt said as Upendera felt empty without his ghostly son on his forehead to talk. Your son is in between them, may be duelling again, I can feel it, he said to his wife as she brought him juice and he was looking outside with some hope. The building was destroyed as a police horn sounded and it was getting worse for the people of the rival forces to resist as most of them had died in the deadly fire blast or the gases sent by the ghosts in the battle closing up the plan.

Pradipta started to do the same as he did the last time he was struck. the ghost flew upwards invisible, turned onto the forest, and started to feel more comfortable. One more time then, Into the woods, Satyarth said, speaking quietly as he charged, telling Praveen to stay back. 'The ghosts of the recently dead can converge. You finish them as I battle with him, he shouted to the friend who let him go reluctantly. Satyarth crossed out a strange line like a message to his father who got it with pride in his thoughts and he had gone to finish the old duel.

I will get support from a certain ghost here, you know, Pradipta said, sending a message as he flew further. Unlucky you, they are not much left here, the word proved true as only two of them could come out. The dagger holder didn't want to fight anymore as he had seen what happened to them in front of fire and light. The old adviser was wise enough not to shake hands with Pradipta as he knew the old tale where the person used to promise land to people in the forest due to which he didn't want mining to happen as his rights would be taken away.

One-on-one, mate, let's face it, a flash of green light hit Pradipta as he sent a white one in response. One more light, this time a yellow one that caused a slash-like mark on the ghost as no blood could come out. Flashes and bolts struck the floor making the bushes glitter but they were not using fire. Pradipta sent a stream like a jet which was turned into fresh air by Satyarth. Their battle started to get intense as the dagger holder started to enjoy alongside the adviser as a spectator. Suddenly Pradipta was turned upside down and there was a sound of a crash like an imprint being hit directly.

The end of your legacy friend, Satyarth whispered, sending a water cannon into the sky with the total force he could muster. It burst into jets of water and caught the struggling shape of Pradipta. It started to cower, just shimmering for a moment and then there was a huge sound of water bursting on trees and the green floor as the imprint had been banished to the world by the positive spirit as the noise started to come from the opposite side of the woods and the victory ghost went pass the remaining party.

Praveen had managed to calm down the place with most of the shapes still burning in the fire. The noise came from the police guards who were not able to clean up the mess and they needed help. Satyarth sent a word to the other ghost and with their hands raised, they conjured one more water cannon that hit the surface directly, and with water spreading all around, it became easy for the guards to mop it up. They looked in heaven to thank the messenger and it was somehow coming close to the wrap-up for the opposite faction as their men and headquarters had been destroyed together by sheer force outnumbered not by men but by the strength of fierce attack.

The ghost of the son simply came back as Upendera had finished the juice and had been walking inside the room where he kept it a secret. The end of the faction Papa I did it, he said in a whisper as the old man raised his hand simply in salute. I am looking for the inscription handed by the spirit, any idea where it is? The ghost pointed towards a bag in the hidden cabinet which only he could reveal. The old man smiled, walked forward, and took out the bag to check the inscription.

What brings you to find it on this brink of the hour? The ghost asked, fixing itself back close to the old man's forehead without effort. I have to find some clues on how the process may work in the ceremony, the father replied finally able to locate the seal and open it to read slowly, 'The time to hand over approaches, You may need to be on the event to do it, the old man smiled tapping it on his forehead so the ghost can consider the statement and he has put it back in the bag pushing it back to the secret cabinet.

Things were not easy in the West as Mahendra had been stopped by a sudden order against him. The officials were not as polite as they may have shown. the pass had been assigned but he could only go either as an American or an Indian born who had been living. the foreigner had been asked to present certain information that could prove he had been living in this country for a decade. It made him angry but he tried to be cool as he searched for his book of passports to attach, his American driving licence, documents to own the estate where he practised, and testimony in the form of signatures of those he had helped.

The documents had been sent to be under the scrutiny of the solicitor's desk as Mahendra had been a high-profile person with his status. He may be frustrated with such terms as he called for some servants to be provided and he did get help as Marun also came back suddenly in the afternoon. However, the fact remains that only after 10 days of scrutiny, he can be permitted to go to India and be part of the function. That makes him fume but he would have to manage such things with time.

Ah, How long did it take you? Look at them, how painful the sight is, he said without much of a start of greeting. Marun agreed looking at the dying plans in the vaces and she went inside and lifted a few mugs and a water barrel to help things over. I wish others could be back before I have to go to India, he smiled as she started to put water into the plants. They had been dry for a long time so one single day's effort might not make them fresh, but there was some hope in them of a Mahendra to have a certain feeling of longing for the place and the way it should be kept.

Evening sir. I am sorry to be late a voice said. Mahendra felt more relaxed to see the coffee maker coming back to work after such a long time. He told about his break up with his girlfriend in the Old City, how sad he had been, and how he did miss the place. We shall get going then before I leave? the owner said, looking at him with excitement and thrills of coffee. Great news. you are also going to India, I guess, he said as with a certain wave of his hands. He took the coffee making machine, the old kettle and went outside to start duties for the boss.

The Indo-American got a call that evening from the cook who said she might not be coming as she felt sorry for her last efforts. She had gone out too after that burnt meal trickery and ever since Mahendra had been either cooking some by himself or he had depended on orders. What can I do for you then? I am doing the cooking myself, he said, scolding the cook who had given him a surprise that his younger sister had just completed her cooking course and would be joining his place from the next morning.

I am sorry that I was ill and didn't manage it, she said, telling him also about a ghost lurking in her home which has now vanished. Mahendra had told his servants how to tackle shadows when they had been most loyal to him. Oh my world, It's fine now? I hope the trick did work, he felt happier as the cook said that she was sorry and with sincere gratitude, the phone disconnected as Mahendra wouldn't have to cook or order from the next day.

One thing remains in his mind that bothers him. it's the permit he may have to get after 10 days. It may be some time to mess around and he told Marun that he is going to visit a local place and may be back at night so she can close all the rooms except one that opens by his fingerprints. The servant agreed and Mahendra went out to a pool in the local area for a search. He had taken his swimming clothes with him and had submerged before any guards could come to ask why he was there

There was a splash from behind as someone caught him. A loud laughter rang in his ears and a few more shapes emerged. We also thought to leave this country if you wish to, one of the figures said as he felt that this might be a trap to trick him. Around 20 underwater spirits surrounded him from up to down as he was swimming and Mahendra felt thankful to his brother as the covering ghosts felt strangely disconnected from the place. OH my inspired soul, the guardian of the coin, I want these spirits to go to the nether world where they belong, he spoke and suddenly all of the shapes collided into each other with a smash and water started to make ripples on the surface with their noises as Mahendra tried to dispatch them.

One more adventure and I may fix this case of watery shadows, Mahendra said, coming out soaking wet and lifting his swimming towel to clear off. He took in the clothes that he had changed before swimming, packed the swimming suit back in the bag, and simply went away. After 20 minutes of walking, he saw a lorry coming which he paid 5 dollars to drop at a local place and he finally arrived at the fearing spot to cover the threat through his skills as he wanted to close the concern once and for all.

He took his swimming suit to go under the water after talking with the locals. I think they are inside as they were reported to have shrunk in numbers, the owner of the pool said as Mahendra decided to go in. One more splash sounded as he went in and this time the power was stronger. The smell of dust, muddy water, and old kerosene made his nostrils feel filled in as it was already not easy to hold his breath inside the water. Three shapes emerged dragging him away from the smell while 4 of them came within the depths. they multiplied suddenly into triple as 21 shapes tried to attack him from all sides speeding within the water zone.

Good for me, the more you are in numbers the easier for me, a strange chemical spread in the area as Mahendra launched it from his swimming suit going at top speed and coming slowly to the upper side of the pool with his strength. There was a crunching sound as the figure started to melt with the positive smell and power of the chemical inside the water. The strange bubble started to emerge as the people watching clapped from outside but Mahendra wasn't able to hear them as he was more focused to finish out the babble inside.

he kept lashing with his spray in water destroying more shapes and in 15 minutes of total effort that made him tired, they all were finished in the waters and the case that pinched him for long had finally come to a close though Scamier was not here to call it a success. I shall be off. thanks all for your love and support, he said soaking as he came out and he was handed a towel and warm soup to get fresh and calm before he left. His efforts in the US were almost at the end and now he can peacefully go home

Mahendra didn't have to knock in the night with his torch held in his hands. He inserted a finger in the hole of the entry gate, the door opened with a click and he was in. The foreigner didn't have to think of any food as those whom he had helped had sent him with a package in honour of what he did for them simply. We are free from the spirits so we shall free you from the effort to cook tonight, they said, handing him the package and he felt quiet as he went inside to wash his hands and get prepared to enjoy a perfect meal after a long time.

Back in England, Andrew sat in an empty room checking his dress for India for the global event. He is fond of white clothes being a doctor but he had to find something that may look good. Get yourself some new dresses, they may suit you uncle the ghost of his nephew had said, chuckling at his appearance abroad. He still had not told his staff or anyone about leaving and he must inform them before they find it out from somewhere else and may bicker on not telling them.

Almost 2 weeks before the event, Andrew called Gelda and Meredith who look after official accounts and surgery in the wards. He asked them to come to his room in the evening and they agreed to come. I need to talk about something private with both of you, he said looking kind rather than harsh as he was shouting most of the time in the wards. they closed the official work just around 8 and after having their drinks, they both went to find Andrew sitting with a letter in his hands

I won't have to say much as you will find this after reading, he said to both of them as the letter was passed to both members and their smiles expanded. This is great news, you are getting the honour to go, they said in whispers so nobody else could hear. it is not whether I am going. To be honest, the thing is the place to manage as You know I may be absent from here, he didn't look disturbed watching people moving and the patients in the hospital who needed help from top doctors.

Both of them looked up with readiness to handle the conditions of the hospital in his absence. I am used to it now, so many times you have helped me sir, Gelda said with kindness as she gave the letter back. I am also ready to handle surgery. You taught me enough to deal with patients, Meredith followed as the main doctor looked proud of both of them. He may have to leave the country which he knows the most and it would take some time for him to adjust to a foreign place.

YOu will come with me, won't you, dear nephew? he said looking for company as the ghost sneered, there will be ghosts I am sure. Though my sources in the community tell me the bad ones are banished by the good ones, it's still a great feeling, the leering laughter of Bernard made him feel pleasure in the darkness and the doctor sat there in night as the orders were quickly passed between the working staff to handle the operations happening in the upper ward by him so there shall be no mistake in doing it.

Ray kept helping Gelda with medicines but they still didn't talk much. He has tried to offer her to come to a hotel or bar to have some time together but she refuses him easily. You know how much work there is left to do, she would complain, showing the empty boxes and cotton pouches. Tell the boss that you may need a free tour, he won't deny you, he said smirking as she waved her hand. You ask him if it is that easy, why don't you? She knew that he didn't dare to go in and ask that so he simply stood up and left as Andrew started to pack for the tour with time for the ceremony coming closer.

There was someone who was not happy with what was going on in India as personal security did come first. A few men stepped out of a small meeting room as they were asked questions about vanishing people. Germans are known to be intelligent, You hear me? the boss asked looking at the list of the missing men with disgust. I give you 3 days to find out what happened to our men, now off you go, he fumed with spit coming out as they said 'yes' and came out in a group to find things out with their network active abroad including India to search for their men.

I am sure magallay did go after the tent, didn't he? one of the explorers said as they traced for images in the Indian local area by their tracking devices on the digital hub. It's not worth going there. I say you request a permit from the boss to indulge in an event taking place there next month and find more, the other 2 ladies whispered as they stood up from their desks closing the hub. it was not easy to convince the boss but in aid of a search, they might get an approval.

People in India were trying to do the best they could to make an event go royal by such efforts. Sports is on the other side of it. the true glory remains with the treasure of getting happier than ever, one of the tent owners said as he was fixing the balloons into the air to decorate them with certain designs flying high in the sky. Yes, it would be all fine if outsiders don't intrude in our efforts, a figure whispered as the police van also took off for one more round into the city to trace any misbehaviour coming from any side.

The boss in Germany had got an invite too as

Germany would also be taking part. The members of the investigation group went in to make an official request to him. it's private, press the bell if you wish to talk with him, the assistant told as one of the cops felt it convenient to disturb him now It urgent, we need to get in, the lady said and the assistant pressed the bell as a noise came from inside to let the visitors in without much a noise from outside as the doors closed.

The group went politely as they were asked to be seated and the talk started to become serious with time. They requested the boss to come along as covering staff for the sports person to search further the case of missing men in Asia or better in India. It may not be easy in the current state to investigate directly in India so they put this as an offer to help the senior out who pondered it over with a glass of coffee ordered for all of them.

This will also help to trace the missing men without any challenge. what say you boss? Elmarda, the elder lady said as he agreed on the subject of it but was told it may be a secret mission. Not a word to anyone, of course, sir, Wilfert said as the boss started to find how many security people may be allowed and he had asked them to leave as he shall see how to manage them with other people going to India. The assistant smiled seeing them leave but he had no idea of what they spoke to him so the meeting was over for the time.

Countries from the developed world, from the developing one, and the farthest corners may be coming and the golden spirit is worried a bit for the security as he knows they are the times when things become the toughest to hold for the locals. We are with you, legend. It is sure that we can keep things under our control, the figures said as they became powerful with the wrong ghosts gone and banished with the help of Satyarth, the security team, and other members.

The mood was certainly high in the area as more people came to see the statue of the legend and stand in front of it to find the right words on its creation and impact. They felt a strange bliss praying to the lord that they get this site to be held in their hearts and they could come back here to get the true wisdom. The moment is not far to come now in the whole country as all of them wait with patience for its arrival and the spirit keeps a close watch to ensure everything remains perfect.

17
BLOOD MOON RISING

It was a calm night with few owls hooting in the forest. Only two ghosts remained as they kept waiting for something to leer or fright anyone off. There was a sudden movement with the sound of feet in the grass. There was a yell, a strange sound of a creature, and the dagger holder went down in delight as it0 had caught something to taste. Nice food it been a while since I had it, the ghost said rushing down to dig its teeth in the bloody wound and it started to sip down enjoying the meal with no one of his friends left to offer them

What kind of food are you having mate now? the adviser ghost had come from the shadows as the dagger holder crushed all the talons away, took care of the body, and started to tear the flesh off. It's the carcass, as no humans were left to hunt being busy for a function in the main city, the holder said looking through the smoke. It's one of the creatures that lurk in the cave. Why did it come here? the adviser ghost said, looking through the dead body onto the floor.

There was some more sound as they were now surrounded. What the hell. Did I make a mistake? the dagger holder said, lifting itself as the creature started to rise in numbers. Few of them saw one of their partners dead on the floor and they started to run off with fury. Go into the city, they must have killed your friend, the adviser started to trick them but they were too angry to hear the invisible voice. One of the creatures jumped high enough to catch out the dagger and it had broken it in pieces before the holder could ask it back from them or protect it.

They broke a few bushes in anger and stampeded like

a hoard unheard of before and it was an absolute mess. The police van came rushing to the spot as the noises became deafening. There were a few gunshots but they didn't work. Only cruel blades or scarring weapons could do the trick as the bullets would hit them and they would stand the force by which they were hit and started to make more noise after being threatened running towards the men to show their absolute anger on them.

Upendera speaking. What's the matter with you? a phone rang in the government quarters. The police chief was on the other side who looked to be totally in pure fit. Strange Creatures in huge numbers. they are making an absolute racket, he said, unable to control his breath Calm down. what would this all do? the old man said as the movement happened in his forehead with his son's ghost coming out ready to fight as he had tipped Praveen earlier that creature would lash someday and they may have to fix it.

I know how to deal with them. leave it to me, the ghost said, whispering something in the air that made the other friendly ghost appear. Time for some more fun dude. Are you ready? The other ghost agreed and Upendera had no choice but to let them fly across As there was no threat from the opposite building now. They passed away simply sending a scent of happiness in the air. Time to take the special weapons out, Satyarth said, summoning a blade from the air as Praveen did the same. They made them crash into each other to find the sharpness and the sound felt pleasing to them as they were ready to crush.

This way, now we shall have to go to the forest first, Satyarth told the news coming from the woods. They flew across watching the creatures running with fury and their sharp talons crushing any human who was trying to fight them off. Here you go. I am your opponent, Praveen did the first strike crushing 4 creatures in one hit and they fell onto the floor. I need that blood, a voice came as the holder came without any dagger in hand anymore. You have lost your weapon, good, you are going to be lost too, Satyarth said, throwing a strange shield sound and the holder finally met its end in the forest.

A light came out from Praveen's blade and the policeman felt dumbstruck to see it going bigger and turning too huge. The light started to expand, became big and it matched the light piercing the hoard from Satyarth's blade in the air. Together they flicked their thumbs and a gigantic blast took place leaving everyone inside the smoke and dust and the men coughing with terror on the floor. Satyarth knew it could cause pain to the cops as humans tried to fight off so he flicked his hands to have a water cannon and everything was clear in the place with it after the burst of water that sounded loud.

NO damage has been done to the trees or plants, but the strange dark creatures were blasted by the light as they could not repel them. The first step of the task, it's done, mate, Praveen said, helping the cops to recover and retreat from the fear. The van had gone with a word of gratitude and Satyarth watched something still lurking. There was a lot of blood left on the grass and he could suspect someone was enjoying it.

Praveen had a naughty smile on his face as he took out a button to do mischief, flicked it and the shadow loomed in front enjoying blood and giving a feel of pure disgust. The ghost of the adviser was drenching with happiness trying to sop up for true relish but it was noticed by the visitors who became angry at it.

The last shape to fall upon in the woods If you ask me, the friend said and with a single pop of the light from the button, the ghost was destroyed as it made a strange sound. Off to the cave then? they can create a serious effect if we don't stop them, Satyarth said as they both still had their blades intact and they had vanished directly appearing on to the entry of the cave. There was no barrier as they had cleared it in the past nor certain ghosts thanks to the security imprint who destroyed them. The only fear was the creatures and they had gone in to face it with light blazing in their blades.

A creature had come followed by his partners who all had 8 legs and 4 eyes looking in all directions. There was a smash of the blade as a few of its partners fell and the leader charged into the air with its tentacle swirling. Praveen's blade repulsed the force and its light hit the creature right on the tentacle as it collapsed onto the stone floor. More rattles had been heard as voices were coming to trace the opponent. Satyarth forces a blue light from its palm and the flying bats run away seeing the strange glow coming towards them. More ghost-like creatures started to duel with them as they planned to go inside the cave.

There was a howl from behind, a roar of the water creature and a demon had come opening its jaw wide enough to fit in the whole area. I see, you are the fear I used to have when I was a human, Praveen said, striking it with a bolt of blue light as it fell. a trap to show that it's fallen, I will give you the final finish, Satyarth blade created a true flash of fire as the demon fell and it was almost done as dwarf ghosts like creatures started to run out but were trapped by the light and were gone by the simple flicker of it.

One more roared this time from the front as two of the bigger creatures had come with blood visible in their mouth open wide. No limit to what level those vampires can go to hidden places, is there? the ghost whispered, creating a sound from the blades and they both got confused. You strike the right one I'll do the left one, Satyarth said with total speed and the blades hit the blood-soaking nuzzles of the wampires who rasped but couldn't figure out the force.

Without wasting time the blades had gone into their bellies and finally, the bloodsuckers had been sent to heaven by them.

Are you ready dude? Praveen said as they almost reached the exit point. yes on the count of 3. 1. 2. 3, go, a water cannon blasted the dig-in place where human corpses were kept by the previous ghostly entities and it turned into perfect water filling fresh with rain water due to the water blast. They both raised their thumbs in true joy, did the process to come out, and the friends of the ghost were also cleared before the ceremony could start in the city.

Mahendra was walking through an airport as things looked somewhat changed in the city. This has happened very quickly, India is changing Indeed, he whispered as he had just arrived in the capital by flight. Excuse me, sir. Your identity pleas, a lady at the exit said as he showed her and she let him pass with his lodging cleared. He went through a few sign boards that read in honour of the grand carnival, he smiled and simply walked away in happiness to see the crowd filling to be part of it.

Are you coming then or had arrived? A voice said in the speaker as Mahendra took the call from Astitva. he told him that he had arrived and it may take him some while to reach as the crowd has been surrounding the visitors. everywhere he could see flags waving, tents on the rise, new shops, and open tables with people on the podium which lifted his mood Finally they are grown-ups now, he said buying a curd sweet package from a shop and took it safely in his bag deciding to eat it back home walking to find a rickshaw to go to quarters and he has finally got it.

It took you late dear. What's the issue after all? Upendera smiled as the foreigner just stepped out from the vehicle reaching the spot. He had a look on the opposite side and there was no certain panic which made him smile NO ghosts now on the opposite side? Good for us, he changed the word as Upendera asked him to go upstairs so he could meet the children there who were waiting with too much noise themselves.

Ah yes, they do deserve a treat from my side as I have brought the joys for them too, he said, climbing the stairs with excitement as Satyarth touched him from behind with a whisper to give a surprise. He whooped in the air and cartwheeled with joy that didn't affect him as he knew his presence and he felt it's more than important.

I am busy with my uncle. It's been a lot to cover around, Nastika said, coming out to touch his feet as the children gathered around. Aisha has started her demands again as her father knows what she wants. He has brought a lot of good moments for them from abroad and they all sat there as Upendera's wife brought a fruit chart for all of them including Astitva who was looking to leave simply. Have this first, You are only called for the official statements, Nastika laughed and the children were having a decent time for themselves chasing their father to get hold of his bag so they could find more sweets.

One more entry happened into the airport as a plane landed. Few doctors and health staff came alongside certain people who wore red and black as they can be considered from England. Welcome to India, a voice said as they all started to check for their bags and luggage. Yes, We have been hoping for a nice welcome, Andrew said, stepping out as the leader of doctors and taking the official process to clear the luggage away with a wave as he saw people showering their wishes and blessings to be part of the event and make some good grabs to be on offer.

Excuse me, sir. this is my bag, if you can let me take that away? a female person from the athletic team said as Andrew knew his niece still didn't know he was with them. I look familiar, don't I? he said with a smile taking his white face cover away and Danika's smile became bigger with a surprise. What a moment. good you are here, she said and they all started to trudge away with laughter in the camp with a lighter mood as Andrew used to be strict when he was in England but now he wants to enjoy here for some time

Hello, my name is Astitva, a man said, wearing pure gold and white as he welcomed the British. Let me show you the quarters where you may be staying for the tournament, come with me sir, he said, asking Andrew to be on the lead reading his expression and they started to walk. After 10 minutes of a quiet tour that had beautiful scenes in it, they were at the place. the players couldn't stop themselves from taking photos due to which it had taken them more time to come. Danika was a bit surprised that her uncle was not shouting, was not in a bad mood and he was letting the wind blow as all of them were laughing louder than ever.

This is the key to the main compartments sir, Astitva said showing Andrew and the health officials the entry For boys, you can go in and out from there, he showed the group players to come in under his guidance simply. For girls, it shall be to the left, and for boys, it may be right. No tricks on sharing bathrooms, it made them laugh as Astitva had the idea of the Western culture and he made a clear wind of their being in the vision of making high standards he had left with a word of gratitude from Andrew who had asked on how to call food service and got the phone to connect the process out

Hello son, what's the news from our country there? Andrew had made an online call to Logan who told him about the frost and weather with regular food service arranged from the local cafeteria. Not much at the outskirts. it is all calm with no ghosts, he laughed as Andrew got reminded of his nephew. Is he there or coming to India then? He asked, having a thought for food, the son gestured that he might fly through soon to India, he must be careful and the father disconnected the call trying one more in the hospital to check the progress in his absence by other staff to be on top.

Hey, sir. How is it going in India? The views are getting better as you start to adjust? The main doctor agreed in the call as Gelda informed him of a damaged pipe that was fixed, some shouts by an outsiders who was fined for not tracing the right way to ask for health service and the surgery expert told of 3 operations done successfully and all being in control there. It all made him feel calm as the food service he had asked had come with a sizzling burger alongside coffee for all of the doctors and they started to talk about their journey as Andrew kept a close watch on them.

Arvind was standing on a dock, his glasses were on and he hadn't forgotten how much he came to learn with the help of Damian. I will teach you how to load ammunition for heavy missions mate, the American had said when they used to work together Sir, he has been retired now, don't you think? one of his men had said but he had waved off. He quietly wades as a helicopter comes down and a naval officer comes out in an old suit stepping out who can be easily recognised as Damian with an old wave of being back at his place with its delights.

Hello, my friend. What a gesture this is, he said laughing loud as Arvind stepped towards him with a warm hug. One for the name of celebrations. Will you Damian? he challenged him like he may not have the appetite left for the beer currently. Not now mate. I travelled. Get me to my reciting place first, Arvind chuckled with a wave of showing off as he had retired but the etiquettes hadn't changed. The subordinates took the foreigner inside a tent and guided him through and he had reached where official party members from abroad had been staying.

I don't need much space to spread. Take these extra couches off, he said, gesturing to the assistant to get him a cover pillow. Would you like to test the underwater fire extinguisher, skip? Arvind asked, giving a hint on testing the water drillers and functioning taps. Na it's all fine. I will get them fixed if they are not working, it made all of them laugh and they understood why Arvind admired him a lot. The receiver call started to sound and the receptionist was told of an official entry which she accepted and it had become a perfect tour to start.

Hello Richard, how are you doing? the American said, walking forward to shake hands and the British obliged. We have Zane from Swiss, Miranda from Bulgaria, and Elmarda from Germany, the British introduced and all of them shook hands as they were from top-level forces arriving in India. Good to see you all here, it's been a true experience if you ask me, Mcqueis a Danish spoke as Richard offered a tip to Damian on how to go outside in the market how much more expensive is it? Our currency speaks the volume, they laughed as Damian said this and the mood had been perfect.

Elmarda was waiting for a gesture from her fellow cops who had not been seen recently. Have you seen my fellow from Germany? she asked, stepping out as the Bulgarian shook her head. A voice made the German turn as it said, HI I am Spretchka from Russia, Any help I can do, the German turned her face in strange emotion as she started to offer and turned away. There was no noise from Richard or Damian as the Russian turned inside, stepped into the Central Asian quarters and she had gone.

She had fear of her gang being captured or in some sort of trouble so she started to go away from the noise in search of them. I will take care of them till they don't reveal the reason, a voice said as she walked it in a dazzling light. A few figures had caught hold ofWilfert and the boss who had been accused of tricking the security in trial or search of lost men but the leader is still missing. How dare you? I ask them to release now, Elmarda said, striking a bullet from her gun into the air but it struck her instead, turning back. don't try, it's absolutely of no use, the figure said, lifting Wilfert and making a slash.

I was watching you from your device a week back, a smaller female figure said, taking care of the ladies and throwing them into the pool before they could say anything. Before the spy girls could say a word, the pool faced a blast and they were all turned into dead bodies ONly Wilfert was left who was again hurt by a brutal slash. There's enough noise here, to be honest. I am going to show what happens to sneak, the figure said, striking a blue bolt as the man paralyzed falling onto the floor.

With no choice but to run, the figures had covered the foreigner and broken his bones severely so he can't stand now. The female figure was looking at the blast and getting impressed with the results. Together they spoke to the dead: Goodbye spies, we shall see your ghosts soon in the city, the figure said and finally, it was the end of them as the boss was also caught by the leading figure who taunted him for playing such a trick on the government. Our men had been lost too. what kind of case do you call it sir? the boss retorted.

There was an announcement from the closely located field as the United States and German football teams started to get ready to face each other for a medal match. They are the ones to make the country proud and people like you are going to be shameful dots in it, the figure said, finally hitting the boss closer to ear as he struggled with pain. We all are paid for doing such stuff, you know that, the figure shook his head wanting to finish him but stopped his hands. We are bound by community rules on not closing out the leaders or you would not be able to speak anymore sir, he said, going off as Germany scored a goal and the crowd roared.

The event had started with matches of football and basketball and the process started to go on after the launch. At the inauguration, the politicians took part as they like to give speeches. A voice also came to everyone that must be from a legend who whispered in the shadows, always be fair to your kind. never try to cross bounds or the consequences are going to be against you no matter how strong you are, the words were welcomed by foreigners as Dixon from Cuba also came who had been close friends of Arvind and Damian enjoying the moments.

they all had started to blend in with the celebrations beginning and people could be seen holding cameras, eating food, or enjoying with friends. The sports events had been getting popular with Germany and the US to face the finals in football as they did so, the figures of security forces had caught intruders to ensure everything remained calm and now it is much better as athletics are starting to happen soon. Nastika is running with her friends behind, talking to new people, and having interviews and her magazine has gotten more popular than before as they keep asking about the ghosts and she keeps talking about the events.

May I request Nastika to reach the main quarters please, it's official and needed urgently, a female voice boomed close to her ears and she asked for an excuse from the Brazilian girls with whom she had made good friends. I will be back shortly. It's my uncle's place, he may want some help, she said, signing off and vanishing before anyone could find where she had gone. It has been easy by vehicles in the past but with so much decoration and crowd, she had to make some effort to find the right way and finally, after 15 hard minutes, she was at the residential place

Thanks, dear, I was expecting you, Astitva had come before finally with Upama smiling at the daughter so no one could ask her for photos or images. He took her back with a word on a coin and she felt pleased to hear it finally. Your uncle has a lot to explain to you, not to me however, he smiled as Upendera could be seen on the balcony, wearing the official suit and looking pleased with everything going to perfection till now as his niece climbed up and the son's ghost also came back with something like an ice cream bowl for her.

Not much time left. How do I look? The old days feel like coming back, won't they? he asked Satyarth, who had a ghost of a smile. all the intruders were crushed by our strong figures. Will they come back as ghosts? he updated Astitvaa in an undertone who shook his head with a smile. He informed of the arrangement of the pandits who are taking care of any bad element in nature. Good, Now we can get cracking, Upenra said, asking all of them to be with him inside his secret room for a moment as he may have to find the coin first.

There was a sound of a tap by the ghost, a cabinet appeared and Upendera was able to reach for his bag to reveal the coin finally in his hands. Test its powers first, astitva said to him in a request. In response, a light came as Upendera lifted the diamond coin in his palms and a figure came out. Finally, my moment to join the next soul has come. I shall be honoured, it said and the figure had gone back inside. There was a jingling softly and coins sparkled in all corners going out from the open windows and turning into beads of rays. The ghost smiled and he told them to bring guards of honour so everything could work.

There was a strange murmur from the woods as the local food service team was passing through. it felt like the ghost may be whispering but Satyarth and Praveen, had seen to it that there should be no such problem March on, it the noise of the coin released from its place, one of the guards said as a few foreigners looked into the sky where shapes of glory were forming with confetti falling everywhere. Where is it? The coin I want to see it, a British man said but he was stopped by Richard as he knew the risk it contained and he stopped the man in his tracks.

I don't want to fall in wait for it a Bulgarian said with the nation's flag in white and red flying up. They say the pressure of the wait is severe to bear upon persons, A Russian said, passing through as Richard's nostrils flared up but he had no intent to fight or argue. Everywhere it was a festive mood as events kept happening either on the podium, at indoor games, or outside in the grounds openly. They were so humble that all things went well and it was certainly going to make India's name rise to the next level.

Let's do it father, a voice spoke not to the crowd but personally close to Upendera quietly. The ghosts started to gather close to the entry of the cave stopping anyone from coming near either by sending a confusion of lights or creating sounds of jingling which people would chase. Satyarth flew past and had been able to find Satvahini; she must stay with the child. Let's take Agnivesh, he is most important, another voice said and the golden spirit came as most of the events were taking place outside or people were enjoying food.

There was a sound of cracking as the royal fire emerged once more. Agnivesh had no fear of it as the child was trying to catch the waves of it rising above. No dear, they are for you. No more pranks here, got it? the mother said as Upendera approached taking the child in his arms. You shall be with the power to bliss, won't you? The child would only babble and the old man looked into the ghost of his son watching from the corner as he was ready to proceed on this great day as everyone was indulged in it with true happiness for the moment.

Oh the grace of heaven, the true honour, the golden spirit as everyone calls you: Please give me the power to transcend the legacy to the next generation as I hand this memory over, Upendera said with his son's ghost raising the fire higher than ever as they lick the stone but didn't burn them as they kept rising. The secret power that resides in the coin comes out in the form of a ghostly shadow and approaches the child. Agnivesh let it come towards him and suddenly it went straight towards his heart with a coin-like sound and out of everyone's sight with a flash.

For a moment those who had been members of the order looked in awe as they gathered for the moment to come finally. They looked in shock for a moment and then they all started to celebrate as Agnivesh took the coin for a moment and handed it back to Upendera with an innocent smile. Now you have the pressure to keep it safe, the old man said with a wave of thanks to the golden spirit which had a shadow of tears in his eyes gleaming with pride and gratitude. we all may go back to the outdoors. Better see what may be happening there, A voice said and they all had dispersed with the ceremony over for them.

The ghost of their son didn't say much but it had the promise to stay with him till the end. I don't care about the future. My word is not clear yet, it said as they were coming out. Upendera had asked him to teach the skills to the newborn and like everyone, he had chosen not to speak it here. I can't wait for the damage if that child may have to certainly face it, he spoke about the matter a few days before the ceremony and the father understood what he meant by it. The bullet that did the worst damage stays as a memory and he doesn't speak about it to the honest ghost as it could hurt him.

Congratulations you did it, Astitva met them on the path to the quarters as they came. I saw it from the lower cave cover, he whispered, so only the family could be part of it. Nastika was not visible as she may be amongst the crowd or may be filling in by using the coupons she had got to let her friends fill in with food. The children were there dancing with some instruments and toys in their hands and it was almost going to be close as the award ceremonies of the events were going on in the open places.

Andrew was delighted to see the gold medal on the chest of his niece who ran in and hugged him as she felt elated for her. Thanks uncle for your guidance, it proved worthwhile, People around her were clapping for her as there was a glow in the shadows by Bernard being happy too. The German football team was surrounded by a few Indian photographers as they tried to crack a few jokes. The Americans were celebrating in the waters as the team had won the yacht contest and Damian kept popping up with his old naval hat back on his head laughing with glee.

Everywhere people were happy, they had a perfect time here and it was time to leave India finally. Russians had done well in boxing and hiking, Bulgarians had succeeded in shooting and athletics apart from races where Danika had won contests and Cuba had done well in the high jump though they got close contests from Swiss and Africans. It was somehow the perfect ending for everyone as Richard shook hands with the other country friends and it was time to go.

As the event may also conclude, It may happen with speeches in the closing ceremony by politicians, the mystery of the coin remains to those who are the guard of true honour with it. it has only sent its spirit to the child but not its complete legacy when it comes to protecting it. It is still Upendera till he lives that the diamond stays with him and he may only hand it once the child grows enough to understand the true power of it as the ghost would come back, spirits may terribly haunt and it may need someone who can banish them.

- The End -